METAL SCREAMED
AGAINST WOOD. . . .

This was it. Vicki was as sure of it as she'd ever been of anything in her life. She started to run. Fifty running paces from the corner something crossed her path. It slipped down the narrow drive between two buildings and when Vicki followed, she could see red taillights burning about a hundred yards away.

It smelled as if something had died at the end of the lane.

Vicki could hear a car engine running, movement against the gravel, and a noise she didn't want to identify.

The evil that had lingered in the subway tunnel had been only the faintest afterimage of the evil that waited for her here.

Something shrieked and the sound drove her back a half dozen steps. Ignoring the cold sweat beading her body and the knot of fear that made each breath a labored fight, Vicki forced herself forward again, turning on her flashlight.

Caught in the beam, a young man crouched, at his feet, a body, blood still draining from its ruined throat. The crouching man stood, his open coat spreading and bracketing him like great black leather wings. And then he was moving toward her. . . .

station. "It was great sex, okay? It was terrific sex! It was . . . What?"

PC West, his fair skin deeply crimson, jumped. "You're blocking the body," he stammered.

Growling an inaudible curse, Celluci jerked back against the wall.

As the gurney rolled by, the contents of the fluorescent orange bag lolling a little from side to side, Vicki curled her hands into fists and contemplated planting one right on Mike Celluci's classically handsome nose. Why did she let him affect her like this? He had a definite knack for poking through carefully constructed shields and stirring up emotions she thought she had under control. *Damn him anyway.* It didn't help that, this time, he was right. A corner of her mouth twitched up. At least they were talking again. . . .

When the gurney had passed, she straightened her fingers, laid her hand on Celluci's arm and said, "Next time, I'll do it by the book."

It was as close to an apology as she was able to make and he knew it.

"Why start now." He sighed. "Look, about leaving the force; you're not blind, Vicki, you could have stayed. . . ."

"Celluci. . . ." She ground his name through clenched teeth. He always pushed it just that one comment too far.

"Never mind." He reached out and pushed her glasses up her nose. "Want a lift downtown?"

She glanced down at her ruined coat. "Why not."

As they followed the gurney up the stairs, he punched her lightly on the arm. "Nice fighting with you again."

She surrendered—the last eight months had been a punitive victory at best—and grinned. "I missed you, too."

* * *

The Monday papers had the murder spread across page one. The tabloid even had a color photograph of the gurney being rolled out of the station, the body bag an obscene splotch of color amid the dark blues and grays. Vicki tossed the paper onto the growing "to be recy-

cled'' pile to the left of her desk and chewed on a thumbnail. Celluci's theory, which he'd grudgingly passed on
while they drove downtown, involved PCPs and some
sort of strap-on claws.

"Like that guy in the movie."

"That was a glove with razor blades, Celluci."

"Whatever."

Vicki didn't buy it and she knew Mike didn't really
either, it was just the best model he could come up with
until he had more facts. His final answer often bore no
resemblance to the theory he'd started with, he just hated
working from zero. She preferred to let the facts fall into
the void and see what they piled up to look like. Trouble
was, this time they just kept right on falling. She needed
more facts.

Her hand was halfway to the phone before she remembered and pulled it back. This had nothing to do with her
any longer. She'd given her statement and that was as far
as her involvement went.

She took off her glasses and scrubbed at one lens with
a fold of her sweatshirt. The edges of her world blurred
until it looked as if she were staring down a foggy tunnel; a wide tunnel, more than adequate for day to day
living. So far, she'd lost about a third of her peripheral
vision. So far. It could only get worse.

The glasses corrected only the nearsightedness. Nothing could correct the rest.

"Okay, this one's Celluci's. Fine. I have a job of my
own to do," she told herself firmly. "One I *can* do." One
she'd better do. Her savings wouldn't last forever and so
far her caseload had been embarrassingly light, her vision
forcing her to turn down more than one potential client.

Teeth gritted, she pulled the massive Toronto white
pages onto her lap. With luck, the F. Chan she was looking for, inheritor of a tidy sum of money from a dead
uncle in Hong Kong, would be one of the twenty-six
listed. If not . . . there were over three full pages of
Chans, sixteen columns, approximately one thousand,
eight hundred and fifty-six names and she'd bet at least
half of those would have a Foo in the family.

Mike Celluci would be looking for a killer right now.

She pushed the thought away.

You couldn't be a cop if you couldn't see.

She'd made her bed. She'd lie in it.

* * *

Terri Neal sagged against the elevator wall, took a number of deep breaths, and, when she thought she'd dredged up a sufficient amount of energy, raised her arm just enough so she could see her watch.

"Twelve seventeen?" she moaned. *Where the hell has Monday gone, and what's the point in going home? I've got to be back here in eight hours.* She felt the weight of the pager against her hip and added a silent prayer that she would actually get the full eight hours. The company had received its pound of flesh already today—the damned beeper had gone off as she'd slid into her car back at 4:20—so maybe, just maybe, they'd leave her alone tonight.

The elevator door hissed open and she dragged herself forward into the underground garage.

"Leaving the office," she murmured, "take two."

Squinting a little under the glare of the fluorescent lights, she started across the almost empty garage, her shadow dancing around her like a demented marionette. She'd always hated the cold, hard light of the fluorescents, the world looked decidedly unfriendly thrown into such sharp-edged relief. And tonight. . . .

She shook her head. Lack of sleep made her think crazy things. Resisting the urge to keep looking over her shoulder, she finally reached the one benefit of all the endless hours of overtime.

"Hi, baby." She rummaged in her pocket for her car keys. "Miss me?"

She flipped open the hatchback, heaved her briefcase— *This damn thing must weigh three hundred pounds!*—up and over the lip, and slid it down into the trunk. Resting her elbows on the weather stripping, she paused, half in and half out of the car, inhaling the scent of new paint, new vinyl, new plastic, and . . . rotting food. Frowning, she straightened.

At least it's coming from outside my car. . . .

Gagging, she pushed the hatchback closed and turned. Let security worry about the smell tomorrow. All she wanted to do was get home.

It took a moment for her to realize she wasn't going to make it.

By the time the scream reached her throat, her throat had been torn away and the scream became a gurgle as her severed trachea filled with blood.

The last thing she saw as her head fell back was the lines of red dribbling darkly down the sides of her new car.

The last thing she heard was the insistent beep, beep, beep of her pager.

And the last thing she felt was a mouth against the ruin of her throat.

* * *

On Tuesday morning, the front page of the tabloid screamed "SLASHER STRIKES AGAIN." A photograph of the coach of the Toronto Maple Leafs stared out from under it, the cutline asking—not for the first time that season—if he should be fired, the Leafs being once again at the very bottom of the worst division in the league. It was the kind of strange layout at which the paper excelled.

"Fire the owner," Vicki muttered, shoving her glasses up her nose and peering at the tiny print under the headline. "Story page two," it said, and on page two, complete with a photo of the underground garage and a hysterical account by the woman who had found the body, was a description of a mutilated corpse that exactly matched the one Vicki had found in the Eglinton West Station.

"Damn."

"Homicide investigator Michael Celluci," the story continued, *"says there is little doubt in his mind that this is not a copycat case and whoever killed Terri Neal also killed Ian Reddick on Sunday night."*

Vicki strongly suspected that was not at all what Mike had said, although it might have been the information he imparted. Mike seldom found it necessary to cooperate with, or even hide his distaste for, the press. And he was never that polite.

She read over the details again and a nameless fear ran icy fingers down her spine. She remembered the lingering presence she'd felt and knew this wouldn't be the end of the killing. She'd dialed the phone almost before she came to a conscious decision to call.

"Mike Celluci, please. What? No, no message."

And what was I going to tell him? she wondered as she hung up. *That I have a hunch this is only the beginning? He'd love that.*

Tossing the tabloid aside, Vicki pulled the other city paper toward her. On page four it ran much the same story, minus about half the adjectives and most of the hysteria.

Neither paper had mentioned that ripping a throat out with a single blow was pretty much impossible.

If I could only remember what was missing from that body. She sighed and rubbed at her eyes.

Meanwhile, she had five Foo Chans to visit. . . .

* * *

There was something moving in the pit. DeVerne Jones leaned against the wire fence and breathed beer fumes into the darkness, wondering what he should do about it. It was his pit. His first as foreman. They'd be starting the frames in the morning so that when spring finally arrived they'd be ready to pour the concrete. He peered around the black lumps of machinery. And there was something down there. In his pit.

Briefly he wished he hadn't decided to swing by the site on his way home from the bar. It was after midnight and the shape he'd seen over by the far wall was probably just some poor wino looking for a warm place to curl up where the cops would leave him alone. The crew could toss the bum out in the morning, no harm done. Except they had a lot of expensive equipment down there and it might be something more.

"Damn."

He dug out his keys and walked over to the gate. The

padlock hung open. In the damp and the cold, it sometimes didn't catch, but he'd been the last man out of the pit and he'd checked it before he left. Hadn't he?

"Damn again." It had just become a very good thing he'd stopped by.

Hinges screaming in protest, the gate swung open.

DeVerne waited for a moment at the top of the ramp, to see if the sound flushed his quarry.

Nothing.

A belly full of beer and you're a hero, he thought, just sober enough to realize he could be walking into trouble and just drunk enough to not really care.

Halfway down into the pit, his eyes growing accustomed to the darkness, he saw it again. Man-shaped, moving too quickly to be a wino, it disappeared behind one of the dozers.

As silently as he was able, DeVerne quickened his pace. He'd catch the son-of-a-bitch in the act. He made a small detour and pulled a three foot length of pipe from a pile of scrap. No sense taking chances, even a cornered rat would fight. The scrape of metal against metal rang out unnaturally loud, echoing off the sides of the pit. His presence announced, he charged around the dozer, bellowing a challenge, weapon raised.

Someone was lying on the ground. DeVerne could see the shoes sticking out of the pool of shadow. In that pool of shadow—or creating it, DeVerne couldn't be sure—crouched another figure.

DeVerne yelled again. The figure straightened and turned, darkness swirling about it.

He didn't realize the figure had moved until the pipe was wrenched from his hand. He barely had time to raise his other hand in a futile attempt to save his life.

There's no such thing! he wailed silently as he died.

*   *   *

Wednesday morning, the tabloid headline, four inches high, read: "VAMPIRE STALKS CITY."

Two

He lifted her arm and ran his tongue down the soft flesh on the inside of her wrist. She moaned, head back, breath coming in labored gasps.

Almost.

He watched her closely and when she began to go into the final climb, when her body began to arch under his, he took the small pulsing vein at the base of her thumb between the sharp points of his teeth and bit down. The slight pain was for her just one more sensation added to a system already overloaded and while she rode the waves of her orgasm, he drank.

They finished at much the same time.

He reached up and gently pushed a strand of damp mahogany hair off her face. "Thank you," he said softly.

"No, thank *you*," she murmured, capturing his hand and placing a kiss on the palm.

They lay quietly for a time; she drifting in and out of sleep, he tracing light patterns on the soft curves of her breasts, his fingertip following the blue lines of veins beneath the white skin. Now that he'd fed, they no longer drove him to distraction. When he was sure that the co-agulant in his saliva had taken effect, and the tiny wound on her wrist would bleed no more, he untangled his legs from hers and padded to the bathroom to clean up.

She roused while he was dressing.

"Henry?"

"I'm still here, Caroline."

"Now. But you're leaving."

"I have work to do." He pulled a sweater over his head and emerged, blinking in the sudden light from the bed-side lamp. Long years of practice kept him from recoiling, but he turned his back to give his sensitive eyes a chance to recover.

"Why can't you work in the daytime, like a normal person," Caroline protested, pulling the comforter up from the foot of the bed and snuggling down under it. "Then you'd have your nights free for me."

He smiled and replied truthfully, "I can't think in the daytime."

"Writers," she sighed.

"Writers," he agreed, bending over and kissing her on the nose. "We're a breed apart."

"Will you call me?"

"As soon as I have the time."

"Men!"

He reached over and snapped off the lamp. "That, too." Deftly avoiding her groping hands, he kissed her good-bye and padded silently out of the bedroom and through the dark apartment. Behind him, he heard her breathing change and knew she slept. Usually, she fell asleep right after they finished, never knowing when he left. It was one of the things he liked best about her, for it meant they seldom had awkward arguments about whether he'd be staying the night.

Retrieving his coat and boots, he let himself out of the apartment, one ear cocked for the sound of the dead bolt snapping home. In many ways, this was the safest time he'd ever lived in. In others, the most dangerous.

Caroline had no suspicion of what he actually was. For her, he was no more than a pleasant interlude, an infrequent companion, sex without guilt. He hadn't even had to work very hard to have it turn out that way.

He frowned at his reflection on the elevator doors. "I want more." The disquiet had been growing for some time, prodding at him, giving him little peace. Feeding had helped ease it but not enough. Choking back a cry of frustration, he whirled and slammed his palm against the plastic wall. The blow sounded like a gunshot in the enclosed space and Henry stared at the pattern of cracks radiating out from under his hand. His palm stung, but the violence seemed to have dulled the point of the disquiet.

No one waited in the lobby to investigate the noise and Henry left the building in an almost jaunty mood.

It was cold out on the street. He tucked his scarf a little more securely around his throat and turned his collar up. His nature made him less susceptible to weather than most, but he still had no liking for a cold wind finding its way down his back. With the bottom of his leather trench coat flapping about his legs, he made his way down the short block to Bloor, turned east, and headed home.

Although it was nearly one o'clock on a Thursday morning, and spring seemed to have decided to make a very late appearance this year, the streets were not yet empty. Traffic still moved steadily along the city's east/west axis and the closer Henry got to Yonge and Bloor, the city's main intersection, the more people he passed on the sidewalk. It was one of the things he liked best about this part of the city, the fact that it never really slept, and it was why he had his home as close to it as he could get. Two blocks past Yonge, he turned into a circular drive and followed the curve around to the door of his building.

In his time, he had lived in castles of every description, a fair number of very private country estates, and even a crypt or two when times were bad, but it had been centuries since he'd had a home that suited him as well as the condominium he'd bought in the heart of Toronto.

"Good evening, Mr. Fitzroy."

"Evening, Greg. Anything happening?"

The security guard smiled and reached for the door release. "Quiet as a tomb, sir."

Henry Fitzroy raised one red-gold eyebrow but waited until he had the door open and the buzzer had ceased its electronic flatulence before asking, "And how would you know?"

Greg grinned. "Used to be a guard at Mount Pleasant Cemetery."

Henry shook his head and smiled as well. "I should've known you'd have an answer."

"Yes, sir, you should've. Good night, sir."

The heavy glass door closed off any further conversation, so as Greg picked up his newspaper Henry waved a silent good night and turned toward the elevators. Then he stopped. And turned back to face the glass.

"VAMPIRE STALKS CITY."

Lips moving as he read, Greg laid the paper flat on his desk, hiding the headline.

His world narrowed to three words, Henry shoved the door open.

"You forget something, Mr. Fitzroy?"

"Your paper. Let me see it."

Startled by the tone but responding to the command, Greg pushed the paper forward until Henry snatched it out from under his hands.

"VAMPIRE STALKS CITY."

Slowly, making no sudden movements, Greg slid his chair back, putting as much distance as possible between himself and the man on the other side of the desk. He wasn't sure why, but in sixty-three years and two wars, he'd never seen an expression like the one Henry Fitzroy now wore. And he hoped he'd never see it again, for the anger was more than human anger and the terror it invoked more than human spirit could stand.

Please, God, don't let him turn it on me. . . .

The minutes stretched and paper tore under tightening fingers.

"Uh, Mr. Fitzroy . . ."

Hazel eyes, like frozen smoke, lifted from their reading. Held by their intensity, the trembling security guard had to swallow once, twice, before he could finish.

". . . you can, uh, keep the paper."

The fear in Greg's voice penetrated through the rage. There was danger in fear. Henry found the carefully constructed civilized veneer that he wore over the predator and forced it back on. "I hate this kind of sensationalism!" He slapped the paper down on the desk.

Greg jumped and his chair hit the back wall, ending retreat.

"This playing on the fears of the public is irresponsible journalism." Henry sighed and covered the anger with a patina of weary annoyance. Four hundred and fifty years of practice made the false face believable regardless of how uncomfortable the fit had grown lately. "They make us all look bad."

Greg sighed in turn and wiped damp palms on his thighs, snatching at the explanation. "I guess writers are kind of sensitive about that," he offered.

"Some of us," Henry agreed. "You sure about the paper? That I can keep it?"

"No problem, Mr. Fitzroy. I checked the hockey scores first thing." His mind had already begun to dull what he had seen, adding rationalizations that made it possible, that made it bearable, but he didn't slide his chair back to the desk until the elevator door had closed and the indicator light had begun to climb.

Muscles knotted with the effort of standing still, Henry concentrated on breathing, on controlling the rage rather than allowing it to control him. In this age his kind survived by blending in, and he'd made a potentially fatal mistake by letting his reaction to the headline show. Allowing his true nature to emerge in the privacy of an empty elevator could do little harm, but doing so before a mortal witness was quite another matter. Not that he expected Greg to suddenly start pointing his finger and screaming vampire. . . .

Helping to dampen the rage was the guilt he felt at terrifying the old man. He liked Greg; in this world of equality and democracy it was good to meet a man willing to serve. The attitude reminded him of the men who'd worked on the estate when he was a boy and took him back, for a little while at least, to a simpler time.

Barriers firmly in place, he got off the elevator at the fourteenth floor, holding the door so Mrs. Hughes and her mastiff could get on. The big dog walked past him stiff-legged, the hairs on the back of his neck up, and a growl rumbling deep in his throat. As always, Mrs. Hughes made apologetic sounds.

"I really don't understand this, Mr. Fitzroy. Owen is usually such a sweet dog. He never . . . Owen!"

The mastiff, trembling with the desire to attack, settled for maneuvering his huge body between his owner and the man in the door, putting as much distance as possible between her and the perceived threat.

"Don't worry about it, Mrs. Hughes." Henry removed his hand and the door began to slide closed. "You can't expect Owen to like everybody." Just before the door shut completely, he smiled down at the dog. The mastiff recognized the baring of teeth for what it was and lunged. Henry managed a slightly more honest smile as the frantic barks faded down toward the lobby.

Ten minutes alone with the dog and they could settle what stood between them. Pack law was simple, the strongest ruled. But Owen always traveled with Mrs. Hughes and Henry doubted Mrs. Hughes would understand. As he had no wish to alienate his neighbor, he put up with the mastiff's animosity. It was a pity. He liked dogs and it would take so little to put Owen in his place.

Once in the condo, with the door safely closed behind him, he looked at the paper again and snarled.

"VAMPIRE STALKS CITY."

The bodies of Terri Neal and DeVerne Jones had been found drained of blood.

The headline appeared to be accurate.

And he knew he wasn't doing it.

With a sudden snap of his wrist he flung the paper across the room and took a minor satisfaction in watching the pages flutter to the floor like wounded birds.

"Damn. Damn. DAMN!"

Crossing to the window, he shrugged out of his coat and tossed it on the couch, then yanked back the curtains that blocked the city from view. Vampires were a solitary breed, not seeking each other out nor keeping track of where their brothers and sisters roamed. Although he suspected he shared his territory with others of his kind, there could be a score moving, living, feeding among the patterns of light and shadow that made up the night and Henry would be no more aware of it than the people they moved among.

And worse, if the killer *was* a vampire, it was a child, one of the newly changed, for only the newly changed needed blood in such amounts and would kill with such brutal abandon.

"Not one of mine," he said to the night, his forehead resting against the cool glass. It was as much a prayer as a statement. Everyone of his kind feared that they would turn loose just such a monster, an accidental child, an accidental change. But *he'd* been careful; never feeding again until the blood had had a chance to renew, never taking the risk that his blood could be passed back. He would have a child someday, but it would change by choice as he had done and he would be there to guide it, to keep it safe.

No, not one of his. But he could not let it continue to terrorize the city. Fear had not changed over the centuries, nor had people's reactions to it and a terrorized city could quickly bring out the torches and sharpened stakes . . . or the twentieth century laboratory equivalent.

"And I no more want to be strapped to a table for the rest of my life than to have my head removed and my mouth stuffed with garlic," he told the night.

He would have to find the child, before the police did and their answer raised more questions than it solved. Find the child and destroy it, for without a blood bond he could not control it.

"And then," he raised his head and bared his teeth, "I will find the parent."

* * *

"Morning, Mrs. Kopolous."

"Hello, darling, you're up early."

"I couldn't sleep," Vicki told her, making her way to the back of the store where the refrigerators hummed, "and I was out of milk."

"Get the bags, they're on sale."

"I don't like the bags." Out of the corner of one eye she saw Mrs. Kopolous expressing a silent and not very favorable opinion of her unwillingness to save forty-nine cents. She grabbed a jug and brought it back to the counter. "Papers not out yet?"

"Yeah, yeah, they're right here, dear." She bent over the bundles, her stocky body hiding the headlines. When she straightened, she slapped one copy of each morning paper down by the cash register.

"SABERS DOWN LEAFS 10–2."

Vicki let out a lungful of air she hadn't known she was holding. If the tabloid made no mention of another murder—besides the slaughter in the division play-offs—it looked like the city had made it safely through the night.

"Those terrible things, you're mixed up in them, aren't you?"

"What terrible things, Mrs. Kopolous?" She scooped up her change, then put it back and grabbed an Easter cream egg instead. What the hell, there was reason to celebrate.

Mrs. Kopolous shook her head, but whether it was at the egg or life in general, Vicki couldn't tell. "You're making faces at the paper like you did when those little girls were killed."

"That was two years ago!" Two years and a lifetime.

"I remember two years. But this time it's not for you to get involved with, these things sucking blood." The register drawer slammed shut with unnecessary force. "This time it's unclean."

"It's never been *clean*," Vicki protested, tucking the papers under her arm.

"You know what I mean."

The tone left no room for argument. "Yeah. I know what you mean." She turned to go, paused, and turned back to the counter. "Mrs. Kopolous, do you believe in vampires?"

The older woman waved an expressive hand. "I don't not believe," she said, her brows drawn down for emphasis. "There are more things in heaven and earth. . . ."

Vicki smiled. "Shakespeare?"

Her expression didn't soften. "Just because it came from a poet, doesn't make it less true."

When Vicki got back to her apartment building, a three-story brownstone in the heart of Chinatown, it was 7:14 and the neighborhood was just beginning to wake up. She considered going for a run, before the carbon monoxide levels rose, but decided against it when an experimental breath plumed in the air. Spring might have officially arrived, but it'd be time enough to start running when the temperature reflected the season. Taking the stairs two at a time, she thanked the lucky genetic combination that gave her a jock's body with a minimum amount of maintenance. Although at thirty-one who knew how much longer that would last. . . .

Minor twinges of guilt sent her through a free weight routine while she listened to the 7:30 news.

By 8:28 she'd skimmed all three newspapers, drunk a pot and a half of tea, and readied the Foo Chan invoice for mailing. Tilting her chair back, she scrubbed at her glasses and let her world narrow into a circle of stucco ceiling. More things in heaven and earth. . . . She didn't know if she believed in vampires, but she definitely believed in her own senses, even if one of them had become less than reliable of late. Something strange had been down that tunnel, and nothing human could have struck that blow. A phrase from Wednesday's newspaper article kept running through her head: *A source in the Coroner's Office reports that the bodies of Terri Neal and DeVerne Jones had been drained of blood.* She knew it was none of her business. . . .

Brandon Singh had always been at his desk at the Coroner's Office every morning at 8:30. He had a cup of tea and a bagel and was, until about 8:45, perfectly approachable.

Although she no longer had any sort of an official position to call from, coroners *were* government appointments and she *was* still a taxpayer. She reached for her address book. *Hell, after Celluci how bad could it be?*

"Dr. Singh, please. Yes, I'll hold." *Why do they ask?* Vicki wondered, shoving at her glasses with her free hand. *It's not like you have a choice.*

"Dr. Singh here."

"Brandon? It's Vicki Nelson."

His weighty Oxford accent—his telephone voice—lightened. "Victoria? Good to hear from you. Been keeping busy since you left the force?"

"Pretty busy," she admitted, swinging her feet up on a corner of the desk. Dr. Brandon Singh was the only person since the death of her maternal grandmother back in the seventies to call her Victoria. She'd never been able to decide whether it was old-world charm or sheer perversity as he knew full well how much she disliked hearing her full name. "I've started my own investigations company."

"I had heard a rumor to that effect, yes. But rumor . . ." In her mind's eye, Vicki could see his long surgeon's hands cutting through the air. ". . . rumor also had you stone blind and selling pencils on a street corner."

"Not. Quite." Anger leached the life from her voice.

Brandon's voice warmed in contrast. "Victoria, I *am* sorry. You know I'm not a tactful man, never had much chance to develop a bedside manner. . . ." It was an old joke, going back to their first meeting over the autopsy of a well-known drug pusher. "Now then," he paused for a swallow of liquid, the sound a discreet distance from the receiver, "what can I do for you?"

Vicki had never found Brandon's habit of getting right to the point with a minimum of small talk disconcerting and she appreciated him never demanding tact when he wouldn't give it. *Don't waste my time, I'm a busy man,* set the tone for every conversation he had. "That article in yesterday's paper, the blood loss in Neal and Jones, was it true?"

The more formal syntax returned. "I hadn't realized you were involved in the case?"

"I'm not, exactly. But I found the first body."

"Tell me."

So she did; information exchange was the coin of favors among city employees even if she no longer exactly qualified.

"And in your professional opinion?" Brandon asked when she finished, his voice carefully neutral.

"In my professional opinion," Vicki echoed both words and tone, "based on three years in homicide, I haven't got a clue what could have caused the wound I saw. Not a single blow ripping through skin and muscle and cartilage."

On the other end of the line, Brandon sighed. "Yes, yes, I know what happened and frankly, I have no more idea than you do. And I've been dealing with this sort of thing considerably longer than three years. To answer your original question, the newspaper story was essentially true; I don't know if it was a vampire or a vacuum cleaner, but Neal and Jones were drained nearly dry.''

"Drained?'' Not just massive blood loss, then, of the kind to be expected with a throat injury that severe. "Oh my God.''

She heard Brandon take another swallow.

"Quite,'' he agreed dryly. "This will, of course, go no further.''

"Of course.''

"Then if you have all the information you require. . . .''

"Yes. Thank you, Brandon.''

"My pleasure, Victoria.''

She sat staring at nothing, considering implications until the phone began to beep, imperiously reminding her she hadn't yet hung up, jerking her out of her daze.

"Drained . . .'' she repeated. "Shit.'' She wondered what the official investigation made of that. *No, be honest. You wonder what Mike Celluci made of it.* Well, she wasn't going to call and find out. Still, it was the sort of thing that friends might discuss if one of them was a cop and one of them used to be. *Except he's sure to say something cutting, especially if he thinks I'm using this whole incident as an excuse to hang around the fringes of the force.*

Was she?

She thought about it while she listened to the three-year-old upstairs running back and forth, back and forth across the living room. It was a soothing, all-is-right-with-the-universe kind of sound and she used its staccato beat to keep her thoughts moving, to keep her from bogging down in the self-pity that had blurred a good part of the last eight months.

No, she decided at last, she was not using these deaths as a way of trying to grab onto some of what she'd had to give up. She was curious, plain and simple. Curious the way anyone would be in a similar circumstance, the difference being that she had a way to satisfy her curiosity.

"And if Celluci doesn't understand that," she muttered as she dialed, "he can fold it sideways and stick it up his. . . . Good morning. Mike Celluci, please. Yes, I'll hold." *Someday,* she tucked the phone under her chin and tried to peel the paper off a very old Life Saver, *I'm going to say no, I won't hold, and send somebody's secretary into strong hysterics.*

"Celluci."

"Morning. It's Vicki."

"Yeah. So?" He definitely didn't sound thrilled. "You complicating my life with another body or is this a social call at . . ."

Vicki checked her watch, during the pause while Celluci checked his.

". . . nine oh two . . ."

"Eight fifty-eight."

He ignored her. ". . . on a Thursday morning?"

"No body, Celluci. I just wondered what you'd come up with so far."

"That's police information, Vicki, and in case you've forgotten, you're not a cop anymore."

The crack hurt but not as much as she expected. Well, two could play at that game.

"Come to a dead end, eh? A full stop?" She flipped over pages of the newspaper loud enough for him to hear the unmistakable rustle. "Paper seems to have come up with an answer." Shaking her head, she held the receiver away from her ear in order not to be deafened by a forcefully expressed opinion of certain reporters, their ancestors, and their descendants. She grinned. She was definitely enjoying this.

"Nice try, Mike, but I called the Coroner's Office and that report was essentially correct."

"Well, why don't I just read *my* report to you over the phone. Or I could send someone over with a copy of the file and no doubt you and your Nancy Drew detective kit can solve the case by lunch."

"Why don't we discuss this like intelligent human beings over dinner?" *Over dinner? Good God, was that my mouth?*

"Dinner?"

Oh, well. In for a penny in for a pound as Granny used to say. "Yeah, dinner, you know, where you sit down in the evening and stuff food in your mouth."

"Oh, dinner. Why didn't you say so?" Vicki could hear the smile in his voice and her mouth curved up in answer. Mike Celluci was the only man she'd ever met whose moods changed as quickly as hers. Maybe that was why. . . . "You buying?" He was also basically a cheap bastard.

"Why not. I'll deduct it as a business expense; consulting with the city's finest."

He snorted. "Took you long enough to remember that. I'll be by about seven."

"I'll be here."

She hung up, pushed her glasses up her nose, and wondered just what she thought she was doing. It had seemed, while they talked—*All right, while we indulged in the verbal sparring that serves us for conversation*—almost like the last eight months and the fights before hadn't happened. Or maybe it was just that their friendship was strong enough to pick up intact from where it had been dropped. Or maybe, just maybe, she'd managed to get a grip on her life.

"And I hope I haven't bitten off more than I can chew," she muttered to the empty apartment.

Three

Stumbling to the right to avoid annihilation by a loaded backpack, Norman Birdwell careened into a stocky young man in a leather York University jacket and found himself back in the corridor outside the lecture hall. Shifting his grip on the plastic handle of his attaché, he squared his narrow shoulders and tried again. He often thought that exiting students should be forced to move in orderly rows through the left side of the double doors so that students arriving early for the next class could enter unopposed through the right.

By sliding sideways between two young women, who, oblivious to Norman's presence, continued discussing the sexist unfairness of birth control and blow-dryers, he made it into the room and headed for his seat.

Norman liked to arrive early so he could sit in the exact center of the third row, his lucky seat ever since he'd written a perfect first year calculus paper in the spot. He was taking this evening sociology class because he'd overheard two jocks in the cafeteria mention it was a great way to meet girls. So far, he wasn't having much luck. Straightening his new leather tie, he wondered if perhaps he shouldn't ask for a jacket.

As he slid into his seat, his attaché jammed between two chair backs in the second row and jerked out of his hand. Bending to free it, his mechanical pencil slid free of his pocket protector and rolled back into the darkness.

"Oh, fuck," he muttered, dropping to his knees. He'd been experimenting with profanity lately, hoping it would make him sound more macho. There'd been no noticeable success.

There were legends about what lurked under the seats

in York University lecture halls but all Norman found, beside his pencil—which he'd only had since Sunday night and didn't want to lose—was a neatly rolled copy of Wednesday's tabloid. Clipping the pencil back where it belonged, Norman spread the paper on his knee. The professor, he knew, would be up to fifteen minutes late; he'd have plenty of time to read the comics.

"VAMPIRE STALKS CITY!"

With trembling fingers, he opened it to the story.

"Get a load of Birdwell." The thick-necked young man elbowed his companion. "He's gone white as a ghost."

Rubbing bruised ribs, the recipient of this tender confidence peered down at the solitary figure in the third row of the hall. "How can you tell?" he grunted. "Ghost, geek; it's all the same."

"I never knew," Norman whispered down at the black type. "I swear to God, I never knew. It wasn't my fault."

He . . . no, it, had said it had to feed. Norman hadn't asked where or how. Maybe, he admitted now, because he hadn't wanted to know. *Don't let anyone see you,* had been his only instruction.

He peeled damp palms up off the newsprint and raised them, smudged and trembling, into the air as he vowed, "Never again, I promise, never again."

* * *

The gong sounded for another order of Peking Duck and while it reverberated through the restaurant, a mellow undertone to the conversations occurring in at least three different languages, Vicki raised a spoonful of hot-and-sour soup to her lips and stared speculatively at Mike Celluci. He'd been almost charming for this, the first half hour of the evening, and she'd had about as much of it as she could take.

She swallowed and gave him her best *don't give me any bullshit, buddy, I'm on to you* smile. "So. Still holding tight to that ridiculous angel dust and Freddy Kruger claws theory?"

Celluci glanced down at his watch. "Thirty-two minutes and seventeen seconds." He shook his head ruefully, a thick brown curl dropping down over his eyes. "And here I bet Dave you couldn't last a half an hour. You just lost me five bucks, Vicki. Is that nice?"

"Quit complaining." She chased a bit of green onion around the edge of her bowl. "After all, I'm paying for dinner. Now, answer the question."

"And here I thought that you were after the pleasure of my company."

She really hated it when his voice picked up that sarcastic edge. Not having heard it for eight months hadn't lessened her dislike. "I'm going to pleasure your company right into the kitchen if you don't answer the question."

"Damn it, Vicki." His spoon slammed into the saucer, "Do we have to discuss this while we eat?"

Eating had nothing to do with it; they'd discussed every case they'd ever had, singly and collectively, over food. Vicki pushed her empty bowl to one side and laced her fingers together. It *was* possible that now she'd left the force he wouldn't discuss the homicides with her. It was possible, but not very likely. At least, she prayed it wasn't very likely. "If you can look me right in the eye," she said quietly, "and tell me you don't want to talk about this with me, I'll lay off."

Technically, he knew he should do exactly that—look her in the eye and tell her he didn't want to talk about it. The Criminal Investigations Bureau took a dim view of investigators who couldn't keep their mouths shut. But Vicki had been one of the best, three accelerated promotions and two citations attested to that, and more importantly, her record of solved crimes had been almost the highest in the department. Honesty forced him to admit, although he admitted it silently, that statistically her record was as good as his, he'd just been at it three years longer. *Do I throw away this resource?* he wondered as the silence lengthened. *Do I refuse to take advantage of talent and skill just because the possessor of those talents and skills has become a civilian?* He tried to keep his personal feelings out of the decision.

He looked her right in the eye and said quietly, "Okay, genius, you got a better idea than PCPs and claws?"

"Difficult to come up with a worse one," she snorted, leaning back to allow their waitress to replace the bowls with steaming platters of food. Grateful for the chance to regain her composure, Vicki toyed with a chopstick and hoped he didn't realize how much this meant to her. She hadn't realized it herself until her heart restarted with his answer and she felt a part of herself she thought had died when she'd left the force slowly begin to come back to life. Her reaction, she knew, would have been invisible to a casual observer but Mike Celucci was anything but that.

Please, God, just let him think he's picking my brain. Don't let him know how much I need this.

For the first time in a long time, God appeared to be listening.

"Your better idea?" Mike asked pointedly when they were alone with their meal.

If he'd noticed her relief, he gave no sign and that was good enough for Vicki. "It's a little hard to hypothesize without all the information," she prodded.

He smiled and she understood, not for the first time, why witnesses of either gender were willing to spill their guts to this man. "Hypothesize. Big word. You been doing crossword puzzles again?"

"Yeah, between tracking down international jewel thieves. Spill it, Celluci."

If anything, there had been fewer clues at the second scene than at the first. No prints save the victim's, no trail, no one who saw the killer enter or exit the underground garage. "And the scene was hours old by the time we arrived. . . ."

"You said the trail at the subway led into a workman's alcove?"

He nodded, scowling at a snow pea. "Blood all over the back wall. The trail led into the alcove, but nothing led out."

"Behind the back wall?"

"You thinking of secret passageways?"

A little sheepishly, she nodded.

"All things considered, *that* would be an answer I could live with." He shook his head and the curl dropped forward again. "Nothing but dirt. We checked."

Although DeVerne Jones had been found with a scrap of torn leather clutched in his fist, dirt was pretty much all they'd found at the third site. Dirt, and a derelict that babbled about the apocalypse.

"Wait a minute . . ." Vicki frowned in concentration, then shoved her disturbed glasses back up her nose. "Didn't the old man at the subway say something about the apocalypse?"

"Nope. Armageddon."

"Same thing."

Celluci sighed with exaggerated force. "You trying to tell me that it's not one guy, it's four guys on horses? Thanks. You've been a lot of help."

"I suppose you've checked for some connection between the victims? Something to hang a motive on?"

"Motive!" He slapped his forehead with the heel of his hand. "Now why didn't I think of that?"

Vicki stabbed at a mushroom and muttered, "Smart ass."

"No, no connections, no discernible motive. We're still looking." He shrugged, a succinct opinion of what the search would turn up.

"Cults?"

"Vicki, I've talked to more weirdos and space cases in the last few days than I have in the last few years." He grinned. "Present company excepted, of course."

They were almost back to her apartment, her hand tucked in the crook of his arm to guide her through the darkness, when she asked, "Have you considered that there might be something in this vampire theory?"

She dug her heels in at his shout of laughter. "I'm serious, Celucci!"

"No, I'm Serious Celluci. You're out of your mind." He dragged her back into step beside him. "Vampires don't exist."

"You're sure of that? 'There are more things . . .' "

"Don't," he warned, "start quoting Shakespeare at me.

I've had the line quoted at me so often lately, I'm beginning to think police brutality is a damned good idea.''

They turned up the path to Vicki's building.

"You've got to admit that a vampire fits all the parameters." Vicki no more believed it was a vampire than Celluci did, but it had always been so easy to rattle his cage. . . .

He snorted. "Right. Something's wandering around the city in a tuxedo muttering, 'I vant to drink your blood.' ''

"You got a better suspect?''

"Yeah. A big guy on PCPs with clip-on claws.''

"You're not back to *that* stupid theory again.''

"Stupid!''

"Yeah. Stupid.''

"You wouldn't recognize a logical progression of facts if they bit you on the butt!''

"At least I'm not so caught up in my own cleverness that I'm blind to outside possibilities!''

"Outside possibilities? You have no idea of what's going on!''

"Neither do you!''

They stood and panted at each other for a few seconds then Vicki shoved her glasses up her nose and dug for her keys. "You staying the night?''

It sounded like a challenge.

"Yeah. I am.''

So did the response.

Sometime later, Vicki shifted to reach a particularly sensitive area and decided, as she got the anticipated inarticulate response, that there were times when you really didn't need to *see* what you were doing and night blindness mattered not in the least.

* * *

Captain Raymond Roxborough looked down at the lithe and cowering form of his cabin boy and wondered how he could have been so blind. Granted, he had thought young Smith very pretty, what with his tousled blue-black curls and his sapphire eyes, but never for a moment had he suspected that the boy was not a boy at all. Although, the captain had to admit, it was a neat solution to the somewhat distressing feelings he'd been having lately.

"I suppose you have an explanation for this," he drawled, leaning back against his cabin door and crossing sun-bronzed arms across his muscular chest.

The young lady—girl, really, for she could have been no more than seventeen—clutched her cotton shirt to the white swell of bosom that had betrayed her and with the other hand pushed damp curls, the other legacy of her interrupted wash, off her face.

"I needed to get to Jamaica," she said proudly, although her low voice held the trace of a quaver, "and this was the only way I could think of."

"You could have paid for your passage," the captain suggested dryly, his gaze traveling appreciatively along the delicate curve of her shoulders.

"I had nothing to pay with."

He straightened and stepped forward, smiling. "I think you underestimate your charms."

"Come on, Smith, kick him right in his windswept desire." Henry Fitzroy leaned back in his chair and rubbed at his temples. Just how much of a shit did he want the captain to be? Should the hero's better nature overcome his wanton lust or did he even have a better nature? And how much of a hero would he be without one?

"And frankly, my dear," he sighed, "I don't give a damn." He saved the night's work, then shut down the system. Usually he enjoyed the opening chapters of a new book, getting to know the characters, warping them to fit the demands of the plot, but this time. . . .

Rolling his chair back from the desk, he stared out his office window at the sleeping city. Somewhere out there, hidden by the darkness, a hunter stalked—blinded, maddened, driven by blood lust and hunger. He'd sworn to stop it, but he hadn't the slightest idea how to start. How could the location of random slaughter be anticipated?

With another sigh, he stood. There'd been twenty-four hours without a death. Maybe the problem had taken care of itself. He grabbed his coat and headed out of the apartment.

The morning paper should be out by now, I'll grab one and . . . Waiting for the elevator, he checked his watch. 6:10. It was much later than he'd thought. . . . *and trust I can make it back inside without igniting.* Sunrise was around 6:30 if he remembered correctly. He wouldn't have much time, but he had to know if there had been another killing. If the load of completely irrational guilt he carried for not finding and stopping the child had gotten any heavier.

The national paper had a box just outside his building. The headline concerned a speech the Prime Minister had just made in the Philippines about north/south relations.

"And I bet he works on the south until at least mid-May." Henry said, drawing his leather trench coat tighter around his throat as a cold wind swept around the building and pulled tears from his eyes.

The tabloid's closest box was down the block and across the street. There wasn't really any need to look for the other local paper, Henry had every faith in the tabloid's headline. He waited at the light while the opening volley of the morning rush hour laid a nearly solid line of moving steel along Bloor Street, then crossed, digging for change.

"LEAFS LOSE BIG."

Death of playoff hopes, perhaps, but not a death Henry need worry about. With a sense of profound relief—lightly tinted with exasperation; the Leafs were in the worst division in the NHL, after all—he tucked the paper under his arm, turned, and realized the sun was about to clear the horizon.

He could feel it trembling on the edge of the world and it took all his strength not to panic.

The elevator, the red light, the headlines, all had taken more time than he had. How he had allowed this to happen after more than four hundred and fifty years of racing the sun to safety was not important now. Regaining the sanctuary of his apartment was the only thing that mattered. He could feel the heat of the sun on the edges of his consciousness, not a physical presence, not yet, although that and the burning would come soon enough, but an awareness of the threat, of how close he stood to death.

The light he needed was red again, a small mocking sun in a box. The pounding of his heart counting off the seconds, Henry flung himself onto the street. Brakes squealed and the fender of a wildly swerving van brushed against his thigh like a caress. He ignored the sudden pain and the driver's curses, slammed his palm against the hood of a car almost small enough to leap, and dove through a space barely a prayer wider than his twisting body.

The sky turned gray, then pink, then gold.

Leather soles slamming against the pavement, Henry raced along shadow, knowing that fire devoured it behind him and lapped at his heels. Terror fought with the lethargy that daylight wrapped around his kind, and terror won. He reached the smoked glass door to his building seconds before the sun.

It touched only the back of one hand, too slowly snatched to safety.

Cradling the blistered hand against his chest, Henry used the pain to goad himself toward the elevator. Although the diffused light could no longer burn, he was still in danger.

"You all right, Mr. Fitzroy?" The guard frowned with concern as he buzzed open the inner door.

Unable to focus, Henry forced his head around to where he knew the guard would be. "Migraine," he whispered and lurched forward.

The purely artificial light in the elevator revived him a little and he managed to walk down the corridor dragging only a part of his weight along the wall. He feared for a moment that the keys were beyond his remaining dexterity, but somehow he got the heavy door open, closed, and locked behind him. Here was safety.

Safety. That word alone carried him into the shelter of the bedroom where thick blinds denied the sun. He swayed, sighed, and finally let go, collapsing across the bed and allowing the day to claim him.

* * *

"Vicki, please!"

Vicki frowned, a visit to the ophthalmologist never put her in what could be called a good mood and all this right-eye, left-eye focusing was giving her a major headache. "What?" she growled through gritted teeth—only incidentally a result of the chin rest.

"You're looking directly at the test target."

"So?"

Dr. Anderson hid a sigh and, with patience developed during the raising of two children, explained, not for the first time, her tone noncommittal and vaguely soothing. "Looking directly at the test target negates the effects of the test and we'll just have to do it all over again."

And they would, too. Over and over again if necessary. Holding back a sharp comment behind the thin line of her lips, Vicki attempted to cooperate.

"Well?" she prodded at last as Dr. Anderson flicked off the perimeter light and motioned for her to raise her head.

"It hasn't gotten any worse. . . ."

Vicki leaned back, watching the doctor's face. "Has it gotten any better?" she asked pointedly.

This time, Dr. Anderson didn't bother to hide the sigh. "Vicki, as I've told you before, retinitis pigmentosa doesn't get better. Ever. It only gets worse. Or," she rolled the perimeter back against the wall, "if you're very lucky, the degeneration reaches a point and goes no further."

"Have I reached that point?"

"Only time will tell. You've been pretty lucky already," she continued, raising a hand to forestall Vicki's next comment, "in many cases, this disease is accompanied by other types of neurodegenerative conditions."

"Deafness, mild retardation, premature senility, and truncal obesity." Vicki snorted. "We went through all this in the beginning, and none of it changes the fact that I have effectively no night vision, the outside edge of my peripheral vision has moved in twenty-five degrees, and I've suddenly become myopic.''

"*That* might have happened anyway.''

Vicki shoved her glasses up her nose. "Very comforting. When can I expect to go blind?''

The nails of Dr. Anderson's right hand beat a tattoo against her prescription pad. "You may *never* go blind and, in spite of your condition, at the moment you have perfectly functional vision. You mustn't let this make you bitter.''

"My condition," Vicki snarled, standing and reaching for her coat, "as you call it, caused me to leave a job I loved that made a difference for the better in the slime-pit this city is becoming and if it's all the same to you, I think I'd rather be bitter.'' She didn't quite slam the door on the way out.

* * *

"What's the matter, darling, you don't look happy?''

"It hasn't been a great day, Mrs. Kopolous.''

The older woman clicked her tongue and shook her head at the family size bag of cheese balls Vicki had laid on the counter. "So I see, so I see. You should eat real food, darling, if you want to feel better. This stuff is no good for you. And it makes your fingers orange.''

Vicki scooped up her change and dropped it into the depths of her purse. Soon she'd have to deal with the small fortune jangling around down there. "Some moods, Mrs. Kopolous, only junk food can handle.''

The phone was ringing when she reached her apartment.

"Yeah, what?''

"There's something about the sound of your dulcet tones that makes this whole wretched day worthwhile.''

"Stuff a sock in it, Celluci.'' Phone balanced under her chin, Vicki struggled out of her coat. "Whadda you want?''

"My, my, sounds like someone's wearing the bishop's shoes.''

Against every inclination, Vicki grinned. His use of

that particular punch line in conversation always did it to her. He knew it, too. "No, I did not get up on the wrong side of the bed this morning," she told him, hooking her office chair over and throwing herself down into it. "As you very well know. But I did just get back from a visit to the ophthalmologist."

"Ah." She could picture him leaning back, his feet up on the desk. Every superior he'd ever had had tried to break him of the habit with no noticeable success. "The eye doctor of doom. Is it any better?"

If he'd sounded sympathetic, she'd have thrown the phone across the room but he only sounded interested. "It doesn't get any better, Celluci."

"Oh, I don't know; I read this article that said large doses of vitamin A and E can improve the visual field and enhance dark adaptation." He was obviously quoting.

Vicki couldn't decide whether to be touched or furious that he'd been reading up. Given her mood. . . . "Do something more useful with your time, Celluci, only abetalipoproteinaemia RP includes biochemical defects," he hadn't been the only one reading up, "and that isn't what I've got."

"Abetalipo*protein*aemia," he corrected her pronunciation, "and excuse me for caring. I also found out that a number of people lead completely normal lives with what you've got." He paused and she heard him take a drink of what was undoubtedly cold coffee. "Not," he continued, his voice picking up an edge, "that you ever lived what could be called a normal life."

She ignored the last comment, picked up a black marker and began venting frustrations with it on the back of her credit card bill. "I'm living a completely normal life," she snapped.

"Running away and hiding?" The tone missed sarcasm but not by very much. "You could've stayed on the force. . . ."

"I *knew* you'd start again." She spat the words from between clenched teeth, but Mike Celluci's angry voice overrode the diatribe she was about to begin and the bitterness in it shut her up.

". . . but oh no, you couldn't stand the thought that you wouldn't be the hot-shit investigator anymore, the fair-haired girl with all the answers, that you'd just be a part of the team. You quit because you couldn't stand not being on the top of the pile and if you weren't on top, if you couldn't be on top, you weren't going to play! So you ran away. You took your pail and your shovel and you fucking quit! You walked out on me, Nelson, not just the job!"

Through all the fights—after the diagnosis and after her resignation—*that* was what he'd wanted to say. It summed up the hours of arguing, the screaming matches, the slammed doors. Vicki knew it, knew it the way she knew when she found the key, the little seemingly insignificant thing that solved the case. Everything about that last sentence said, *this is it*.

"You'd have done the same thing, Celluci," she said quietly and although her knuckles were white around the receiver, she set it gently back on the phone. Then she threw the marker in her other hand across the room.

Her anger went with it.

He really cares about you, Vicki. Why is that such a problem?

Because lovers are easy to get and friends good enough to scream at are a lot rarer.

Running both hands through her hair, she sighed. He was right and she'd admitted as much by her response. As soon as he realized she was right as well, they could go on building the new parameters of their relationship. Unless, it suddenly occurred to her, last night had been the farewell performance that enabled him to finally come clean.

If it was, she pushed her glasses up her nose, *at least I had the last word*. As such things went, it wasn't much of a comfort.

* * *

"Well, if it isn't old Norman. How you doing, Norman? Mind if we sit down?" Without waiting for an answer the young man hooked a chair out from under the table and sat. The four other members of his party noisily followed his lead.

When the scramble for space ended, Norman found himself crammed between the broad shoulders of two jocks he knew only as Roger and Bill, the three of them staring across the round table at three young ladies. He recognized the blonde—he usually saw her hanging on Roger's arm—and as the girl next to Bill was being awfully friendly he supposed she was with him. That left one extra. He grinned wolfishly at her. He'd been practicing the grin in his bathroom mirror.

She looked puzzled, then snorted and turned away.

"It was real nice of old Norman to keep this table for us, wasn't it, Bill?"

"It sure was." Bill leaned a little closer and Norman gasped for breath as his available space narrowed drastically. "If it wasn't for old Norman, we'd be sitting on the floor."

Norman looked around. The Friday night crowd at the Cock and Bull had filled the basement pub. "Well, I, uh. . . ." He shrugged. "I, uh, knew you were coming."

"Of course you did," Bill grinned at him, a little disconcerted to find that the Birdwell-nerd was at least as tall as he was. "I was saying to Roger here before we came in, it wouldn't be Friday night if we didn't spend part of it with old Norman."

Roger laughed and all three of the girls grinned. Norman didn't get the joke, but he preened at the attention.

He bought the first round of beer. "After all, it's my table."

"And the only empty one in the place," the blonde muttered.

He bought the second round as well. "Because I've got lots and lots of money." The wad of twenties he pulled out of the pocket of his windbreaker—five thousand dollars in small unmarked bills had been the third thing he'd asked for—caused a simultaneous dropping of jaws around the table.

"Jesus Christ, Norman, what did you do, rob a bank?"

"I didn't have to," Norman said airily. "And there's plenty more where that came from."

He insisted on buying the third and fourth rounds and on switching to imported beer. "Imported beer is classier," he confided to the shoulder of Roger's leather jacket, Roger having moved his ear out of range. "It really gets the chicks."

"Chicks?" The echo had a dangerous edge to it.

"Consider the source, Helen." Bill deftly removed the glass from her hand—both hand and glass having been threateningly raised—and drained it. "You'd just be wasting the beer."

The five burst out laughing again and again, not understanding, Norman joined in. No one would think he wasn't with it.

When they started getting up, he rose with them. The room swayed. He'd never had four beers in quick succession before. In fact, he wasn't entirely certain he'd ever had four beers before. "Where we going?"

"*We* are going to a private party," Bill told him, a beefy hand pushing him back into his seat.

"You just stay here, Norman," Roger patted him on the other shoulder.

Confused, Norman looked from one to the other. They were leaving without him?

"Jesus, it's like kicking a puppy," Bill muttered.

Roger nodded in agreement. "Uh, look, Norman, it's invitation only. We'd bring you if we could. . . ."

They *were* leaving without him. He pointed across the table, his voice an accusatory whine, "But she's supposed to be for me."

Expressions of guilty sympathy changed to disgust and Norman quickly found himself alone, Helen's voice drifting back from the door, somehow audible in spite of the noise level in the pub. "I'd give him back his beer if I didn't hate vomiting so much."

Trying unsuccessfully to flag the waitress, Norman scowled into the beer rings on the table. She *was* supposed to be for him. He knew she was. They were cheating him. With the tip of a shaking finger, he drew a five pointed star in the spilled liquid on the tabletop, his vows of the day before forgotten. He'd show them.

His stomach protested suddenly and he lurched toward the bathrooms, hand clutched over his mouth.

I'll show them, he thought, his head dangling over the toilet. *But maybe . . . not tonight.*

* * *

Henry handed the young man seated just inside the door a twenty. "What's on for tonight?" He didn't quite have to yell to make himself heard over the music but, then, the night was young.

"The usual." Three rolls of tickets were pulled from the cavernous left pocket of the oversized suit jacket while the money slid into the right. A number of after-hours clubs had been switching to tickets so that if, or more likely when, they were busted they could argue that they hadn't been selling drinks. Just tickets.

"Guess it'll have to be a usual, then."

"Right. Two trendy waters." The pair of tickets changed hands. "You know, Henry, you're paying a hell of a lot for piss and bubbles."

Henry grinned down at him and swept an arm around the loft. "I'm paying for the ambience, Thomas."

"Ambience my ass," Thomas snorted genially. "Hey, I just remembered, Alex got a case of halfway decent burgundy. . . ."

It wouldn't have taken a stronger man than Henry Fitzroy to resist. "No thanks, Thomas, I don't drink . . . wine." He turned to face the room and, just for a moment, saw another gathering.

The clothes, peacock bright velvets, satins, and laces turned the length of the room into a glittering kaleidoscope of color. He hated coming to Court and would appear only when his father demanded it. The false flattery, the constant jockeying for position and power, the soul destroying balancing act that must be performed to keep both the block and the pyre at bay; all this set the young Duke of Richmond's teeth on edge.

As he made his way across the salon, each face that

turned to greet him wore an identical expression—a mask of brittle gaiety over ennui, suspicion, and fear in about an equal mix.

Then the heavy metal beat of Anthrax drove "Greensleeves" back into the past. The velvet and jewels spun away into black leather, paste, and plastic. The brittle gaiety now covered ennui alone. Henry supposed it was an improvement.

I should be on the street, he thought, making his way to the kitchen/bar, brushing past discussions of the recent killings and the creatures they had been attributed to. *I will not find the child up here. . . .* But the child hadn't fed since Tuesday night and so perhaps had passed through the frenzy and moved to the next part of its metamorphosis. *But the parent. . . .* His hands clenched into fists, the right pulling painfully against the bandage and the blisters beneath it. *The parent must still be found.* That he could do up here. Twice before in Alex's loft he had tasted another predator in the air. Then, he had let it go, the blood scent of so many people made tracking a competitor a waste of time. Tonight, if it happened again, he would waste the time.

Suddenly, he noticed that a path was opening before him as he made his way across the crowded room and he hastily schooled his expression. The men and women gathered here, with faces painted and precious metals dangling, were still close enough to their primitive beginnings to recognize a hunter walking among them.

That's three times now; the guard, the sun, and this. You'll bring the stakes down on yourself if you're not more careful, you fool. What was the matter with him lately?

"Hey, Henry, long time since you bin by." Alex, the owner of the loft wrapped a long, bare arm around Henry's shoulders, shoved an open bottle of water into his hand, and steered him deftly away from the bar. "I got someone who needs to see you, mon."

"Someone who *needs* to see me?" Henry allowed himself to be steered. It was the way most people dealt with Alex, resistance just took too much energy. "Who?"

Alex grinned down from his six-foot-four vantage point and winked broadly. "Ah, now, that would be tellin'. Whach you do to your hand?"

Henry glanced down at the bandage. Even in the dim light of the studio it seemed to glow against the black leather of his cuff. "Burned myself."

"Burns is bad stuff, mon. Were you cookin'?"

"You could say that." His lips twitched although he sternly told himself it wasn't funny.

"What's the joke?"

"It'd take too long to explain. How about you explaining something to me?"

"You ahsk, mon. I answer."

"Why the fake Jamaican accent?"

"Fake?" Alex's voice rose above the music and a half a dozen people ducked as he windmilled his free arm. "Fake? There's nothing fake about this accent, mon. I'm gettin' back to my roots."

"Alex, you're from Halifax."

"I got deeper roots than that, you betcha." He gave the shorter man a push forward and, dropping the accent, added, "Here you go, shrimp, delivered as ordered."

The woman sitting on the steps to Alex's locked studio stood considerably shorter even than Henry's five six. Her lack of height, combined with baggy jeans and an oversized sweater, gave her a waiflike quality completely at odds with the cropped platinum hair and the intensity of her expression.

Sliding out from Alex's arm, Henry executed a perfect sixteenth century court bow—not that anyone in the room could identify it as such. "Isabelle," he intoned gravely.

Isabelle snorted, reached out, grabbed his lapels, and yanked his mouth against hers.

Henry returned the kiss enthusiastically, skillfully parrying her tongue away from the sharp points of his teeth. He hadn't been certain he was going to feed tonight. He was certain now.

"Well, if you two are going to indulge in such rampant heterosexuality, in *my* house yet, I'm going." With an exaggerated limp-wristed wave, Alex sashayed off into the crowd.

"He'll change personalities again before he gets to the door," Henry observed settling himself on the step. The length of their thighs touched and he could feel his hunger growing.

"Alex has more masks than anyone I know," Isabelle agreed, retrieving her beer bottle and picking at the label.

Henry stroked one finger along the curve of her brow. It had been bleached near white to match her hair. "We all wear masks."

Isabelle raised the brow out from under his finger. "How profound. And do we all unmask at midnight?"

"No." He couldn't stop the melancholy from sounding in his voice as he realized the source of his recent discontent. It had been so long, so very long, since he'd been able to trust someone with the reality of what he was and all that meant. So long since he'd been able to find a mortal he could build a bond with based on more than sex and blood. And that a child could be created out of the deepest bond that vampire and mortal could share, then abandoned, sharpened his loneliness to a cutting edge.

He felt Isabelle's hand stroke his cheek, saw the puzzled compassion on her face, and with an inward curse realized his mask had slipped for the second time that night. If he didn't find someone who could accept him soon, he feared the choice would be taken from him, his need exposing him whether he willed it or not.

"So," with an effort, he brought himself back to the moment, "how was the gig?"

"It was March. It was Sudbury." She shrugged, returning to the moment with him, if that was how he wanted it. "Not much else to add."

If you can't share the reality, there are worse things than having someone to share the masks. His gaze dropped to a faint line of blue disappearing beneath the edge of her sweater and the thought of the blood moving so close beneath the surface quickened his breath. It was hunger, not lust, but he supposed in the end they were much the same thing. "How long will you be in town?"

"Only tonight and tomorrow."

"Then we shouldn't waste the time we have."

She twined her fingers in his, carefully ignoring the bandage, and pulled him with her as she stood. "I thought you'd never ask."

* * *

Saturday night, at 11:15, Norman realized he was out of charcoal for the hibachi and the only local store he'd been able to find it in had closed at nine. He considered substitutions and then decided he'd better not mess with a system that worked.

Saturday night passed quietly.

Sunday night. . . .

* * *

"Damn. Damn! DAMN!"

Mrs. Kopolous clicked her tongue and frowned. Not at Vicki's profanity, as she might have on any other day, but at the headline of the tabloid now lying on her counter.

"VAMPIRE KILLS STUDENT; Young man found drained in York Mills."

Four

"Good God, would you look at old Norman."

"Why?" Roger pulled his head out of his locker and turned around. He could feel his jaw quite literally drop. " 'Good God' doesn't quite cover it, my man. I wish Bill were here to see this."

"Where is he?"

Roger shrugged, not taking his eyes from the sartorial splendor of Norman Birdwell. "Beats me. But he'll shit if he misses this."

Norman, conscious of eyes upon him, threw a bit more of a swagger into his walk. The chain hanging from his new black leather jacket chimed softly against the small of his back. He squinted down at the sterling silver toe caps on his authentic style cowboy boots and wondered if maybe he shouldn't have gotten spurs as well. His new black jeans, tighter than he'd ever worn before, made an almost smug shik shik sound as the inseams rubbed together.

He'd shown them. Thought he wasn't cool, did they? Thought he was some kind of a nerd, did they? Well, they'd be thinking differently now. Norman's chin went up. They wanted cool? He'd show them *cold*. Tonight he was going to ask for a red Porsche. He'd learn to drive later.

"What the hell is that?"

Roger grinned. "Now aren't you glad you weren't any later?" he asked, shoving a friendly elbow into Bill's ribs. "Kinda takes your breath away, doesn't it?"

"If you mean it makes me want to gag, you're close." Bill sagged against his locker and shook his head. "How the hell is he paying for all of that?"

"So go ask him."

"Why not. . . ." Bill straightened and stepped away from his locker just as Norman passed by.

Norman saw him, allowed their eyes to meet for a second, then moved on, chortling silently to himself, *"Ha! Snubbed you. Let's see how you like it."*

The question of payment dead in his mouth, Bill stood staring until Roger moved up beside him and slugged him in the arm.

"Hey, what's wrong?"

Bill shook his head. "There's something different about Birdwell."

Roger snorted. "Yeah, new threads and an attitude. But underneath he's the same old Norman the Nerd."

"Yeah, I guess you're right." But he wasn't. And it wasn't something Bill could explain. He felt as though he'd reached under the bed and something rotten had squished through his fingers—a normal, everyday action gone horribly awry.

Norman, aware he'd made an impression—Norman, who in a fit of pique had decided he didn't care if a stranger had to die—Norman strutted on.

* * *

"Victoria Nelson?"

"Yes?" Vicki peered down at the young woman—*girl, really, if she's out of her teens it's by hours only*—standing outside her apartment door. "If you're selling something. . . ."

"Victoria Nelson, the Private Investigator?"

Vicki considered it a moment before answering and then said slowly, "Yes. . . ."

"I have a job for you."

The words were delivered with the intensity only the very young can muster and Vicki found herself hiding a smile.

The girl tossed unnaturally brilliant red curls back off her face. "I can pay, if that's what you're worried about."

As the question of money hadn't even begun to cross Vicki's mind, she grunted noncommittally. They locked eyes for a moment—*Tinted contacts, I thought so. Well they go with the hair.*—then she added, in much the same noncommittal tone, "Most people call first."

"I thought about it." The shrug was so minimal as to be almost nonexistent and her voice was completely non-apologetic. "I figured the case would be harder to turn down in person."

Vicki found herself holding he door open wider. "I suppose you'd better come in." Work wasn't so scarce she had to take jobs from children, but it wouldn't hurt to hear what the girl had to say. "Another thirty seconds in the hall and Mr. Chin'll be showing up to see what's going on."

"Mr. Chin?"

"The old man who lives downstairs likes to know what's going on, likes to pretend he doesn't speak English."

Sliding past Vicki in the narrow hall, the girl sniffed, obviously disapproving. "Maybe he *doesn't* speak English," she pointed out.

This time, Vicki didn't bother to hide her smile. "Mr. Chin has been speaking English a lot longer than both of us have been alive. His parents came to Vancouver in the late 1880s. He used to teach high school. He still teaches English as a Second Language at the Chinese Community Center."

Bright green eyes narrowed accusingly and the girl glared up at Vicki. "I don't like being patronized," she said.

Vicki nodded as she closed the door. "Neither do I."

During the silence that followed, Vicki could almost hear their conversation being replayed, each phrase, each word tested for nuance.

"Oh," the girl said at last. "Sorry." Then her brow unfurrowed and she grinned as she offered a compro-mise. "I won't do it anymore if you'd don't."

"Deal." Vicki led the way through her tiny living room, pushing her leather recliner back upright as she passed, to her equally tiny office. She'd never actually had a client, or potential client, in the office before and there were a couple of unanticipated problems. "I'll, uh, get another chair from the kitchen."

"It's okay. This is fine." Shrugging out of her coat she settled both herself and it on Vicki's weight bench. "Now, about this job. . . ."

"Not yet." Vicki pulled her own chair out from the desk and sat down. "First, about you. Your name is?"

"Coreen, Coreen Fergus." She continued on the same breath, obviously feeling that her name covered all the necessary details. "And I want you to find that vampire that's been terrorizing the city."

"Right." It was too early on a Monday and the latest death was too close. "Did Michael Celluci put you up to this?"

"Who?"

"Never mind." Shaking her head, Vicki stood. "Look, I don't know *who* put you up to this but you can go back to them and. . . ."

"Ian Reddick was my . . ." She frowned, searching for a word that would give the relationship its proper weight. ". . . lover."

"Ian Reddick," Vicki repeated and sat down again. Ian Reddick, the first victim. The body she'd found mutilated in the Eglinton West subway station.

"I want you to find the thing that killed him."

"Look, Coreen," her voice dropped into the professional "comfort tone" that police officers worldwide had to master, "I recognize how upset you must be, but don't you think that's a job for the authorities?"

"No."

There was something utterly intractable in that "no." Vicki pushed her glasses up her nose and searched for a response while Coreen continued.

"They insist on looking for a man, refusing to acknowledge that the paper might be right; refusing to consider anything outside their narrow little world view."

"Refusing to consider that the killer might actually be a vampire?"

"Right."

"The paper doesn't really believe it's a vampire either, you know."

Coreen tossed her hair back off her face. "So? The facts still fit. The blood is still missing. I bet Ian would have been drained dry if he hadn't been found so quickly."

She doesn't know it was me. Thank God. And again she saw him, his face a clichéd mask of terror above the gaping red wound that was his throat. Gaping red wound . . . no, more as though the whole front of his throat had been ripped away. Not ripped through, ripped away. *That* was what had been missing; the incongruity that had been nagging at her for over a week now. Where was the front of Ian Reddick's throat?

". . . so will you?"

Vicki slowly surfaced from memory. "Let me get this straight. You want me to find Ian's killer, working under the assumption that it really is a vampire? Bats, coffins, the whole bit."

"Yes."

"And once I've found it, I drive a stake through its heart?"

"Creatures of the night can hardly be brought to trial," Coreen pointed out reasonably but with a martial light in her eye. "Ian must be avenged."

Don't get sad, get even. It was a classic solution to grief and one Vicki didn't altogether disapprove of. "Why me?" she asked.

Coreen sat up straighter. "You were the only female private investigator in the yellow pages."

That, at least, made sense and explained the eerie coincidence of Coreen showing up in the office of the woman who'd found Ian's body. *"Out of all the gin joints in all the. . . ."* She couldn't remember the rest of the quote but she was beginning to understand how Bogart had felt. "It wouldn't be cheap." *What am I cautioning her for? I am not going vampire hunting.*

"I can afford the best. Daddy pays me a phenomenal amount of guilt money. He ran off with his executive assistant when I was in junior high."

Vicki shook her head. "Mine ran off with his secretary when I was in sixth grade and I never got a cent out of him. Times change. Was she young and pretty?"

"He," Coreen corrected. "And yes, very pretty. They've opened a new law practice in the Bahamas."

"As I said, times change." Vicki pushed her glasses up her nose and sighed. Vampire hunting. Except it wouldn't have to be that. Just find whoever, or whatever, killed Ian Reddick. Exactly what she'd be doing if she were still on the force. Lord knew they were undermannned and could use the help.

Coreen, who had kept her gaze locked on the older woman's face, smiled triumphantly and dug for her checkbook.

* * *

"Michael Celluci, please."

"One moment."

Vicki tapped her nails against the side of the phone as she waited for the call to be put through. Ian Reddick's throat had been missing and Celluci, the arrogant shit, hadn't thought to mention whether it had been found or if the other bodies were in the same condition. She didn't really care at this point if he wasn't speaking to her 'cause she was bloody well going to speak to him.

"Criminal Investigation Bureau, Detective-Sergeant Graham."

"Dave? It's Vicki Nelson. I need to talk to Celluci."

"He's not here right now, Vicki. Can I help?"

From her brief experience with him, Vicki knew Dave to be, if possible, a worse liar than she was. And if he couldn't lie convincingly for important things he certainly couldn't do it just to protect his partner's ass. Trust Celluci to get out before the heat came down. "I need a favor."

"Shoot."

The wording became crucial here. It had to sound like she knew more than she did or Dave might clam up and retreat to the official party line. Although, with luck, the acquired habit of answering her questions could last around the department for years. "The hunk of throat missing from the first body, did anyone ever find it?"

"Nope."

So far so good. "What about the others?"

"Not a sign."

"Not even last night's?"

"Not yet anyway. Why?"

"Just sitting here wondering. Thanks, Dave. Tell your partner from me that he's a tight-lipped horse's ass." She hung up and stared at the far wall. Maybe Celluci had been holding the information back to ensure he had bargaining power in the future. Maybe. Maybe he quite honestly forgot to tell her. Ha! Maybe pigs would fly, but she doubted it.

Right now, she had more important things to consider. Like what kind of creature walked off with six square inches of throat as well as twelve pints of blood?

The subway roared out of Eglinton West toward Lawrence and, with the station momentarily deserted, Vicki strode purposefully for the workman's access at the southern end of the northbound platform. This was now her case and she couldn't stand working with secondhand information. She'd see the alcove where the killer allegedly disappeared for herself.

At the top of the short flight of concrete stairs, she paused, her blood pounding unnaturally loudly in her ears. She had always considered herself immune to foolish superstitions, race memories, and night terrors, but faced with the tunnel, stretching dark and seemingly endless like the lair of some great worm, she was suddenly incapable of taking the final step off the platform. The hair on the back of her neck rose as she remembered how, on the night Ian Reddick had died, she'd been certain that something deadly lingered in the tunnel. The feeling itself hadn't returned, but the memory replayed with enough strength to hold her.

This is ridiculous. Pull yourself together, Nelson. There's nothing down in that tunnel that could hurt you. Her right foot slid forward half a step. *The worst thing you're likely to run into is a TTC official and a trespassing charge.* Her left foot moved up and passed the right. *Good God, you're acting like some stupid teenager in a horror movie.* Then she stood on the first step. The second. The third. Then she was on the narrow concrete strip that provided a safe passage along the outside rail.

See. Nothing to it. She wiped suddenly sweaty palms on her coat and dug in her purse for her flashlight, then, with the satisfyingly solid weight of it in her hand, flooded the tunnel with light. She would have preferred not to use it, away from the harsh fluorescents of the station, the tunnel existed more in a surreal twilight than a true darkness, but her night-sight had deteriorated to the point where even twilight had become impenetrable. The anger her condition always caused wiped away the last of the fear.

She rather hoped something was skulking in her path. For starters, she'd feed it the flashlight.

Pushing her glasses up her nose, her gaze locked on the beam of light, Vicki moved carefully along the access path. If the trains were on schedule—and while the TTC wasn't up to Mussolini, it did all right—the next one wouldn't be along for another, she checked the glowing dial of her watch, eight minutes. Plenty of time.

She reached the first workman's alcove with six minutes remaining and sniffed disapprovingly at the evidence of police investigation. "Sure, boys," she muttered, playing the light around the concrete walls, "mess it up for the next person."

The hole Celluci's team had dug was about waist level in the center of the back wall and about eight inches in diameter. Stepping over chips of concrete, Vicki leaned forward for a better look. There was, as Celluci said, nothing but dirt behind the excavation.

"So if he didn't come in here," she frowned, "where did he. . . ." Then she noticed the crack that ran the length of the wall, into and out of the exploratory hole. A closer look brought her nose practically in contact with the concrete. The faint hint of a familiar smell had her digging for her Swiss army knife and carefully scraping the edges of the dark recess.

The flakes on the edge of the stainless steel blade showed red-brown in the flashlight beam. They could have been rust. Vicki touched one to the tip of her tongue. They could have been rust, but they weren't. She had a pretty good idea whose blood she'd found but brushed the remaining flakes into a plastic sandwich bag anyway. Then she squatted and ran the blade up under the crack at the top edge of the hole.

Even as she did it, she wasn't sure why. Most of Ian's blood had been sprayed over the subway station wall. There could not have been enough blood on the killer's clothes to have soaked all the way through a crack in six inches of concrete even if he'd been wearing paper towels and had remained plastered against the wall for the entire night.

When she pulled out the knife, mixed in with dirt and bits of cement, were similar red-brown flakes. These went into another bag and then she quickly repeated the procedure at the bottom edge of the hole with the same results.

The roar of the subway became a welcome, normal kind of terror for the only explanation Vicki could come up with, as the alcove shook and a hundred tons of steel hurtled past, was that whatever killed Ian Reddick had somehow passed through the crack in the concrete wall.

And *that* was patently ridiculous.

Wasn't it?

As the largest producer and wholesaler of polyester clothing, Sigman's Incorporated didn't exactly run a high security building. Since the murder of Terri Neal in the underground parking lot, they'd tried to tighten things up.

In spite of four and a half pages of new admittance regulations, the guard in the lobby glanced up as Vicki strode past, then went back to his book. In gray corduroy pants, black desert boots, and her navy pea jacket she could have been any one of the hundreds of women who came through the area every day and he was neither expected nor encouraged to stop all of them. She certainly wasn't the press—the guard had grown adept at spotting the ladies and gentlemen of the fifth estate and herding them off to the proper authorities. She didn't look like a cop, and besides, cops always checked in. She looked like she knew where she was going, so the guard decided not to interfere. In his opinion, the world could use a few more people who knew where they were going.

At 2:30 in the afternoon, the underground parking garage was empty of people which explained pretty much exactly why Vicki was there at that time. She stepped off the elevator and frowned up at the whining fluorescent lights. *Why the hell don't they have security cameras down here?* she wondered as the echoes of her footsteps bounced off the stained concrete walls.

Even without the scuffed and faded chalk marks she could tell where the body had fallen. The surrounding cars had been crammed together, leaving an open area over three spaces wide, as if violent death were somehow contagious.

She found what she'd come looking for tucked almost under an ancient rust and blue sedan. Her lower lip caught between her teeth, she pulled out her knife and knelt beside the crack. The blade slid in its full six inches, but the bottom of the crack was deeper still. The red-brown flakes that came up on the steel had most certainly not dropped off the wreck.

She sat back on her heels and frowned. "I really, really don't like the looks of this."

Fishing a marble from the bottom of her bag, she placed it on one of the remaining chalk marks and gave it a little push. It rolled toward the wall, moving away from the crack at almost a forty-five degree angle. Further experiments produced similar results. Blood, or for that matter anything else, could not have traveled from the body to the crack in any way that might be called natural.

"Not that there's anything even remotely natural about any of this," she muttered, tucking this third sandwich bag of dried blood in beside the others and crawling after her marble.

Rather than go back through the building, she climbed up the steeply graded driveway and out onto St. Clair Avenue West.

"Excuse me!"

The attendant in the booth looked up from his magazine.

Vicki waved a hand back down the drive in the general direction of the underground garage. "Do you know what's under the bottom layer of concrete?"

He looked in the direction she indicated, looked back at her, and repeated, "Under the concrete?"

"Yeah."

"Dirt, lady."

She smiled and eased around the barricade. "Thanks. You've been a great help. I'll show myself out."

The chain link fence protested slightly and sagged forward under Vicki's weight as she peered down into the construction site. It was, at the moment, little more than a huge hole in the ground filled with smaller holes, filled with muddy water. All the machinery appeared to have been removed and work stopped. Whether because of the murder or the weather, Vicki had no way of knowing.

"Well," she shoved her hands down into the pockets of her coat, "there's definitely dirt." If there was any blood, it was beyond finding.

"No problem, Vicki." Rajeet Mohadevan tucked the three sandwich bags into the pocket of her lab coat. "I can run them through before I head home tonight with no one the wiser. Are you going to be around the building?"

"No." Vicki saw the flicker of sympathy across the researcher's face but decided to ignore it. Rajeet was doing her a favor, after all. "If I'm not at home, you can leave a message on the machine."

"Same number?"

"Same number."

Rajeet grinned. "Same message?"

Vicki found herself grinning back. The last time the police lab had called her at home had been in the worst of the fights between her and Celluci. "Different message."

"Pity." Rajeet gave an exaggerated sigh of disappointment as Vicki headed for the door. "I've forgotten a few of the places you told him to stuff his occurrence book." She sketched a salute—a reminder of the old days, when

Vicki had been an *intense* young woman in a uniform—
and returned to the report she'd been filling out before
the interruption.

Walking down the hall, the familiar white tiles of the
corridor wrapping around her like an old friend, Vicki
considered heading through the tunnel to headquarters
and checking to see if Celluci were at his desk. She could
tell him about the cracks, find out if he'd been withholding any more information from her, and . . . no. Given
his mood the last time they'd talked and given that he
hadn't called over the weekend, if she showed up now
she'd just interfere with his work and that was something
neither of them ever did. The work being what it was,
the work came first and the cracks were added questions,
not answers.

She was out of the building entirely when she realized
that the thought of seeing another cop sitting at what had
been *her* desk had not influenced her decision one way
or another. Feeling vaguely like she'd betrayed her past,
she hunched her shoulders against the late afternoon chill
and started for home.

For years Vicki had been promising to buy herself a
really good encyclopedia set. For years she'd been putting it off. The set she had, she'd bought at the grocery
store for five dollars and ninety-nine cents a volume with
every ten dollars worth of groceries. It didn't have a lot
to say about vampires.

"Legendary creatures, uh huh, central Europe, Vlad
the Impaler, Bram Stoker. . . ." Vicki pushed her glasses
up her nose and tried to remember the characteristics of
Stoker's Dracula. She'd seen the play years ago and
thought she might have read the book in high school—
only a lifetime or two back.

"He was stronger, faster, his senses were more
acute. . . ." She flicked the points off on her fingertips.
"He slept all day, came out at night, and he hung around
with a guy who ate flies. And spiders." Making a dis-
gusted face she turned back to the encyclopedia.

The vampire," she read, *"was said to be able to turn
into bats, wolves, mist, or vapor."* The ability to turn to

mist or vapor would explain the cracks, she realized. The victim's blood, being heavier, would precipitate out to coat the narrow passageway. "And a creature that rises from the grave should have no trouble moving through earth." Marking her place with an old phone bill, she heaved herself out of the recliner and turned the television on, suddenly needing sound in the apartment.

"This is crazy," she muttered, opening the book again and reading while she paced. Fantasy and reality were moving just a little too close for comfort, definitely too close for sitting still.

The remainder of the entry listed the various ways of dealing with the creatures, from ash stakes through mustard seed to the crucifix, going on in great detail about staking, beheading, and burning.

Vicki allowed the slender volume to fall closed and raised her head to look out the window. In spite of the street light glowing less than three meters from her apartment, she was very conscious of the darkness pressing against the glass. For a legendary creature, the methods of its destruction seemed to be taken very seriously indeed.

* * *

Behind the police barricade, something crouched low over the piece of sidewalk where the fourth body had been found. Although the night could hide no secrets from him and, unlike the others who had searched, he knew what to search for, he found nothing.

"Nothing," Henry murmured to himself as he stood. "And yet there should be something here." A child of his kind might be able to hide its tracks from human hunters but not from kin. He lifted his head and his nostrils flared to check the breeze. A cat—no, two—on hunts of their own, rain that would fall before morning, and. . . .

He frowned, brows drawing down into a deep vee. And what? He knew the smell of death in all its many manifestations and laid over the residue of this morning's slaying was a faint miasma of something older, more foul, almost familiar.

His memories stretched back over four hundred and fifty years. Somewhere in there. . . .

The police car was almost up on him before he saw it and the tiny sun in the heart of the searchlight had begun to glow before he moved.

"Holy shit! Did you see that?"

"See what?" Auxiliary Police Constable Wojtowicz stared out her window at the broad fan of light spilling out from the top of the slowly moving car.

"I don't know." PC Harper leaned forward over the steering wheel and peered past his partner. "I could've sworn I saw a man standing inside the barricades just as I flipped the light on."

Wojtowicz snorted. "Then we'd still be able to see him. Nobody moves that fast. And besides," she waved a hand at the view out the window, "there's nowhere to hide in that." That included the sidewalk, the barricades, and an expanse of muddy lawn. Although black shadows streamed away from every irregularity, none were large enough to hide a man.

"Think we should get out and look around?"

"You're the boss."

"Well. . . ." Nothing moved amid the stark contrast of light and shadow. Harper shook his head. The night had been making him jumpy lately; exposing nerves and plucking at them. "I guess you're right. There's nothing there."

"Of course I'm right." The car continued down the block and she reached over to shut the searchlight off. "You're just letting all this vampire stuff in the press get to you."

"You don't believe in vampires, do you?"

"Course not." Wojtowicz settled more comfortably into her seat. "Don't tell me you do?"

It was Harper's turn to snort. "I," he told her dryly, "have been audited."

Back on the lawn, one of the shadows lay, face pressed against the dirt, and remembered. The scent was stronger

here, mixed a third part with earth and blood, and it
brushed away the centuries.

It was London, 1593. Elizabeth was on the throne and
had been for some time. He'd been dead for fifty-seven
years. He'd been walking back from the theater, having
just seen the premiere presentation of *Richard the Third*.
On the whole, he'd enjoyed himself although he had a
feeling the playwright had taken a few liberties with the
personality of the king.

Out of a refuse-strewn alleyway, a young man had
stumbled—thin and disheveled but darkly handsome, very
drunk, and, clinging about him like his own personal bit
of fog, had been that same smell.

Henry had already fed from a whore behind the theater, but even if he hadn't, he would not have fed from
this man. The scent alone was enough to make him wary,
the not quite sane glitter in the dark eyes had only added
further warning.

"Most humbly, I beg your pardon." His voice, the
voice of an educated man, had been slurred almost beyond understanding. "But I have been in Hell this night
and am having some small difficulty in returning." He'd
giggled then, and executed a shaky bow in Henry's direction. "Christopher Marlowe at your service, milord.
Can you spare a few coppers for a drink?"

"Christopher Marlowe," Henry repeated softly into a
night more than four hundred years after that unhappy
man had died. He rolled onto his back and gazed up at
the clouds closing ranks over the stars. Although he had
read the play just after its posthumous publication in
1604, he wondered tonight for the first time just how
much research Marlowe had done before writing *The
Tragical History of Dr. Faustus.*

* * *

"Vicki, it's Rajeet. Sorry to call so late—uh, it's 11:15,
Monday night, I guess you've gone to bed—but I figured
you'd want to know the results of the tests. You have
positive matches with both Ian Reddick and Terri Neal.
I don't know what you've found, but I hope it helps."

Five

". . . although the police department refuses to issue a statement at this time, the Coroner's Office has confirmed that Mark Thompson, the fifth victim, has also been drained of blood. A resident, who wishes to remain nameless, living in the area of Don Mills Road and St. Dennis Drive, swears he saw a giant bat fly past his balcony just moments before the body was found. Jesus H. Christ." Vicki punched the paper down into a tightly wadded mass and flung it at the far wall. "Giant bats! No surprise he wants to remain nameless. Shit!"

The sudden shrill demand of the phone lifted her about four inches out of her chair. Scowling, she turned on it but at the last instant remembered that the call might be business and modified her response accordingly. A snarled, "What!" seldom impressed potential clients.

"Private investigations, Nelson speaking."

"Have you seen this morning's paper?!"

The voice was young, female, and not instantly identifiable. "Who is this, please?"

"It's me. Coreen Fergus. *Have* you seen this morning's paper?"

"Yes, Coreen, I have, but. . . ."

"Well, that proves it then, doesn't it."

"Proves what?" Tucking the phone under her chin, Vicki reached for her coffee. She had a feeling she was going to need it.

"About the vampire. There's a witness. Someone saw it!" Coreen's voice had picked up a triumphant tone.

Vicki took a deep breath. "A giant bat could be anything, Coreen. A blowing garbage bag, the shadow of an airplane, laundry falling off another balcony."

"And it could also be a giant bat. You are going to talk to this person, aren't you?"

It wasn't really a question and although Vicki had been deliberately not thinking about trying to find an unnamed source in the rabbit warren of apartments and townhouses around St. Dennis Drive, talking to "this person" was the next logical step. She reassured Coreen, promised to call the moment she had any results, and hung up.

"Like looking for a needle in a haystack." But it had to be done; a witness could break the case wide open.

She finished her coffee and checked her watch. There was one thing she wanted to check before she hit the pavement. 8:43. Cutting it close, but Brandon should still be at his desk.

He was.

After greetings were exchanged—perfunctory on one side at least—Vicki slid in the reason for her call. ". . . and you and I both know you've found things that you haven't told the papers."

"That's very true, Victoria." The coroner didn't even pretend not to understand. "But, as you know very well, I won't be able to tell these *things* to you either. I'm sorry, but you're no longer a member of the constabulary."

"But I have been hired to work on the case." Quickly, she outlined the pertinent parts of Coreen's visit for him, leaving out any mention of the young lady's personal belief as to the supernatural identity of the killer as well as the latest phone call.

"You've been hired as a private citizen, Victoria, and as such you have no more right to information than any other private citizen."

Vicki stifled a sigh and considered how best to approach this. When Brandon Singh meant no, he said it, straight out with no frills. And then he hung up. As long as he remained willing to talk he remained willing to be convinced. "Look, Brandon, you know my record. You know I have as good a chance as anyone in the city of solving this case. And you *know* you want it solved. I'll stand a better chance if I have all available information."

"Granted, but somehow this smacks of vigilantism."

"Vigilantism? Trust me, Brandon, I am not going to dress up in some silly costume and leap around making the city safe for decent people." She doodled a bat symbol on her notepad, then hastily crumpled the page up and tossed it away. Under the circumstances, bats were not a particularly apt motif. "All I'm doing is investigating. I swear I'll hand over everything I turn up to Violent Crimes."

"I believe you, Victoria." He paused and Vicki, fidgeting with impatience, jumped into the silence.

"With a killer of this caliber on the loose, can the city afford not to have me on the case, even in an auxiliary position?"

"Think highly of yourself, don't you?"

She heard the smile in his voice and knew she had him. Dr. Brandon Singh believed in using every available resource and while he personally might have preferred a less intuitive approach than hers, he had to admit that "Victory" Nelson represented a valuable resource indeed. If she thought highly of herself, it wasn't without cause.

"Very well," he said at last, his tone even more portentous than usual as though to make up for his earlier lapse. "But there's very little the papers don't have and I don't know what use you'll be able to make of it." He took a deep breath and even the ambient noise on the phone line seemed to fall silent to listen. "We found, in all but the first wound, a substance very like saliva. . . ."

"Very like saliva?" Vicki interjected. "How could something be *very like saliva?*"

"Something can't. But this was. What's more, every body so far, including that of young Reddick, has been missing the front half of the throat."

"I'd already discovered that."

"Indeed." For a moment, Vicki was afraid he'd taken offense at her interruption, but he continued. "The only other item kept from the press concerns the third body—the large man, DeVerne Jones. He was clutching a torn piece of thin membrane in his hand."

"Membrane?"

"Yes."

"Like a bat wing?"

"Remarkably similar, yes."

It was Vicki's turn to breathe deeply. Something very like saliva and a bat wing. "I can see why you didn't tell the papers."

* * *

Celluci hung up the phone and reached for the paper. He couldn't decide whether the apology had been made easier because Vicki was out of her apartment or harder because he'd had to talk to her damned machine. Whatever. It was done and the next move was hers.

A second later Dave Graham barely managed to snatch his coffee out of harm's way as his partner slammed the paper down on the desk.

"Did you see this bullshit?" Celluci demanded.

"The, uh, giant bat?"

"Fuck the bat! Those bastards found a witness and didn't see fit to let us know!"

"But we were heading out to St. Dennis this morning. . . ."

"Yeah," Celluci shrugged into his jacket and glared Dave up out of his chair, "but we're heading down to the paper first. A witness could blow this case wide open and I don't want to piss away my time if they've got a name."

"A name of someone who sees giant bats," Dave muttered, but he scrambled into his own coat and followed his partner out into the hall. "You think it really could be a vampire?" he asked as he caught up.

Celluci didn't even break stride. "Don't you start," he growled.

"Who is it?"

"It's the police, Mr. Bowan. We need to talk to you." Celluci held his badge up in line with the spy-eye and waited. After a long moment, he heard a chain being pulled free and two—no, three—locks snapped off. He stepped back beside his partner as the door slowly opened.

The old man peered up at them through rheumy eyes. "You Detective-Sergeant Michael Celluci?"

"Yes, but . . ." Surely the old man's eyesight hadn't been good enough to read that off his ID.

"She said you'd probably show up this morning." He opened the door wider and moved back out of the way. "Come in, come in."

The detectives exchanged puzzled looks as they entered the tiny apartment. While the old man relocked the door, Celluci looked around. Heavy blankets had been tacked up along one wall, over the windows and the balcony door, and every light in the place was on. There was a Bible on the coffee table and a water glass beside it that smelled of Scotch. Whatever the old man had seen, it had caused him to put up the barricades and reach for reassurance.

Dave settled himself carefully on the sagging couch. "Who said we'd be here this morning, Mr. Bowan?"

"Young lady who just left. In fact, I'm surprised you didn't pass her in the parking lot. Nice girl, real friendly."

"Did this nice, real friendly girl have a name?" Celluci asked through clenched teeth.

The old man managed a wheezy laugh. "She said you'd react like that." Shaking his head, he picked a business card off his kitchen table and dropped it into Celluci's hand.

Leaning over his partner's shoulder, Dave barely had a chance to read it before Celluci closed his fist.

"What else did Ms. Nelson say?"

"Oh, she seemed real concerned that I cooperate with you gentlemen. That I tell you everything I told her. Course I had no intention of doing otherwise, though I've got no idea what the police can do. More a job for an exorcist or maybe a pri. . . ." A yawn that threatened to split his face in half cut off the flow of words. "S'cuse me, but I didn't get much sleep last night. Can I get either of you a cup of tea? Pot's still hot." When both men declined, he settled himself down in a worn armchair and looked expectantly from one to the other. "You going to ask me questions or you just want me to start at the beginning and tell it in my own words?"

"Start at the beginning and tell it in your own words." Celluci had heard Vicki give that instruction a thousand times and had no doubt he was hearing her echo now. His anger had faded into a reluctant appreciation of her ability with a witness. Whatever mood Vicki had found him in, she'd left Mr. Bowan well primed for their visit. "Use your own words, we'll ask questions if we need to."

"Okay." Mr. Bowan rubbed his hands together, obviously enjoying his second captive audience of the morning in spite of his fright of the night before. "It was just after midnight, I know that 'cause I turned the TV off at midnight like I always do. Well, I was on my way to bed so I turned off the lights, then I thought I might better step out on the balcony to have a look around the building, just in case. Sometimes," he confided, leaning forward, "we get kids fooling around in the bushes down there."

While Dave nodded in understanding, Celluci hid a grin. Mr. Bowan, no doubt, spent a great deal of time out on his balcony checking out the neighborhood . . . and the neighbors. The binocular case on the floor by the armchair bore mute witness.

Last night, he'd barely stepped outside before he knew something was wrong. "It was the smell. Like rotten eggs, only worse. Then there it was, big as life and twice as ugly and so close I could've reached out and touched it—if I was as senile as my daughter-in-law seems to think I am. The wings were spread out seven or eight feet." He paused for effect. "The giant bat. Nosferatu. Vampire. You find his crypt, gentlemen, and you'll find your killer."

"Can you describe the creature?"

"If you mean could I pick it out in a lineup, no. Tell you the truth, it went by so awfully fast I saw mostly outline. But I'll tell you this much," his voice grew serious and a note of terror crept in, "that thing had eyes like I've never seen on any living creature and I hope to God never to see again. Yellow they were and cold, and

I knew that if they looked back at me I wouldn't last much beyond the first glance. It was evil, gentlemen, real evil, not the diluted kind of evil humanity is prey to but the cold uncaring kind that comes from old Nick himself. Now, I'm old and death and me's gotten pretty chummy over the last few years; nothing much scares me anymore but this, this scared the holy bejesus out of me.'' He swallowed heavily and searched both their faces. ''You can believe me or not—that reporter fella didn't when I went down to see what the sirens were about—but I know what I saw and I know what I felt.''

As much as he wanted to side with the reporter, who had described Mr. Bowan as an entertaining old coot, Celluci found himself unable to dismiss what the old man had seen. And what the old man had felt. Something in his voice or his expression raised the hair on the back of Celluci's neck and although intellect argued against it, instinct trembled on the edge of belief.

He wished he could talk this over with Vicki, but he wouldn't give her the satisfaction.

* * *

''God, I hate these machines.'' The heavy, exaggerated sigh that followed had been recorded in its annoyed entirety. ''Okay. I'd have reacted much the same way. Probably been an equal pain in the ass. So, I'm right, you're right, we're both right, let's start over.'' The tape hissed quietly for a few seconds while background noises—the rumble of two deep voices arguing, the staccato beat of an old, manual typewriter, and the constant ringing of other phones—grew louder. Then Celluci's voice returned, bearing just enough edge to show he meant what he said. ''And stop hustling my partner for classified information. He's a nice man, not that you'd recognize nice, and you give him palpitations.'' He hung up without saying good-bye.

Vicki grinned down at her answering machine. Mike Celluci was no better at apologizing than she was. For him, that was positively gracious. And it had obviously been left before he talked to Mr. Bowan and found she'd

been there first. Any messages left *after* that would have
had a very different tone.

Finding the tabloid's unnamed source had actually been
surprisingly easy. The first person she'd spoken to had
snorted and said, "You want old man Bowan. If anyone
sees anything around here it's him. Never minds his own
fucking business." Then he'd jerked his head at 25 St.
Dennis with enough force to throw his mohawk down
over his eyes.

As to what old man Bowan had seen. . . . As much as
Vicki hated to admit it, she was beginning to think Coreen might not be as far out in left field as first impressions indicated.

She wondered if she should call Celluci. They could
share their impressions of Mr. Bowan and his close en-
counter. "Nah." She shook her head. Better give him
time to cool off first. Spreading the detailed map of Toronto she'd just bought out over her kitchen table, she
decided to call him later. Right now, she had work to do.

It was easy to forget just how big Toronto was. It had
devoured any number of smaller places as it grew, and it
showed no signs of stopping. The downtown core, the
image everyone carried of the city, made up a very small
part of the whole.

Vicki drew a red circle around the Eglinton West subway station, another around the approximate position of
the Sigman's building on St. Clair West, and a third
around the construction site on Symington Avenue where
DeVerne Jones had died. Then she frowned and drew a
straight line through all three. Allowing for small inac-
curacies in placing the second and third positions, the
line bisected all three circles, running southwest to
northeast across the city.

The two new deaths appeared to have no connection to
the first three but seemed to be starting a line of their own.

And there was more.

"No one could be that stupid," Vicki muttered, digging in her desk for a ruler.

The first two deaths were essentially the same distance
apart as the fourth and the fifth; far from exact by math-
ematical standards but too close to be mere coincidence.

"No one could be that stupid," she said again, smacking the ruler against her palm. The second line ran northwest to southeast and it measured out in a circle that centered at Woodbine and Mortimer. Vicki was willing to bet any odds that between midnight and dawn a sixth body would turn up to end the line.

Just west of York University, the lines crossed.

"X marks the spot." Vicki pushed her glasses up her nose, frowned, and pushed them up again. It was too easy. There had to be a catch.

"All right. . . ." Tossing the ruler onto the map, she ticked off points on her fingers. "First possibility; the killer wants to be found. Second possibility; the killer is just as capable of drawing lines on a map as I am, has set up the pattern to mean nothing at all, and is sitting in Scarborough busting a gut laughing at the damn fool police who fell for it." For purposes of this exercise, she and the police were essentially the same. "Possibility three"; she stared at the third finger as though it might have an answer, "we're hunting a vampire even as the vampire is hunting us and who the hell knows how a vampire thinks."

Celucci was as capable as she of drawing lines on a map, but she reached for the phone anyway. Occasionally, the obvious escaped him. To her surprise, he was in. His reaction came as no surprise at all.

"Teach your grandmother to suck eggs, Vicki."

"So can I assume Toronto's finest will be gathered tonight at Mortimer and Woodbine?"

"You can assume whatever you want, I've never been able to stop you, but if you think you and your little Nancy Drew detective kit are going to be anywhere near there, think again."

"What are you going to do?" How dare he dictate to her. "Arrest me?"

"If I have to, yes." His tone said he'd do exactly that. "You are no longer on the force, you are virtually blind at night, and you are more likely to end up as the corpse than the hero."

"I don't need you babying me, Celluci!"

"Then act like an adult and stay home!"

They slammed the receivers down practically simultaneously. He knew she'd be there and she knew he knew it. Moreover, she had no doubt that if their paths crossed he'd lock her away on trumped up charges for her own safety. Better than even odds said that, having been forewarned, he'd lock her up now if he thought he could get away with it.

He was right. She was virtually blind at night.

But the police were hunting a man and Vicki no longer really believed a man had anything to do with these deaths. Blind or not, if she was there, she might even the odds.

Now, what to do until dark? Maybe it was time to do a little detecting and find out what the word was on the street.

"At least he didn't scream about Mr. Bowan," she muttered as she shrugged back into her coat.

"Yo, Victory, long time no see."

"Yeah, it's been a couple of months. How've you been, Tony?"

Tony shrugged thin shoulders under his jean jacket. "I've been okay."

"You clean?"

He shot her a look out of the corner of one pale blue eye. "I hear you ain't a cop no more. I don't got to tell you."

Vicki shrugged in turn. "No. You don't."

They walked in silence for a moment, threading their way through the crowds that surged up and down Yonge Street. When they stopped at the Wellesley lights, Tony sighed. "Okay, I'm clean. You happy now? You going to bugger off and leave me alone?"

She grinned. "Is it ever that easy?"

"Not with you it ain't. Listen," he waved a hand at a corner restaurant, less trendy than most of its competitors, "you're going to take up my time, you can buy me lunch."

She bought him lunch, but not the beer he wanted, and asked him about the feeling on the street.

"Feeling about what?" he asked, stuffing a huge forkful of mashed potatoes into his mouth. "Sex? Drugs? Rock'n'roll?"

"Things that go bump in the night."

He threw his arm up in the classic Hammer films tradition. "Ah, the wampyre."

Vicki took a swallow of tepid coffee, wondered how she'd survived drinking it all those years on the force, and waited. Tony had been her best set of eyes and ears on the street. He wasn't exactly a snitch, more a barometer really, hooked into moods and feelings, and although he never mentioned specifics, he'd pointed her in the right direction more than once. He was nineteen now. He'd been fifteen when she first brought him in.

"Feelin' on the street. . . ." He methodically spread the last roll a quarter inch thick with butter. "Feelin' on the street says, paper's right with this one."

"A vampire?"

He peered up at her from under the thick fringe of his eyelashes. "Killer ain't human, that's what the street says. Sucks blood, don't it? Vampire's a good enough name for it. Cops won't catch it 'cause they're lookin' for a guy." He grinned. "Cops in this city ain't worth shit anyway. Not like they used to be."

"Well, thank you very much." She watched him scrape his plate clean, then asked, "Tony, do *you* believe in vampires?"

He flicked a tiny crucifix out from inside his shirt. "I believe in stayin' alive."

Outside the restaurant, turning collars up against the wind, she asked him if he needed money. She couldn't get him off the street, he wouldn't accept her help, so she gave him what he'd take. Celluci called it white-middle-class-guilt-money. While admitting he was probably right, Vicki ignored him.

"Nah," Tony pushed a lock of pale brown hair back off his face. "I'm doing okay for cash."

"You hooking?"

"Why? You can't arrest me anymore; you wanna hire me?"

"I want to smack you. Haven't you heard there's an epidemic going on?"

He danced back out of her range. "Hey, I'm careful. Like I said," and just for an instant he looked much, much older than his years, "I believe in stayin' alive."

"Vicki, I don't care what your curbside guru says and I don't care what the 'feeling on the street is'; there are no such thing as vampires and you are losing your mind."

Vicki got the phone away from her ear before Celluci slammed his receiver down. Shaking her head, she hung up her own phone considerably more gently. All right, she'd told him. She'd done it against her better judgment and knowing full well what his reaction would be. No matter what went down tonight, *her* conscience was clear.

"And it's not that *I* believe in vampires," she pointed out to the empty apartment, pushing back to extend the recliner. "*I* believe in keeping an open mind." *And,* she added silently, grimly, her mind on Tony and his crucifix, *I, too, believe in stayin' alive.* Beside the chair, her bag bulged with the afternoon's purchases.

At 11:48, Vicki stepped off the northbound Woodbine bus at Mortimer. For a moment, she leaned against the window of the small garden store on the corner, giving herself time to grow used to the darkness. There, under the street lamp, her vision was functional. A few meters away, where the overlap of two lights created a double-shadowed twilight, she knew she wouldn't be able to trust it. It would be worse off the main street. She fished her flashlight out of her bag and held it ready, just in case.

Across a shadow-filled distance, she saw a traffic signal work through its tiny spectrum and decided to cross the street. For no reason really, the creature could appear on the east side of Woodbine just as easily as on the west, but it seemed like the thing to do. Moving had always been infinitely preferable to waiting around.

Terry's Milk Mart on the north side of Mortimer appeared to be open—it was the only building in the immediate neighborhood still brightly lit—so she crossed toward it.

I can ask a few questions. Buy a bag of chips. Find out. . . . SHIT! Two men from homicide were in the store talking to a surly looking teenager she could only assume was not the proprietor. Eyes streaming from the sudden glare of the fluorescents, she backed down the six stairs much more quickly than she'd gone up them. She spotted the unmarked car south across Mortimer in the Brewers Retail parking lot—*trust the government to light a square of asphalt at almost midnight*—and headed in the opposite direction, willing to bet long odds that Celluci had included her in his instructions to his men.

If she remembered correctly, the houses that lined the street were small, virtually identical, detached, two-story, single family dwellings. *Not the sort of neighborhood you'd think would attract a vampire.* Not that she expected the creature to actually put in an appearance on Woodbine; the street was too well lit, too well traveled, with too great a possibility of witnesses. No, she was putting her money on one of the quiet residential streets tucked in behind.

At Holborne, for no reason she could think of, she turned west. The streetlights were farther apart here and she hurried from one island of sight to the next, trusting to bureaucracy and city planning to keep the sidewalk under her feet. She slipped at one point on a pile of dirt, her bag sliding off her shoulder and slamming hard edges against her knees. Her flashlight beam played over a tiny construction site where a skinny house was rising to fill what had once no doubt been a no larger than average side yard. The creature had killed under circumstances like these once before, but somehow she knew it wouldn't again. She moved on.

The sudden scream of a siren sent her heart up into her throat and she spun around, flashlight raised like a weapon. Back at the corner, a fire engine roared from the station and, tires squealing, turned north up Woodbine.

"Nerves a bit shot, are they, Vicki?" she muttered to herself taking a long, calming breath. Blood pounded in her ears almost loud enough to echo and sweat glued her gloves to her palms. Still a bit shaky with reaction, she made her way to the next streetlight and leaned back against the pole.

The spill of light reached almost to the house, not quite

far enough for Vicki to see the building. The bit of lawn she could see looked well cared for—in spite of the spring mud—and along one edge roses, clipped short to survive the cold, waited for spring. It was a working class neighborhood, she knew, and, given the lawn, Vicki was willing to bet that most of the families were Italian or Portuguese as both cultures cared about—and for—the land. If that was the case, many of the houses would be decorated with painted icons of saints, or of the Madonna, or of Christ himself.

She wondered how much protection those icons would offer when the killer came.

Up the street, two golden circles marked a slow moving car. To Vicki, they looked like the eyes of some great beast for the darkness hid the form that followed and the headlights were all she could see. But then, she didn't need to see more to identify it as a police car. Only police on surveillance ever drove at that precise, unchanging speed. She'd done it herself too many times to mistake it now. Fighting the urge to dive out of sight, she turned and strode confidently up the walk toward the house, digging in her bag for an imaginary set of keys.

The car purred by behind her.

Making her way back to the sidewalk, Vicki doubted that her luck could last. Celluci had to have saturated this area with his men. Sooner or later, she had to run into someone she knew—probably Celluci himself—and she wasn't looking forward to explaining just what she was doing roaming about in the middle of a police manhunt.

She continued west along Holborne, marshaling her arguments. *I thought you could use an extra pair of eyes.* But then, so could she. *I doubted you'd be prepared to deal with a vampire.* True, but it'd go over like rats in the drunk tank. *You have no right to keep me away.* Except that they/he did. Every right. It was why there were laws against suicide.

So what am I doing out here anyway? And is this more or less stupid than charging down into a subway station to single-handedly challenge God knows what. The darkness pressed close around her, waiting for an answer. *What am I trying to prove?*

That in spite of everything I can still be a fully functioning member of society. She snorted. *On the other hand, there're a number of fully functioning members of society I'm not likely to run into out here tonight.*

Which brought the silent interrogation back around to "just what was she trying to prove," and Vicki decided to leave it there. Things were tough enough without bogging them down further in introspection.

At the corner of Woodmount, she paused. The triple line of streetlights disappeared into the distance to either side and straight ahead. The suspended golden globes were all she could see. Casting about like a hound for a scent, she drew in a deep lungful of the cold night air. All she could smell was earth, damp and musty, freshly exposed by the end of winter. Normally, she liked the smell. Tonight, it reminded her of the grave and she pulled her jacket tighter around her to ward off a sudden chill. In the distance, there was the sound of traffic and farther off still, a dog barked.

There seemed little to choose between the directions, so she turned to her left and headed carefully back south.

A car door slammed.

Vicki's heart slammed up against her ribs in response. This was it. She was as sure of it as she'd ever been of anything in her life.

She started to run. Slowly at first, well aware that a misstep would result in a fall or worse. Her flashlight remained off; she needed the stations of the streetlights to guide her and the flashlight beam confined her sight. At Baker Street, she rocked to a halt.

Where now? Her other senses strained to make up for near blindness.

Metal screamed against wood; nails forced to release their hold.

East. She turned and raced toward it, stumbled, fell, recovered, and went on, trusting her feet to find a path she couldn't see. Fifty running paces from the corner, shadow sight marked something crossing her path. It slipped down the narrow drive between two buildings and when Vicki followed, responding to the instinct of the chase, she could see red taillights burning about a hundred yards away.

It smelled as if something had died at the end of the lane. Like the old lady who'd been found the third week of last August but who'd been killed in her small, airless room around the first of July.

She could hear the car engine running, movement against the gravel, and a noise she didn't want to identify.

The evil that had lingered in the subway tunnel had been only the faintest afterimage of the evil that waited for her here.

A shadow, its parameters undefined, passed between Vicki and the taillight.

Her left hand trailing along a wall of fake brick siding and her right holding the flashlight out before her like the handle of a lance, Vicki pounded up the drive paying no attention to the small, shrill voice of reason that demanded to know just what the hell she thought she was doing.

Something shrieked and the sound drove her back a half dozen steps.

Every dog in the neighborhood began to howl.

Ignoring the cold sweat beading her body and the knot of fear that made each breath a labored fight, Vicki forced herself to move forward again; the six steps regained, then six more. . . .

Half sprawled across the trunk of the car, she turned on the flashlight.

Horror flickered just beyond the beam's farthest edge where a wooden garage door swung haphazardly from a single twisted hinge. Darkness seemed to move within the darkness and Vicki's mind shied away from it so quickly and with such blind panic that it convinced her nothing lingered there at all.

Caught in the light, a young man crouched, one arm flung up to shield his eyes from the glare. At his feet, a body; a bearded man, late thirties, early forties, blood still draining from the ruined throat, thickening and congealing against the gravel. He had been dead before he hit the ground, for only the dead fall with that complete disregard of self that gives them the look of discarded marionettes.

All this Vicki took in at glance. Then the crouching

man stood, his open coat spreading and bracketing him like great black leather wings. He took a step toward her, face distorted and eyes squinted nearly shut. Blood had stained his palms and fingers a glistening crimson.

Scrambling in her purse for the heavy silver crucifix she'd acquired that afternoon—and not really, God help her, expected to need—Vicki drew breath to scream for backup. Or maybe just to scream. She never found out which for he took another step toward her and that was all she saw for some time.

Henry caught the young woman as she fell and eased her gently to the gravel. He hadn't wanted to do that, but he couldn't allow her to scream. There were too many things he couldn't explain to the police.

She saw me bending over the body, he thought as he snapped off the flashlight and shoved it into her purse. His too sensitive eyes welcomed the return of night. They felt as though they'd been impaled with hot irons. *Got a good look at me, too. Damn.* Common sense said he should kill her before she had a chance to expose him. He had strength enough to make it look no different from the other deaths. He would be safe again then.

Henry turned and looked past the body—meat now, nothing more—into the torn earthen floor of the garage where the killer had fled. This night had proven the deaths were in no way his responsibility.

"Damn!" He said it aloud this time as approaching sirens and a car door slamming at the end of the drive reminded him of the need for immediate action. Dropping to one knee, he heaved the unconscious young woman over a shoulder and grabbed up her bag in his free hand. The weight posed no problem; like all of his kind he was disproportionately strong, but her dangling height was dangerously awkward.

"Too damn tall in this century," he muttered, vaulted the chain link fence that bordered the back of the yard, and disappeared with his burden into the night.

Six

Dumping the contents of the huge black purse out on his coffee table, Henry dropped to his knees and rummaged through the mess for something that looked like ID; a wallet, a card case, anything. Nothing.

Nothing? Impossible. These days no one traveled without identification, not even those who traveled only the night. He found both card case and wallet at last in the bag itself, tucked in a side pocket, accessible without having to delve through the main compartment.

"Victoria Nelson, Private Investigator." He let out a breath he hadn't been aware of holding as he went through the rest of her papers. *A private investigator, thank God.* He'd been afraid he'd run off with some sort of ununiformed police officer, thereby instigating a citywide manhunt. He'd observed, over the centuries that the police, whatever else their failings, took care of their own. A private investigator, though, was a private citizen and as such had probably not yet been missed.

Rising to his feet, Henry looked down at the unconscious woman on his couch. Although he found it distasteful, he would kill to protect himself. Hopefully, this time, it wouldn't be necessary. He shrugged out of his coat and began to compose what he'd say to her when she woke up . . .

. . . if she woke up.

Her heartbeat filled the apartment, its rhythm almost twice as fast as his own. It called to him to feed, but he held the hunger in check.

He glanced at his watch. 2:13. Sunrise in four hours. If she was concussed. . . .

He hadn't wanted to hit her. Knocking someone out

with a single blow wasn't easy no matter what movies and television suggested. Sporadic practice over the years had taught him where and how to strike, but no expertise could change the fact that a head blow slammed the brain back and forth within the skull, mashing soft tissue against bone.

And it's quite an attractive skull, too, he noted, taking a closer look. *Although there's a definite hint of obstinacy about the width of that jaw.* He checked her ID again. Thirty-one. Her short dark blond/light brown hair—he frowned, unable to make up his mind—had no touch of gray but tiny laugh wrinkles had begun to form around her eyes. When he'd been "alive," thirty-one had been middle-aged. Now, it seemed to be barely adult.

She wore no makeup, he approved of that, and the delicate, pale gold down on her cheeks made her skin look like velvet.

And feel like velvet. . . . He drew back his hand and clamped the hunger tighter. It was want, not need, and he would not let it control him.

The tiny muscles of her face shifted and her eyes opened. Like her hair, they were neither one color nor the other; neither blue, nor gray, nor green. The tip of her tongue moistened dry lips and she met his gaze without fear.

"Son of a bitch," she said clearly, and winced.

Vicki came up out of darkness scrambling desperately for information, but the sound of blood pounding in her ears kept drowning out coherent thought. She fought against it. Pain—and, oh God, it hurt—meant danger. She had to know where she was, how she'd gotten there. . . .

A man's face swam into view inches above her own, a man's face she recognized.

"Son of a bitch," she said, and winced. The words, the movement of her jaw, sent fresh shards of pain up into her head. She did what she could to ignore them. The last time she'd seen that face, and the body it was no doubt attached to, it had risen from slaughter and attacked her. Although she had no memory of it, he had obviously knocked her out and brought her here; wherever here was.

She tried to look past him, to get some idea of her surroundings, but the room, if room it was, was too dark. Did she know *anything* she could use?

I'm fully clothed, lying on a couch in the company of an insane killer and, although the rest of my body appears to be functional, my head feels like it's taken too many shots on goal. There seemed to be only one thing she could do. She threw herself off the couch.

Unfortunately, gravity proved stronger than the idea.

When she hit the floor, a brilliant fireworks display left afterimages of green and gold and red on the inside of her eyelids and then she sank into darkness again.

The second time Vicki regained consciousness, it happened more quickly than the first and the line between one state and the next was more clearly delineated. This time, she kept her eyes closed.

"That was a stupid thing to do," a man's voice observed from somewhere above her right shoulder. She didn't argue. "It's entirely possible you won't believe this," he continued, "but I don't want to hurt you."

To her surprise, she did believe him. Maybe it was the tone, or the timbre, or the ice pack he held against her jaw. Maybe her brains had been scrambled, which seemed more likely.

"I never did want to hurt you. I'm sorry about," she felt the ice pack shift slightly, "this, but I didn't think I had time to explain."

Vicki cracked open first one eye and then the other. "Explain what?" The pale oval of his face appeared to float in the dim light. She wished she could see him better.

"I didn't kill that man. I arrived at the body just before you did."

"Yeah?" She realized suddenly what was wrong. "Where are my glasses?"

"Your . . . oh." The oval swiveled away and returned a moment later.

She waited, eyes closed, as he pushed the ends in over her ears, approximately where they belonged, and settled the bridge gently against her nose. When she opened her eyes again, things hadn't changed significantly. "Could you turn on a light?"

Vicki could sense his bemusement as he rose. So she wasn't reacting as he expected; if he wanted terror, she'd have to try for it later, at present her head hurt too much to make the effort. And besides, if it turned out he was the killer, there wasn't a damn thing she could do about it now.

The light, although it wasn't strong enough to banish shadows from far corners, helped. From where she lay, she could see an expensive stereo system and the edge of a bookshelf with glass doors. Slowly, balancing her head like an egg in a spoon, she sat up.

"Are you sure that's wise?"

She wasn't. But she wasn't going to admit it. "I'm fine," she snapped, closing her throat on a wave of nausea and successfully fighting it back down. Peeling off her gloves, she studied her captor from under beetled brows.

He didn't look like an insane killer. *Okay, Vicki, you're so smart, in twenty-five words or less, describe an insane killer.* She couldn't tell what color his eyes were, though an educated guess said light hazel, but his brows and lashes were redder than his strawberry-blond hair— coloring that freckled in the sun. His face was broad, without being in the least bit fat—the kind of face that got labeled honest—and his mouth held just the smallest hint of a cupid's bow. *Definitely attractive.* She measured his height against the stereo and added, *But short.*

"So," she said, settling carefully back against the sofa cushions, keeping her tone conversational. *Talk to them,* said the rule book. *Get their trust.* "Why should I believe you had nothing to do with ripping that man's throat out?"

Henry stepped forward and handed her the ice pack. "You were right behind me," he told her quietly. "You must have seen. . . ."

Seen what? She'd seen the body, him bending over it, the lights of the car, the ruined garage door and the darkness beyond it. *Darkness swirled against darkness and was gone.* No. She shook her head, the physical pain the action caused a secondary consideration. *Darkness swirled against darkness and was gone.* She couldn't catch her breath and began to struggle against the strong hands that held her. "No. . . ."

"Yes."

Gradually, under the strength of his gaze and his touch, she calmed. "What . . ." She wet dry lips and tried again. "What was it?"

"A demon."

"Demons don't . . ." *Darkness swirled against darkness and was gone.* "Oh."

Straightening, Henry almost smiled. He could practically see her turning the facts over, accepting the evidence, and adjusting her worldview to fit. She didn't look happy about it, but she did it anyway. He was impressed.

Vicki took a deep breath. *Okay, a demon.* It certainly answered all the questions and made a kind of horrific sense. "Why were *you* there?" She was pleased to note her voice sounded almost normal.

What should he tell her? Although she wasn't exactly receptive—not that he blamed her—she wasn't openly hostile either. The truth, then, or as much of it as seemed safe.

"I was hunting the demon. I was just a little too late. I kept it from feeding but couldn't stop the kill." He frowned slightly. "Why were *you* there, Ms. Nelson?"

So he's found my ID. For the first time, Vicki became aware that the contents of her bag were spread out over the smoked glass top of the coffee table. The garlic, the package of mustard seed, the Bible, the crucifix—all spread out in plain, ridiculous sight. She snorted gently. "I was hunting a vampire."

To her surprise, after one incredulous glance down at the contents of her bag, as if he, too, were seeing them for the first time, her captor, the demon-hunter, threw back his head and roared with laughter.

* * *

Henry, Duke of Richmond, had felt her speculative gaze on him all through the meal. Whenever he glanced her way she was staring at him, but every time he tried to actually catch her eye she'd drop her lids and look demurely at her plate, the long sweep of her lashes—lashes so black he was sure they must be tinted—lying against the curve of an alabaster cheek. He thought she smiled once, but that could have been a trick of the light.

While Sir Thomas, seated to his left, prated on about sheep, he rolled a grape between his fingers and tried to figure out just who the lady could be. She had to be a member of the local nobility invited to Sheriffhuton for the day for surely he would have remembered her if she'd been with the household on the journey north from London. The little bit he could see of her gown was black. Was she a widow, then, or did she wear the color only because she knew how beautifully it became her and was there a husband lurking in the background?

For the first time in weeks he was glad that Surrey had decided against journeying to Sheriffhuton with him. *Women never look at me when he's around.*

There, she smiled. I'm sure of it. He wiped the crushed grape off against his hose and reached for his wine, emptying the delicate Venetian glass in one frantic swallow. He couldn't stand it any longer.

"Sir Thomas."

". . . of course, the best ram for the purpose is. . . . Yes milord?"

Henry leaned closer to the elderly knight; he didn't want the rest of the table to hear, he got enough teasing as it was. He'd barely managed to live down the ditty his father's fool, Will Sommers, had written about him; *Though he may have his sire's face/He cannot keep the royal pace.*

"Sir Thomas, who is that woman seated next to Sir Giles and his lady?"

"Woman, milord?"

"Yes, woman." It took an effort, but the young duke kept his voice level and calm. Sir Thomas was a valued retainer, had been a faithful chamberlain at Sheriffhuton all the long years he'd been away in France, and by age alone deserved his respect. "The one in black. Next to Sir Giles and his lady."

"Ah, next to Sir Giles. . . ." Sir Thomas leaned forward and squinted. The lady in question looked demurely at her plate. "Why that's old Beswick's relic."

"Beswick?" This beautiful creature had been married to Beswick? Why the baron was Sir Thomas' age at least. Henry couldn't believe it. "But he's old!"

"He's dead, milord." Sir Thomas snickered. "But he met his maker a happy man, I fancy. She's a sweet thing though, and seemed to take the old goat's death hard. Saw little enough of her when he was alive and less now."

"How long were they married?"

"Month . . . no, two."

"And she lives at Beswick Castle?"

Sir Thomas snorted. "If you can call that moldering ruin a castle, yes, milord."

"If you can call this heap a castle," Henry waved a hand at the great hall, relatively unchanged since the twelfth century, "you can call anything a castle."

"This is a royal residence," Sir Thomas protested huffily.

She did smile. I saw her clearly. She smiled. At me. "And where *she* dwells, it would be heaven come to earth," Henry murmured dreamily, forgetting for a moment where he was, losing himself in that smile.

Sir Thomas gave a great guffaw of laughter, choked on a mouthful of ale, and had to be vigorously pounded on the back, attracting the attention Henry had been hoping to avoid.

"You should be more careful of excitement, good sir knight," chided the Archbishop of York as those who had hurried to the rescue moved back to their places.

"Not me, your Grace," Sir Thomas told the prelate piously, "it's our good duke who finds his codpiece tied too tightly."

As he felt his face redden, Henry cursed the Tudor coloring that showed every blush as though he were a maiden and not a man full sixteen summers old.

Later, when the musicians began to play up in the old minstrel's gallery, Henry walked among his guests, trying, he thought successfully, to hide his ultimate goal. They'd be watching him now and one or two, he knew, reported back to his father.

As he at last crossed the hall toward her, she gathered her black and silver skirts in one hand and headed for the open doors and the castle courtyard. Henry followed. She was waiting for him, as he knew she would be, on the second of the broad steps; far enough away from the door to be in darkness, close enough for him to find her.

"It, uh, it is hot in the hall, isn't it?"

She turned toward him, her face and bosom glimmering pale white. "It *is* August."

"Yes, uh, it is." They weren't, in fact, the only couple to seek a respite from the stifling, smoky hall but the others discreetly moved away when they saw the duke appear. "You, uh, aren't afraid of night chills?"

"No. I love the night."

Her voice reminded him of the sea, and he suspected it could sweep him away as easily. Inside, under torchlight, he had thought her not much older than he, but outside, under starlight, she seemed ageless. He wet lips gone suddenly dry and searched for something more to say.

"You weren't at the hunt today."

"No."

"You don't hunt, then?"

In spite of the darkness, her eyes caught and held his. "Oh, but I do."

Henry swallowed hard and shifted uncomfortably—his codpiece was now, indeed, too tight. If three years at the French Court had taught him nothing else, he had learned to recognize an invitation from a beautiful woman. Hoping his palm had not gone damp, he held out a hand.

"Have you a name?" he asked as she laid cool fingers across his.

"Christina."

"Vampire?" Henry stared at Christina in astonishment. "I was making a joke."

"Were you?" She turned from the window, arms crossed under her breasts. "It is what Norfolk calls me."

"Norfolk is a jealous fool." Henry suspected his father had sent the Duke of Norfolk to keep an eye on him, to discover why he continued at Sheriffhuton, a residence he made no pretense of liking, into September. He also suspected that the only reason he hadn't been ordered back to Court was because his father secretly approved of his dalliance with an older, and very beautiful, widow. He wasn't fool enough to think his father didn't know.

"Is he? Perhaps." Ebony brows drew down into a frown. "Have you never wondered, Henry, why you only see me at night?"

"As long as I get to see you. . . ."

"Have you never wondered why you have never seen me eat or drink?"

"You've been to banquets," Henry protested, confused. He had only been making a joke.

"But you have never seen me eat or drink," Christina insisted. "And, this very night, you yourself commented on my strength."

"Why are you telling me this?" His life had come to revolve around the hours they spent in his great canopied bed. She was perfect. He wouldn't see her otherwise.

"Norfolk has named me vampire." Her eyes caught his and held them although he tried to break away. "The next step will be to prove it. He will say to you, if I am not as he names me, then surely I will come to you by day." She paused and her voice grew cold. "And you, wondering, will order it. And either I will flee and never see you again, or I will die."

"I, I would never order you. . . ."

"You would, if you did not believe me vampire. This is why I tell you."

Henry's mouth opened and closed in stunned silence, and when he finally spoke his voice came out a shrill caricature of his normal tone. "But I've seen you receive the sacrament."

"I'm as good a Catholic as you are, Henry. Better perhaps, as you have more to lose while the king's favor wanes toward the Mass." She smiled, a little sadly. "I am not a creature of the devil. I was born of two mortal parents."

He had never seen her in daylight. He had never seen her eat or drink. She possessed strength far beyond her sex or size. But she received the sacraments and she filled his nights with glory. "Born," his voice had almost returned to normal, "when?"

"Thirteen twenty-seven, the year that Edward the Third came to the throne. Your grandfather's grandfather had not yet been conceived."

It wasn't hard to think of her as an ageless beauty, forever unchanging down through the centuries. From there, it wasn't hard to believe the rest.

Vampire.

She saw the acceptance on his face and spread her arms wide. The loose robe she wore dropped to the floor and she allowed him to look away now that she was sure he would not. "Will you banish me?" she asked softly, casting the net of her beauty over him. "Will you give me to the pyre? Or will you have the strength to love me and be loved in return?"

The firelight threw her shadow against the tapestries on the wall. Angel or demon, Henry didn't really care. He was hers and if that damned his soul to hell so be it.

He opened his arms in answer.

As she buried herself in his embrace, he pressed his lips against the scented ebony of her hair and whispered, "Why have you never fed from me?"

"But I have. I do."

He frowned. "I've never borne your mark upon my throat. . . ."

"Throats are too public." He could feel her smile against his chest. "And your throat is not the only part of your body I have put my mouth against."

Even as he reddened, she slid down to prove her point and somehow, knowing that she fed as she pleasured him lifted him to such heights that he thought he could not bear the ecstasy. Hell would be worth it.

"This was your idea, wasn't it?"

The Duke of Norfolk inclined his head. His eyes were sunk in shadow and the deep lines that bracketed his mouth had not been there a month before. "Yes," he admitted heavily, "but it is for your own good, Henry."

"My own good?" Henry gave a bitter bark of laughter. "For your good more like. It does move you that much closer to the throne." He saw the older man wince and was glad. He didn't really believe Norfolk used him to get closer to the throne; the duke had proven his friendship any number of times, but Henry had just come from a painful interview with his father and he wanted to lash out.

"You will wed Mary, Norfolk's daughter, before the end of this month. You will spend Christmas with the Court and then you will retire to your estates at Richmond and you will never go to Sheriffhuton again."

Norfolk sighed and laid a weary hand on Henry's shoulder. His own interview with the young duke's father had been anything but pleasant. "What he does not know, he suspects; I offered this as your only way out."

Henry shook the hand free. Never to go to Sheriffhuton again. Never to see her again. Never to hear her laugh or feel her touch. Never to touch her in return. He clenched his teeth on the howl that threatened to break free. "You don't understand," he growled out instead, and strode off down the corridor before the tears he could feel building shamed him.

"Christina!" He ran forward, threw himself to his knees, and buried his head in her lap. For a time, the world became the touch of her hands and the sound of her voice. When at last he had the strength to pull away, it was only far enough to see her face. "What are you doing here? Father and Norfolk, at least, suspect and if they find you. . . ."

She stroked cool fingers across his brow. "They won't find me. I have a safe haven for the daylight hours and we will not have so many nights together that they will discover us." She paused and cupped his cheek in her palm. "I am going away, but I could not leave without saying good-bye."

"Going away?" Henry repeated stupidly.

She nodded, her unbound hair falling forward. "It has become too dangerous for me in England."

"But where. . . ."

"France, I think. For now."

He caught up her hands in both of his. "Take me with you. I cannot live without you."

A wry smile curved her lips. "You cannot exactly *live* with me," she reminded him.

"Live, die, unlive, undie." He leapt to his feet and threw his arms wide. "I don't care as long as I'm with you."

"You're very young."

The words lacked conviction and he could see the indecision on her face. She wanted him! Oh, blessed Jesu and all the saints, she wanted him. "How old were you when you died?" he demanded.

She bit her lip. "Seventeen."

"I shall be seventeen in two months." He threw himself back on his knees. "Can't you wait that long?"

"Two months. . . ."

"Just two." He couldn't keep the triumph from his voice. "Then you will have me for all eternity."

She laughed then and pulled him to her breast. "You think highly of yourself, milord."

"I do," he agreed, his voice a little muffled.

"If your lady wife should come in. . . ."

"Mary? She has rooms of her own and is happy to stay in them." Still on his knees, he pulled her to the bed.

Two months later, she began to feed nightly, taking as much as he could bear each night.

Norfolk posted guards on his room. Henry ordered them away, for the first time in his life his father's son.

Two months after that, while revered doctors scratched their heads and wondered at his failing, while Norfolk tore the neighborhood apart in a fruitless search, she pulled him to her breast again and he suckled the blood of eternal life.

* * *

"Let me get this straight; you're the bastard son of Henry VIII?"

"That's right." Henry Fitzroy, once Duke of Richmond and Somerset, Earl of Nottingham, and Knight of the Garter, leaned his forehead against the cool glass of the window and looked down at the lights of Toronto. It had been a long time since he'd told the story; he'd forgotten how drained it left him.

Vicki looked down at the book of the Tudor age, spread open on her lap, and tapped a paragraph. "It says here you died at seventeen."

Shaking off his lethargy, Henry turned to face her. "Yes, well, I got better."

"You don't look seventeen." She frowned. "Midtwenties I'd say, no younger."

He shrugged. "We age, but we age slowly."

"It doesn't say so here, but wasn't there some mystery about your funeral?" One corner of her mouth quirked up at his surprised expression, the best she could manage considering the condition of her jaw. "I have a BA in History."

"Isn't that an unusual degree for a person in your line of work?"

He meant for a private investigator, she realized, but it had been just as unusual for a cop. If she had a nickel for every time someone, usually a superior officer, had dragged out that hoary old chestnut, *those who fail to learn from history are doomed to repeat it,* she'd be a rich woman. "It hasn't slowed me down," she told him a little pointedly. "The funeral?"

"Yes, well, it wasn't what I'd been expecting, that's for certain." He clasped his hands together to still their shaking and although he fought it, the memories caught him up again. . . .

* * *

Waking—confused and disoriented. Slowly, he became aware of his heartbeat and allowed it to pull him back to full consciousness. He'd never been in a darkness so complete and, in spite of Christina's remembered reassurance, he began to panic. The panic grew when he tried to push the lid off the crypt and found he couldn't move. Not stone above him, but rough wood embracing him so closely that the rise and fall of his chest brushed against the boards. All around, the smell of earth.

Not a noble's tomb but a common grave.

Screaming until his throat was raw, he twisted and thrashed through the little movement he had but, although the wood creaked once or twice, the weight of earth was absolute.

He stopped then, for he realized that to destroy the coffin and lie covered only in the earth would be infinitely worse. That was when the hunger began. He had no idea how long he lay, paralyzed with terror, frenzied need clawing at his gut, but his sanity hung by a thread when he heard a shovel blade bite into the dirt above him.

* * *

"You know," he said, scrubbing a hand across his face, terror still echoing faintly behind the words, "there's a very good reason most vampires come from the nobility; a crypt is a great deal easier to get out of. I'd been buried good and deep and it took Christina three days to find me and dig me free." Sometimes, even four centuries later, when he woke in the evening, he was back there. Alone. In the dark. Facing eternity.

"So your father," Vicki paused, she had trouble with this next bit, "Henry VIII, really did suspect?"

Henry laughed, but the sound had little humor. "Oh, he more than suspected. I discovered later that he'd ordered a stake driven through my heart, my mouth stuffed with garlic and the lips sewn shut, then my head removed and buried separately. Thank God, Norfolk remained a true friend until the end."

"You saw him again?"

"A couple of times. He understood better than I thought."

"What happened to Christina?"

"She guided me through the frenzy that follows the change. She guarded me during the year I slept as my body adapted to its new condition. She taught me how to feed without killing. And then she left.''

''She left?'' Vicki's brows flew almost to her hairline. ''After all that, she left?''

Henry turned again to look out at the lights of the city. She could be out there, he'd never know. Nor, he had to admit a little sadly, would he care. ''When the parent/child link is over, we prefer to hunt alone. Our closest bonds are formed when we feed and we can't feed from each other.'' He rested his hand against the glass. ''The emotional bond, the love if you will, that causes us to offer our blood to a mortal never survives the change.''

''But you could still. . . .''

''Yes, but it isn't the same.'' He shook himself free of the melancholy and faced her again. ''That also is tied too closely to feeding.''

''Oh. Then the stories about vampiric . . . uh . . . .''

''Prowess?'' Henry supplied with a grin. ''Are true. But then, we get a lot of time to practice.''

Vicki felt the heat rise in her face and she had to drop her gaze. Four hundred and fifty years of practice. . . . Involuntarily, she clenched her teeth and the sudden sharp pain from her jaw came as a welcome distraction. *Not tonight, I've got a headache.* She closed the book on her lap and carefully set it aside, glancing down at her watch as she did. 4:43. *I've heard some interesting confessions in my time, but this one. . . .* The option, of course, existed to disbelieve everything she'd heard. To get out of the apartment and away from a certified nut case and call for the people in the white coats to lock Mr. Fitzroy, bastard son of Henry VIII, etcetera, etcetera, away where he belonged. Except, she did believe and trying to convince herself she didn't would be trying to convince herself of a lie.

''Why did you tell me all this?'' she asked at last.

Henry shrugged. ''The way I saw it, I had two options. I could trust you or I could kill you. If I trusted you first,'' he spread his hands, ''and discovered it was a bad idea, I could still kill you before you could do me any harm.''

''Now wait a minute,'' Vicki bridled. ''I'm not that

easy to kill!'' He was standing at the window; ten, maybe twelve feet away. Less than a heartbeat later he sat beside her on the couch, both hands resting lightly around her neck. She couldn't have stopped him. She hadn't even seen him move. ''Oh,'' she said.

He removed his hands and continued as though she hadn't interrupted. ''But if I killed you first, well, that would be that. And I think we can help each other.''

''How?'' Up close, he became a little overwhelming and she had to fight the desire to move away. Or move closer. *Four hundred and fifty years develops a forceful personality,* she observed, shifting her gaze to the white velvet upholstery.

''The demon hunts at night. So do I. But the one who calls the demon is mortal and must live his life during the day.''

''You're suggesting that we team up?''

''Until the demon is captured, yes.''

She brushed the nap of the velvet back and forth, back and forth, and then looked up at him again. *Light hazel eyes. I was right.* ''Why do you care?''

''About catching the demon?'' Henry stood and paced back to the window. ''I don't, not specifically, but the papers are blaming the killings on vampires and are putting us all in danger.'' Down below, the headlights of a lone car sped up Jarvis Street. ''Until just recently, even I thought it was one of my kind; a child, abandoned, untrained.''

''What, purposefully left to fend for itself?''

''Perhaps. Perhaps the parent had no idea there was a child at all.''

''I thought you said there had to be an emotional bond.''

''No, I said the emotional bond did not survive past the change, I didn't say that it had to exist. My kind can create children for as many bad or accidental reasons as yours. Technically, all that is needed is for the vampire to feed too deeply and for the mortal to feed in return.''

''For the mortal to feed in return? How the hell would that happen?''

He turned to face her. "I take it," he said dryly, "you don't bite."

Vicki felt her cheeks burn and hurriedly changed the subject. "You were looking for the child?"

"Tonight?" Henry shook his head. "No, tonight I knew and I was looking for the demon." He walked to the couch and leaned over it toward her, hands braced against the pale wood inlaid in the arm. "When the killings stop, the stories will stop and vampires will retreat back into myth and race memory. We prefer it that way. In fact, we work very hard to keep it that way. If the papers convince their readers we are real, they can find us—our habits are too well known." He caught her gaze, held it, and grimly bared his teeth. "I, for one, don't intend to end up staked for something I didn't do."

When he released her—and she refused to kid herself, she couldn't have looked away if he hadn't allowed it— Vicki swept the stuff on the coffee table back into her bag and stood. Although she faced him, she focused on the area just over his right shoulder.

"I have to think about this." She kept her voice as neutral as she could. "What you've told me . . . well, I have to think about it." Lame, but the best she could do.

Henry nodded. "I understand."

"Then I can go?"

"You can go."

She nodded in turn and reaching into her pocket for her gloves, made her way to the door.

"Victoria."

Vicki had never believed that names held power nor that speaking names transferred that power to another, but she couldn't stop herself from pivoting slowly around to face him again.

"Thank you for not suggesting I tell all this to the police."

She snorted. "The police? Do I look stupid?"

He smiled. "No, you don't."

He's had a long time to perfect that smile, she reminded herself, trying to calm the sudden erratic beating of her heart. She fumbled behind her for the door, got it open, and made her escape. Despite proximity, she took a moment on the other side to catch her breath. *Vampires. Demons. They don't teach you about this sort of shit at the police academy. . . .*

Seven

Because the streets in the inner city were far from dark, and as she'd managed so well out at Woodbine with much less light, Vicki decided to walk home. She turned her collar up against the wind, shoved her gloved hands deep in her pockets, more out of habit than for additional warmth, and started west along Bloor Street. It wasn't that far and she needed to think.

The cool air felt good against her jaw and seemed to be easing the pounding in her head. Although she had to be careful about how heavily her heels struck the pavement, walking remained infinitely preferable to the jostling she'd receive in the back of a cab.

And she needed to think.

Vampires and demons; or *a* vampire and *a* demon at least. In eight years on the police force, she'd seen a lot of strangeness and been forced to believe in the existence of things that most sane people—police officers and social workers excepted—preferred to ignore. Next to some of the cruelties the strong inflicted on the weak, vampires and demons weren't that hard to swallow. And the vampire seemed to be one of the good guys.

She saw him smile again and sternly stopped herself from responding to the memory.

At Yonge Street, she turned south, waiting for the green more out of habit than necessity. While not exactly ablaze with light, the intersection was far from dark and the traffic was still infrequent. She wasn't the only person around, Yonge Street never completely emptied, but the others whose business or lifestyle kept them out in the hours between midnight and dawn stayed carefully, unobtrusively, out of her way.

"It's 'cause you walk like a cop," Tony had explained once. "After a while, you guys all develop the same look. In uniform, out of uniform; it doesn't matter any more."

Vicki saw no reason to disbelieve him, she'd seen the effect for herself. Just as she saw no reason to disbelieve Henry Fitzroy; she'd seen the demon for herself as well.

Darkness swirled in darkness and was gone. She'd seen no more than the hint of a shape sinking into the earth, and for that she gave thanks. The vague outline she remembered held horror enough and her mind kept shying away from the memory. The smell of decay, however, she remembered perfectly.

It had been neither sight nor smell that had convinced her Henry spoke the truth. Both could be faked, although she had no idea of how or why. Her own reaction convinced her. Her own terror. Her mind's refusal to clearly recall what she had seen. The feeling of evil, cloying and cold, emanating out of the darkness.

Vicki pulled her jacket tighter, the chill that pebbled her flesh having nothing to do with the temperature of the night.

Demon. At least now they knew what they were looking for. They knew? No, *she* knew. She cracked a smile as she thought of explaining all this to Mike Celluci. He hadn't been there, he'd think she was out of her mind. *Hell, if I hadn't been there, I'd think I was out of my mind.* Besides, she couldn't tell Celluci without betraying Henry. . . .

Henry. Vampire. If he wasn't what he claimed, why would he go to all the trouble of creating such a complicated story?

Never mind, she chided herself. *Stupid question.* She'd known pathological liars, had arrested a couple, had worked with one, and why was never a question they concerned themselves with.

Henry's story had been so complicated, it had to be the truth. Didn't it?

At College Street, she paused on the corner. Only a block to the west, she could see the lights of police headquarters. She could go in, grab a coffee, talk to someone who understood. *About demons and vampires, right.*

Suddenly, the headquarters building seemed very far away.

She could walk past it, keep walking west to Huron Street and home, but, in spite of everything, she wasn't tired and didn't want to enclose herself with walls until she had banished all the dark on dark from the shadows. She watched a streetcar rattle by, the capsule of warmth and light empty save for the driver, and continued south to Dundas.

Approaching the glass and concrete bulk of the Eaton's Center, she heard the bells of St. Michael's Cathedral sound the hour. In the daytime, the ambient noise of the city masked their call but in the still, quiet time before dawn they reverberated throughout the downtown core. Lesser bells added their notes, but the bells of St. Michael's dominated.

Not really sure why, Vicki followed the sound. She'd chased a pusher up the steps of the cathedral once, years ago when she'd still been in uniform. He'd grabbed at the doors claiming sanctuary. The doors had been locked. Apparently, not even God trusted the night in the heart of a large city. The pusher had fought all the way back to the car and he hadn't thought it at all funny when Vicki and her partner insisted on referring to him as Quasimodo.

She expected the heavy wooden doors to be locked again, but to her surprise they swung silently open. Just as silently, she slipped inside and pulled them closed behind her.

Quiet please, warned a cardboard sign, mounted in a gleaming brass floor stand, *Holy Week Vigil in progress.*

Her rubber soled shoes squeaking faintly against the floor, Vicki moved into the sanctum. Only about half of the lights were on, creating an unreal, almost mythical twilight in the church. Vicki could see, but only just and only because she didn't attempt to focus on anything outside the specific. A priest knelt at the altar and the first few rows of pews held a scattering of stocky women dressed in black, looking as though they'd been punched out of the same mold. The faint murmur of voices, lifted in what Vicki assumed was prayer, and the fainter click of beads, did nothing to disturb the heavy hush that hung over the building. Waiting; it felt like they were waiting. For what, Vicki had no idea.

The flickering of open flame caught her eye and she slipped down a side aisle until she could see into an alcove off the south wall. Three or four tiers of candles in red glass jars rose up to a mural that gleamed under a single spotlight. The Madonna, draped in blue and white, held her arms wide as though to embrace a weary world. Her smile offered comfort and the artist had captured a certain sadness around the eyes.

Like many of her generation, Vicki had been raised vaguely Christian. She could recognize the symbols of the church, and she knew the historical story, but that was about it. Not for the first time, she wondered if maybe she hadn't missed out on something important. Peeling off her gloves, she slid into a pew.

I don't even know if I believe in God, she admitted apologetically to the mural. *But then, I didn't believe in vampires before tonight.*

It was warm in the cathedral and the nap she'd had that afternoon seemed very far away. Slowly she slid down against the polished wood and slowly the Madonna's face began to blur. . . .

In the distance something shattered with the hard, definite crash that suggested to an experienced ear it had been thrown violently to the floor. Vicki stirred, opened her eyes, but couldn't seem to gather enough energy to move. She sat slumped in the pew, caught in a curious assitude while the sounds of destruction grew closer. She could hear men's voices shouting, more self-satisfied than angry, but she couldn't catch the words.

In the alcove the spotlight appeared to have burned out. Wrapped in shadow, illuminated only by the tiers of flickering candles, the Madonna continued to smile sadly, holding her arms out to the world. Vicki frowned. The candles were squat and white, the wax dribbling down irregular sides to pool and harden in the metal holders and on the stone floor.

But the candles were enclosed . . . and the floor, the floor was carpeted. . . .

A crash, louder and closer than the others, actually caused her to jerk but didn't break the inertia holding her in the pew.

She saw the ax head first, then the shaft, then the man holding it. He charged up the side aisle from the front of the church, from the altar. His dark clothes were marked with plaster dust and through the gaping front of his bulging leather vest Vicki thought she saw the glint of gold. Candlelight glittered off colored bits of broken glass caught in the folded tops of his wide boots. Sweat had darkened his short hair, blunt cut to follow the curve of his head, and his lips were drawn back to reveal the yellow slabs of his teeth.

He rocked to a halt at the entrance to the alcove, caught his breath, and raised the ax.

It stopped short of the Madonna's smile, the haft slapping into the upraised hand of the young man who had suddenly appeared in its path. The axman swore and tried to yank the weapon free. The ax stayed exactly where it was.

From Vicki's point of view it appeared that the young man twisted his wrist a gentle half turn and then lowered his arm, but he must have done more for the axman swore again, lost his grip, and almost lost his footing. He stumbled back and Vicki got her first good look at the young man now holding the ax across his body.

Henry. The tiers of flickering candle flame behind him brought out the red-gold highlights in his hair and created almost a halo around his head. He wore the colors of the Madonna; wide bands of snowy white lace at collar and cuff, a white shirt billowing through the slashed sleeves of his pale blue jacket. His eyes, deep in shadow, narrowed and his hands jerked up.

The ax haft snapped. The sound of its shattering reverberated through the alcove, closely followed by the rattle of both pieces striking the floor. Vicki didn't see Henry move, but the next thing she knew he had the axman hanging from his fist by the front of his vest, feet dangling a foot off the marble floor.

"The Blessed Virgin is under my protection," he said, and the quiet words held more menace than any weapon.

The axman's mouth opened and closed, but no sound emerged. He hung limp and terrified. When dropped, he collapsed to his knees, apparently unable to take his eyes from Henry's face.

To Vicki, the vampire looked like an avenging angel, ready to draw a flaming sword at any moment and strike down the enemies of God. The axman apparently agreed, for he moaned softly and raised trembling hands in entreaty.

Henry stepped back and allowed his captive to look away. "Go," he commanded.

Still on his knees, the axman went, scrambling backward until he moved from Vicki's line of sight. Henry watched him go a moment longer, than turned, made the sign of the cross, and knelt. Above his bowed head, VIcki met the painted eyes of the Madonna. Her own grew heavy and, of their own volition, slid slowly closed.

When she opened them again a second later, the spotlight had returned, the candles were back in their red glass containers, and a red-gold head remained bowed beneath the mural.

The inability to move seemed gone, so she pulled herself to her feet and slid out of the pew heading toward the alcove. "Henry. . . ."

At the sound of his name, he crossed himself, stood, and turned to face her, pulling closed his black leather trenchcoat as he moved.

"Wha . . ."

He shook his head, put his finger to his lips, and taking her arm gently in one hand, led her out of the sanctum.

"Did you have a pleasant nap?" he asked, releasing her arm as the heavy wooden door closed behind them.

"Nap?" Vicki repeated, running a hand up through her hair. "I, I guess I did."

Henry peered up into her face with a worried frown. "Are you all right? Your head took a nasty blow earlier."

"No, I'm fine." Obviously, it had been a dream. "You don't have an accent." He'd had one in the dream.

"I lost it years ago. I came to Canada just after World War I. Are you sure you're all right?"

"I told you, I'm fine." She started down the cathedral steps.

Henry sighed and followed. He seemed to remember reading that sleeping after a concussion was not necessarily a good thing, but he'd entered the church right behind her and she hadn't been asleep very long.

It was just a dream, Vicki told herself firmly as the two of them headed north. *Vampires and demons I can handle, but holy visions are out.* Although why she should dream about Henry Fitzroy defending a painting of the Virgin Mary from what looked like one of Cromwell's roundheads she had no idea. *Maybe it was a sign.* Maybe it *was* the blow she'd taken on the head. Either way, her few remaining doubts about his ex-royal bastard highness seemed to have vanished and while she was more willing to bet on her subconscious working it out than on God intervening, she decided to keep an open mind. Just in case. *Wait a minute. . . .*

"You followed me!"

Henry smiled guardedly. "I'd just told you a secret that could get me killed. I had to see how you were dealing with it."

In spite of her pique, Vicki had to admit he made sense. "And?"

He shrugged. "You tell me."

Vicki pushed the strap of her bag back up on her shoulder. "I think," she said slowly, "that you're right. We could accomplish more working together. So, for now, you've got yourself a partner." She stumbled over a dark crack in the pavement, righted herself before Henry could help, and added dryly, "But I think you should know that generally, I only work days." It wasn't the time to tell him why. Not yet.

Henry nodded. "Days are fine. I myself, being a little sensitive to sunlight, prefer to work nights. Between us, we have the entire twenty-four hours covered. And speaking of days," he shot a quick glance to the east where he could feel dawn approaching, "I have to go. Can we discuss this tomorrow evening?"

"When?"

"About two hours after sunset? It'll give me time to grab a bite."

He was gone before she had time to react. Or agree.

"We'll see who plays straight man to whom tomorrow night," she snorted and turned west toward home.

The sun had cracked the horizon by the time she reached her apartment, and with yawns threatening to rip her jaw from her face, she fell straight into bed.

Only to be rudely awakened about forty-five minutes later. . . .

"Where! Have! You! Been!" Celluci punctuated each word with a vigorous shake.

Vicki, whose reactions had never been particularly fast when first roused from sleep, actually let him finish the sentence before bringing her arms up between his and breaking his grip on her shoulders.

"What the hell are you talking about, Celluci?" she demanded, shielding her eyes against the glare from the overhead light with one hand and grabbing her glasses off the bedside table with the other.

"One of the uniforms saw a women who looked like you being bundled into a late model BMW, just after midnight, and not more than five blocks from the latest body. You want to tell me you weren't in the Woodbine area tonight?"

Vicki leaned back and sighed, pushing her glasses up her nose. "What makes that any business of yours?" There was no point in trying to reason with Celluci until he calmed down.

"I'll tell you what makes it my business." He threw himself off the bed and began to pace the length of the bedroom; three steps and turn, three steps and turn. "You were in the middle of a police investigation, that's what makes it my business. You were. . . ." Suddenly, he stopped. His eyes narrowed and he jabbed an accusing finger in Vicki's direction. "What hit you?"

"Nothing."

"Nothing does not put a black and blue lump the size of a grapefruit on your jaw," Celluci growled. "It was him, wasn't it? The guy loading you into his car." He sat back down on the bed and reached out to turn Vicki's face into the light.

"You are out of your mind!" She knocked his hand away. "Since you obviously aren't going to let me get back to sleep until you satisfy your completely irrational curiosity; I *was* in the area. And, as you keep telling me, I don't see so well in the dark." She smiled with scorpion sweetness. "You were right about something. Make you feel better?"

He responded with an identical smile and growled, "Get on with it."

"I went with a friend. When I walked my face into a post, he took me back to his place to make sure I was all right. All right?" She waved a hand at the door and threw herself back on the pillows. "Now get out!"

"The hell it's all right." He slammed his palm against the bed. "Next to my partner, you are the world's worst liar and you are throwing some grade A bullshit in my direction. Who's this friend?"

"None of your business."

"Where did he take you?"

"Also none of your business." She sat back up and shoved her face close to his. "You jealous, Celluci?"

"Jealous? Damn it, Vicki!" He raised his hands as if to shake her again but let them fall as her eyes narrowed and her own hands came up. "I've got six dead bodies out there. I don't want you to be the seventh!"

Her voice dropped dangerously low. "But *you* should be able to throw yourself in the line of fire?"

"What does that have to do with anything? I had half the fucking force out there with me. You were alone!"

"Oh." She grabbed the front of his jacket and dragged him suddenly forward until their noses touched. "So you were worried?" she ground the words out through clenched teeth. It hurt her jaw, but at least it kept her from ripping his throat out.

"Of course, I was worried."

"THEN WHY DIDN'T YOU SAY SO INSTEAD OF ALTERNATELY ASSAULTING AND ACCUSING ME!" She pushed him backward so hard she flung him off the bed and he had to scramble to get his feet under him.

"Well?" she prodded when he'd regained his balance again.

He pushed the heavy curl of hair off his forehead and shrugged, actually looking a little sheepish. "It . . . I . . . I don't know."

Folding her arms over her breasts, Vicki settled carefully back against the pillows. Given that she'd have done exactly the same thing under similar circumstances she supposed she'd have to let it pass. Besides, her jaw hurt, her whole head hurt, and now she had enough adrenaline in her system to keep her awake for a week.

"You been home yet?" she asked.

Celluci rubbed a weary hand across his eyes. "No. Not yet."

Settling her glasses back on the bedside table, she patted the sheet beside her.

A little later, something occurred to her.

"Wait a minute—watch my jaw—you gave me back your key to my apartment months ago." He'd thrown it at her as a matter of fact.

"I had a copy made."

"You told me there were no copies!"

"Vicki, *you* are a lousy liar. *I* am a very good one. Ow, that hurt!"

"It was supposed to."

"No, Mom, I'm not sick. I was just up late last night working on a case." Vicki wedged the phone between her shoulder and her ear and poured herself a mug of coffee.

On the other end of the line she heard her mother sigh deeply. "You know, Vicki, I had hoped that when you left the force I'd be able to stop worrying about you. And here it is, three in the afternoon and you're not out of bed yet."

What the second observation had to do with the first, escaped Vicki entirely. "Mom, I'm up. I'm drinking coffee." She took a noisy swallow. "I'm talking to you. What more do you want?"

"I want you to get a normal job."

As Vicki was well aware how proud her mother had been of her two police citations, she let this pass. She knew that in time, if it hadn't happened already, the phrase "my daughter the private investigator" would begin peppering her mother's conversations much the way "my daughter the homicide investigator" had.

"And what's more, Vicki, your voice sounds funny."

"I walked my face into a post. I got a bit of a bump on my chin. It hurts a little when I talk."

"Did this happen last night?"

"Yes, Mom."

"You know you can't see in the dark. . . ."

It was Vicki's turn to sigh. "Mom, you're beginning to sound like Celluci." On cue, Celluci came out of the bedroom, tucking his shirt into his pants. Vicki waved him at the coffeepot, but he shook his head and stuffed his arms into his overcoat. "Hold on for a minute, Mom." She covered the receiver with one hand and looked him over critically. "If we're going to keep this up, you'd better bring a razor back over. You look like a terrorist."

He scratched at his chin and shrugged. "I have a razor at the office."

"And a change of clothes?"

"They can live with yesterday's shirt for a few hours." He bent down and kissed her gently, careful not to put too much pressure on the spreading green and purple bruise. "I don't suppose you'll listen if I ask you to be careful?"

She returned the kiss as enthusiastically as she was able to and said, "I don't suppose you'll listen if I ask you to stop being a patronizing son of a bitch?"

He scowled. "Because I ask you to be careful?"

"Because you assume I won't be. Because you assume I'm going to do something stupid."

"All right." He spread his arms in surrender. "How about, don't do anything I wouldn't do?"

She considered saying, *"I'm paying a call on a vampire tonight, how do you feel about that?"* but decided against it and said instead, "I thought you didn't want me to do anything stupid?"

He smiled. "I'll call you," he told her, and left.

"You still there, Mom?"

"They won't let me go home until five, dear. Where else would I be? What was that all about?"

"Mike Celluci was just leaving." She tucked the phone under her arm and with the extra long cord trailing behind her, got up to make toast.

"So you're seeing him again?"

The last piece of bread was a little moldy around the edges. She tossed it in the garbage and settled for a bag of no-name chocolate chip cookies. "I seem to be."

"Well, you know what they say about spring and a young man's fancy."

She sounded doubtful, so Vicki changed the subject. Her mother had liked Celluci well enough the few times they'd met, she just thought that temperamentally they'd both be better off with someone calmer. "It's spring?" Gusts of wind slapped what could've been rain but looked more like sleet against the windows.

"It's April, dear. That makes it spring."

"Yeah, what's your weather like?"

Her mother laughed. "It's snowing."

Vicki brushed cookie crumbs off her sweatshirt and got herself more coffee. "Look, Mom, this is going to be costing the department a fortune." Her mother had worked for eighteen years as the private secretary of the head of Life Sciences at Queen's University, Kingston and she abused the privileges that had accumulated as often as possible. "Although you know I enjoy talking to you, did you have an actual reason for calling?"

"Well, I was wondering if you might be coming down for Easter."

"Easter?"

"It's this weekend. I won't be working tomorrow or Monday, we could have four whole days together."

Darkness, demons, vampires, and six bodies, the life violently ripped from them.

"I don't think so, Mom. The case I'm on could break at any time. . . ."

After listening to a few more platitudes and promising to stay in touch, Vicki hung up and went to her weight bench to work off equal parts of cookies and guilt.

* * *

"Henry, it's Caroline. I've got tickets to the *Phantom* for May fourth. You said you wanted to see it and now's your chance. Give me a call in the next couple of days if you're free."

It was the only message on the machine. Henry shook his head at his vague sense of disappointment. There was no reason for Vicki Nelson to call. No reason he should want her to.

"All right," he glared at his reflection in the antique mirror over the telephone table, "you tell me why I trusted her. Circumstance?" He shook his head. "No. Circumstance said I should have disposed of her. A much neater solution with much less risk. Try again. She reminded you of someone? If you live long enough, and you will, *everyone* will remind you of someone."

Turning away from the mirror, he sighed and ran his fingers through his hair. He could deny it all he wanted but she did remind him of someone, not in form perhaps but in manner.

Ginevra Treschi had been the first mortal he had trusted after the change. There had been others with whom he had played at trust but in her arms he was himself, not needing to be anything more. Or less.

When he found he could not live in Elizabeth's England—it was both too like and too unlike the England he had known—he had moved south, to Italy and finally to Venice. Venice had much to offer one of his kind for the ancient city came alive at night and in its shadows he could feed as he chose.

It had been carnival, he remembered, and Ginevra had been standing by San Marco, at the edge of the square, watching the crowd surging back and forth before her like a living kaleidoscope. She'd seemed so very real amidst all the posturing that he'd moved closer. When she left, he followed her back to her father's house then spent the rest of the night discovering her name and situation.

"Ginevra Treschi." Even three hundred years and many mortals later it still sounded in his mouth like a benediction.

The next night, while the servants slept and the house was quiet and dark, he'd slipped into her room. Her heartbeat had drawn him to the bed and he'd gently pulled the covers back. Almost thirty and three years a widow, she wasn't beautiful, but she was so alive—even asleep—that he'd found himself staring. Only to find, a few moments later, that she was staring back at him.

"I don't wish to hurry your decision," she'd said dryly. "But I'm getting chilled and I'd like to know if I should scream."

He'd intended to convince her he was only a dream but he found he couldn't.

They had almost a year of nights together.

"A convent?" Henry raised himself up on one elbow, disentangling a long strand of ebony hair from around the back of his neck. "If you'll forgive me saying so, *bella,* I don't think you'd enjoy convent life."

"I'm not making a joke, Enrico. I go with the Benedictine Sisters tomorrow after early Mass."

For a moment, Henry couldn't speak. The thought of his Ginevra locked away from the world struck him as close to a physical blow. "Why?" he managed at last.

She sat up, wrapping her arms around her knees. "I had a choice, the Sisters or Giuseppe Lemmo." Her lips pursed as though she tasted something sour. "The convent seemed the better course."

"But why choose at all?"

She smiled and shook her head. "In your years out of the world you have forgotten a few things, my love. My father wishes me for Signore Lemmo, but he will graciously allow me to go to God if only to get his overly educated daughter out of his house." Her voice grew serious and she stroked a finger down the length of Henry's bare chest. "He fears the Inquisition, Enrico. Fears that I will bring the Papal Hounds down upon the family.'' Her lips twisted. ''Or that he will be forced to denounce me.''

Henry stared at her in astonishment. ''The Inquisition? But you've done nothing. . . .''

Both her eyebrows rose. ''I am lying with you and for some, even not knowing what you are, that would be enough. If they knew that I willingly give myself to an Angel of Darkness . . .'' She turned her wrist so that the small puncture wound became visible. ''. . . burning would be too good for me.'' A finger laid against his lips stopped him when he tried to speak. ''Yes, yes, no one knows but I am also a woman who dares to use her mind and that is enough for these times. If my husband had died and left me rich or if I had borne a son to carry on his name. . . .'' Her shoulder's lifted and fell. ''Unfortunately . . .''

He caught up her hand. ''You have another choice.''

''No.'' She sighed. The breath quavered as she released it. ''I have thought long and hard on this, Enrico, and I cannot take your path. It is my need to live as I am that places me in danger now, I simply could not exist behind the masks you must wear to survive.''

It was the truth and he knew it, but that made it no easier to bear. ''When I was changed . . .''

''When you were changed,'' she interrupted, ''from what you have told me, the passion was so great it left no room for rational thought, no room to consider what would happen after. Although I am fond of passion,'' her hand slid down between his legs, ''I cannot lose myself in it.''

He pushed her back onto the pillow, trapping her beneath him. ''This doesn't have to end.''

She laughed. ''I know you, Enrico.'' Her eyes half closed and she thrust her hips up against him. ''Could you do *this* with a nun?''

After a moment of shock, he laughed as well and bent his mouth to hers. ''If you are sure,'' he murmured against her lips.

''I am. If I must give up my freedom, better to God than to man.''

All he could do was respect her decision.

It hurt to lose her, but in the months that followed the hurt eased and it was enough to know that the Sisters kept her safe. Although he thought of leaving, Henry lingered in Venice, not wanting to cut the final tie.

Chance alone brought him news that the Sisters had not been able to keep her safe enough. Hushed whispers overheard in a dark café said the Hounds had come for Ginevra Treschi, taken her right from the convent, said she had been consorting with the devil, said they were going to make an example of her. She had been with them three weeks.

Three weeks with fire and iron and pain.

He wanted to storm their citadel like Christ at the gates of hell, but he forced himself to contain his rage. He could not save her if he threw himself into the Inquisitor's embrace.

If anything remained of her to be saved.

They had taken over a wing of the Doge's palace—the Doge being more than willing to cooperate with Rome. The smell of death rolled through the halls like fog and the blood scent left a trail so thick a mortal could have followed it.

He found her hanging as they'd left her. Her wrists had been tightly bound behind her back, a coarse rope threaded through the lashing and used to hoist her into the air. Heavy iron weights hung from her burned ankles. They had obviously begun with flogging and had added greater and more painful persuasions over time. She had been dead only a few hours.

". . . confessed to having relations with the devil, was forgiven, and gave her soul up to God." He rubbed his fingers in his beard. "Very satisfactory all around. Shall we return the body to the Sisters or to her family?"

The older Dominican shrugged. "I cannot see that it makes any difference, she. . . . Who are you?"

Henry smiled. "I am vengeance," he said, closing the door behind him and bolting it.

* * *

"Vengeance." Henry sighed and wiped damp palms on his jeans. The Papal Hounds had died in terror, begging for their lives, but it hadn't brought Ginevra back. Nothing had, until Vicki had prodded at the memories. She was as real in her own world as Ginevra had been and unless he was very careful, she was about to become as real in his.

He'd wanted this, hadn't he? Someone to trust. Someone who could see beneath the masks.

He turned again to face his reflection in the mirror. The others, men and women whose lives he'd entered over the years since Ginevra, had never touched him like this.

"Keep her at a distance," he warned himself. "At least until the demon is defeated." His reflection looked dubious and he sighed. "I only hope I'm up to it."

* * *

The girl darted behind the heavy table, sapphire eyes flashing. "I thought you were a gentleman, sir!"

"You are exactly right, Smith." The captain bowed with a feline grace, never taking his mocking gaze from his quarry. "Or should that be Miss Smith? Never mind. As you pointed out, I was a gentleman. You'll find I surrendered the title some time ago." He lunged, but she twisted lithely out of his way.

"If you make one more move toward me, I shall scream."

"Scream away." Roxborough settled one slim hip against the table. "I shan't stop you. Although it would pain me to have to share such a lovely prize with my crew."

"Fitzroy, what is this shit?"

"Henry, please, not Fitzroy." He saved the file and shut off the computer. "And this shit," he told her, straightening, "is my new book."

"Your what?" Vicki asked, pushing her glasses up her nose. She'd followed him from the door of the condo into the tiny office even though he'd requested that she wait a minute in the living room. If he was going back to close his coffin, she had to see it. "You actually read this stuff?"

Henry sighed, pulled a paperback off the shelf above the desk, and handed it to her. "No. I actually write the stuff."

"Oh." Across the cover of the book, a partially unclothed young woman was being passionately yet discreetly embraced by an entirely unclothed young man. The cover copy announced the date of the romance as "the late 1800s" but both characters had distinctly out of period hair and makeup. Cursive lavender script delineated both the title and the author's name; *Destiny's Master* by Elizabeth Fitzroy.

"Elizabeth Fitzroy?" Vicki asked, returning the book.

Henry slid it back on the shelf, rolled the chair out from the desk, and stood, smiling sardonically. "Why *not* Elizabeth Fitzroy? She certainly had as much right to the name as I do."

The prefix "Fitz" was a bastard's name and was given to acknowledged accidental children. The "roy" identified the father as the king. "You didn't agree with the divorce?"

The smile twisted further. "I was always a loyal subject of the king, my father." He paused and frowned as though trying to remember. He sounded less mocking when he started speaking again. "I liked her Gracious Majesty Queen Catherine. She was kind to a very confused little boy who'd been dumped into a situation he didn't understand and he didn't ever much care for. Mary, the Princess Royal, who could have ignored me or done worse, accepted me as her brother." His voice picked up an edge. "I did not like Elizabeth's mother and the feeling was most definitely mutual. Given that all parties concerned have now passed to their eternal reward; no, I did not agree with the divorce."

Vicki glanced back at the shelf of paperbacks as Henry politely but inexorably ushered her out of his office. "I suppose you've got a lot of material to use for plots," she muttered dubiously.

"I do," Henry agreed, wondering why some people

had less trouble handling the idea of a vampire than they did a romance writer.

"I suppose you can get even with any number of people in your past this way." Of all the strange scenarios Vicki had imagined occurring during this evening's conference with the over four century old, vampiric, bastard son of Henry VIII, none had included discovering that he was a writer of—*What was the term?*—bodice rippers.

He grinned and shook his head. "If you're thinking of my relatives, I got even with most of them. I'm still alive. But that's not why I write. I'm good at it, I make a very good living doing it, and most of the time I enjoy it." He waved her to the couch and sat down at the opposite end. "I could exist from feeding to feeding—and I have—but I infinitely prefer living in comfort than in some rat-infested mausoleum."

"But if you've been around for so long," Vicki wondered, settling down into the same corner she'd vacated early that morning, "why aren't you rich?"

"Rich?"

Vicki found his throaty chuckle very attractive and also found herself speculating about. . . . A mental smack brought her wandering mind back to the business at hand.

"Oh, sure," he continued, "I could've bought IBM for pennies in nineteen-oh-whenever, but who knew? I'm a vampire, I'm not clairvoyant. Now," he picked a piece of lint off his jeans, "may I ask you a question?"

"Be my guest."

"Why did you believe what I told you?"

"Because I saw the demon and you had no logical reason to lie to me." There was no need to tell him about the dream—or vision—in the church. It hadn't had much to do with her decision anyway.

"That's it?"

"I'm an uncomplicated sort of a person. Now," she mimicked his tone, "enough about us. How *do* we catch a demon?"

Very well, Henry agreed silently. *If that's how you want it, enough about us.*

"We don't. I do." He inclined his head toward her

end of the couch. "You catch the man or woman calling it up."

"Fine." Tackling the source made perfect sense to Vicki and the farther she could stay from that repulsive bit of darkness the happier she'd be. She perched her right foot on her left knee and clasped both hands around the ankle. "How come you're so sure we're dealing with a single person, not a coven or a cult?"

"Focused desire is a large part of what pulls the demon through and most groups just can't achieve the necessary single-mindedness." He shrugged. "Given the success rate, the odds are good it's just one person."

She mirrored his shrug. "Then we go with the odds. Any distinguishing characteristics I should look for?"

Henry stretched his arm out and drummed his fingers against the upholstery. "If you're asking does a certain type of person call up demons, no. Well," he frowned as he reconsidered, "in a way, yes. Without exception, they're people looking for an easy answer, a way to get what they want without working for it."

"You just described a way of life for millions of people," Vicki told him dryly. "Could you be a little more specific?"

"The demon is being asked for material goods; it wouldn't need to kill if it remained trapped in the pentagram answering questions. Look for someone who's suddenly acquired great wealth, money, cars. And demons can't create so all that has to come from somewhere."

"We could catch him for possession of stolen goods?" They couldn't mark every bit of cash in existence, but luxury cars, jewels, and stocks all were traceable. Vicki's pulse began to quicken as she ran over the possibilities now open to investigation. *Yes!* Her hands curled into fists and punched the air triumphantly. It was only a matter of time. They had him. Or her.

"One more thing," Henry warned, trying not to smile at her—What did they call it? Shadow boxing? "The more contact this person has with demonkind, the more unstable he or she is going to get."

"Yeah? Well, it's another trait to look for, but you've

got to be pretty damned unstable to stand out these days. What about the demon?''

"The demon isn't very powerful."

Vicki snorted. "You might be able to rip a person's throat out with a single blow . . ." She paused and Henry nodded, answering the not-quite-asked question. ". . . but no one else I know could. This demon is plenty powerful enough."

Henry shook his head. "Not as demons go. It has to feed every time it's called in order to have an effect on things in this world."

"So the deaths were it feeding? Completely random?"

"They didn't mean anything to the person controlling the demon if that's what you're asking. If the demon had been killing business or personal rivals of a single person, the police would have found him or her by now. No, the demon chose where and whom to feed on."

Vicki frowned. "But there *was* a definite external pattern."

"My guess is that the demon being called is under the control of another, more powerful demon and has been attempting to form that demon's name on the city."

"Oh."

Henry waited patiently while Vicki absorbed this new bit of information.

"Why?" Actually, she wasn't sure she wanted to know. Or that she needed to ask.

"Access; uncontrolled access for the more powerful demon and however many more of its kind it might want to bring through."

"And how many more deaths until the name is completed?"

"No way of knowing."

"One? Two? You must have some idea," she snapped. With one hand he gave her hope, with the other he took it away. The son of a bitch. "How many deaths in a demon's name?"

"It depends on the demon." As Vicki scowled, he rose, walked to the bookcase, and slid open one of the glass doors. The book he removed was about the size of a dictionary, bound in leather that might have once been red before years of handling had darkened it to a worn and greasy black. He sat back down, closer this time, twisted the darkly patinaed clasp, and opened the book to a double page spread.

"It's hand-written," Vicki marveled, touching the corner of a page. She withdrew her finger quickly. The parchment had felt warm, like she'd just touched something obscenely alive.

"It's very old." Henry ignored her reaction; his had been much the same the first time he'd touched the book. "These are the demonic names. There're twenty-seven of them and no way of knowing if the author discovered them all."

The names, written in thick black ink in an unpleasantly angular script, were for the most part seven or eight letters long. "The demon can't be anywhere near finished," she said thankfully. She still had time to find the bastard behind this.

Henry shook his head, hating to dampen her enthusiasm. "It wouldn't be laying out the entire name, just the symbol for it." He flipped ahead a few pages. The list of names was repeated and beside each was a corresponding geometrical sign. Some were very simple. "Literacy is a fairly recent phenomenon," Henry murmured. "The signs are all that are really needed."

Vicki swallowed. Her mouth had gone suddenly dry. Some of the signs were *very* simple.

Silently, Henry closed the book and replaced it on the shelf. When he turned to face her again, he spread his arms in a helpless gesture. "Unfortunately," he said, "I can't stop the demon until after it kills again."

"Why not?"

"Because I have to be there ready for it. And last night it completed the second part of the pattern."

"Then it could have completed . . ."

"No. We'd know if it had."

"But the next death, the death that starts the pattern again, it could complete . . ."

"No, not yet. Not even the least complicated of the names could be finished so quickly."

"You were ready for it last night." He'd been there,

just as she had. "Why didn't you stop it, then?" But then, why didn't she?

"Stop it?" The laugh had little humor in it. "It moved so fast I barely saw it. But the time after next, now that I know what I'm facing, I'll be waiting for it. I can trap it and destroy it."

That sounded encouraging, if there *was* a time after next. "You've done this before?"

She needed reassurance but Henry, who knew he could make her believe anything he chose to tell her, found he couldn't lie. "Well, no." He'd never been able to lie to Ginevra either, another similarity between the two women he'd just as soon not have found.

Vicki took a deep breath and picked at the edge of her sweater. "Henry, how bad will it get if the named demon gets free?"

"How bad?" He sighed and sagged back against the bookcase. "At the risk of being considered facetious, all hell will break loose."

Eight

Norman glanced around the Cock and Bull and frowned. Thursday, Friday, and Saturday nights, the nights he'd set aside for seriously trying to pick up chicks, he arrived early to be sure of getting a table. So far, this had meant by 9:30 or 10:00, someone would have to share with him. Tonight, the Thursday before the long Easter weekend, the student pub was so empty it looked as if he'd have no company all night.

It isn't cool to go home for Easter, he thought smugly, running a finger up and down the condensation on his glass of diet ginger ale. His parents had been disappointed, but he'd been adamant. The really cool guys hung out around the university all weekend and Norman Birdwell was now really cool.

He sighed. They didn't, however, apparently hang out at the Cock and Bull. He'd have given up and gone home long ago except for the redhead who held court at the table in the corner. She was absolutely beautiful, everything Norman had ever wanted in a woman, and he had long adored her from across the room in their Comparative Religions class. She wasn't very tall, but her flaming hair gave her a presence and inches in other areas made up for her lack of height. Norman could imagine ripping off her shirt and just gazing at the softly mounded flesh beneath. She'd smile at him in rapt adoration and he'd gently reach out to touch. His imagination wasn't up to much beyond that, so he replayed the scene over and over as he stared across the room.

A beer or two later and voices at the corner table began to rise.

"But I'm telling you there's evidence," the redhead exclaimed, "for the killer being a creature of the night."

"Get real, Coreen!"

Her name was Coreen! Norman's heart picked up an irregular rhythm and he leaned forward, straining to hear more clearly.

"What about the missing blood?" Coreen demanded. "Every victim sucked dry."

"A pyscho," snorted one of her companions.

"A giant leech," suggested another. "A giant leech that slimes along the streets of the city until it finds a victim and then . . . SLURP!" He sucked back a beer, suiting the action to the word. The group at the table groaned and buried him in thrown napkins and then Coreen's voice rose over the babble.

"I'm telling you there was nothing natural about these deaths!"

"Nothing natural about giant leeches either," muttered a tall, blonde woman in a bright pink flannel shirt.

Coreen turned on her. "You know what I mean, Janet. And I'm not the only person who thinks so either!"

"You're talking about the stories in the newspapers? Vampire stalks city and all that?" Janet sighed expansively and shook her head. "Coreen, they don't believe that bullshit, they're just trying to sell papers."

"It isn't bullshit!" Coreen insisted, slamming her empty mug down on the table. "Ian was killed by a vampire!" Her mouth thinned into an obstinate line and the others at the table exchanged speaking glances. One by one, they made excuses and drifted away.

Coreen didn't even look up as Norman sat down in Janet's recently vacated chair. She was thinking of how foolish all her so-called friends would look when her private investigator found the vampire and destroyed him. They'd soon stop laughing at her then.

Norman, after taking a few moments to work out the best things to say, tried a tentative, "Hi." The icy stare he received in response discouraged him a little, but he swallowed and went on. He might never get another chance like this. "I just, uh, wanted you to know that, uh, I believe you."

"Believe what?" The question was only slightly less icy than the stare.

"Believe, well, you. About the vampires." Norman lowered his voice. "And stuff."

The way he said *"and stuff"* sent chills down Coreen's back. She took a closer look and thought she might vaguely remember him from one of her classes, although she couldn't place which one. Nor could she be sure if her lack of clear memory had more to do with him or with the pitcher of beer she'd just finished.

"I know," he continued, glancing around to be sure that no one would overhear, "that there's more to the world than most people think. And I know what it's like to be laughed at." He ground out the last words with such feeling that she had to believe them and believing them, to believe the rest.

"It doesn't matter what we know." She poked him in the chest with a fingernail only a slightly less brilliant red than her hair. "We can't prove anything."

"I can. I've got completely incontestable proof in my apartment." He grinned at her look of surprise and nodded, adding emphasis. *And the best part of it is,* he thought, almost rubbing his hands in anticipation, *it isn't a line. I do have the proof and when I show her, she'll fall into my arms and. . . .* Once again, his imagination balked but he didn't care that fantasy failed him; soon he'd have the reality.

"You can help me prove that a vampire murdered Ian?" The brilliant green eyes blazed and Norman, transfixed, found himself stammering.

"V-vampire. . . ." Caught up in the proof he could offer her, he'd forgotten she expected vampires.

Coreen took the repetition as an affirmation. "Good." She practically dragged him to his feet and then out of the Cock and Bull. She wasn't very big, Norman discovered, but she was pretty strong. "We'll take my car. It's out in the lot."

Her headlong charge slowed a little as they reached the doors and stopped completely by the row of pay phones. She frowned and came to a sudden decision.

"You got a quarter?"

Norman dug one out of his pocket and handed it over. He wanted to give her the world; what was twenty-five cents? As Coreen dialed, he inched toward her until by the time she started to speak he stood close enough to hear perfectly.

"Hi, it's Coreen Fergus. Oh, I'm sorry, were you asleep?" She twisted to look at her watch. "Yeah, I guess. But you've gotta hear this. Of course, it's about the vampire. Why else would I call you? Look, I met a guy who says he had incontestable proof . . . in his apartment. . . . Give me a break. You're my detective, not my mother." The receiver missed being slammed back onto its cradle by the narrowest of margins.

"Some people," she muttered, "are just so bitchy when you wake them up. Come on." She gave him a little push in the direction of the parking lot. "Ian's death will be avenged even if I have to do it all myself."

Norman, suddenly realizing that he and not the vampire Coreen seemed fixated on had been in some small part responsible for Ian's death, wondered what he should do next. *Nothing,* he decided, hurriedly buckling his seat beat as Coreen pulled out with a squeal of rubber. *She's coming to my apartment, that's the main thing. Once she's there, I can handle the rest.* His chest puffed out as he thought of what he'd achieved. *When I show her, she'll be so impressed she'll forget about the vampire and Ian both.*

Norman's apartment was in a cluster of identical high rises perched on the flatland west of York University and completely out of sync with their surroundings. He pointed out the visitors' parking and with one eye on the York Regional Police car that had been following her for the last quarter mile Coreen pulled into the first empty spot and shut the motor off. The police car kept going and Coreen, well aware she shouldn't have been driving at all after sharing three pitchers of beer, heaved a sigh of relief.

While Norman fumbled with his keys, she stared through the glass doors at the beige and brown lobby and wondered how he could tell he was in the right building.

In the elevator, she drummed her fingers against the stainless steel wall. If she hadn't been feeling so sorry for herself back in the pub that her mind had been on hold, she'd have never gone anywhere with Norman Birdwell. She'd realized who he was the moment she saw him under the bright lights in the parking lot. If York University had a definitive geek, he was it.

Except . . . She frowned, remembering. Except he'd really sounded like he knew something, and for Ian's sake she had to follow every lead. Maybe there was more to him than met the eye. She glanced at Norman, who was smiling at her in a way she didn't like, and realized suddenly where he fit in. He was the vampire's Renfield! The human servant who not only eased his master's way in the modern world but who, on occasion, procured. . . .

Her hand went to her throat and the tiny gold crucifix her grandfather had given her at her first communion. If Norman "the geek" Birdwell thought he was procuring her as a late night snack for his undead master, he was in for a bit of a surprise. She patted her purse and the comforting bulge of a squirt gun filled with holy water. She wasn't afraid to use it either and she'd seen enough vampire movies to know what the effect would be. Holy water wouldn't affect Norman, of course, but then Norman wasn't much of a threat.

"When I started this, I wanted to change to the fourteenth floor," Norman told her, managing to get his keys in the lock in spite of his trembling hands. *I'm actually bringing a girl back to my apartment!* "Because the fourteenth floor is really the thirteenth, but they didn't have any empties so I'm still on nine."

"There's a lot of psychic significance in the number nine," Coreen muttered, pushing past him into the apartment. The entrance way, with its coat closet and plastic mat, opened into one big room that didn't appear to contain a coffin. An old sofa, covered in a handmade afghan, was pushed up against one wall and a blue, metal trunk served as a coffee table. Tucked over in a corner, by the door that led to the balcony, was a square plastic fan and a tiny desk buried beneath computer equipment. At the other end of the room, stove, fridge, and sink made a half turn around a chrome and vinyl table with two matching chairs.

Coreen's nose wrinkled. The whole place looked spotless but there was a distinctly funny smell. Then she noticed that every available flat surface held at least one solid air freshener; little plastic mushrooms, shells, and fake crystal candy dishes. The combined effect was somewhat overpowering.

"Can I take your coat?" He had to raise his voice to be heard over the noise of the stereo in the apartment upstairs.

"No." She sneezed and dug a tissue out of her pocket. "Do you have a bathroom?" All the beer seemed to have suddenly passed through her system.

"Oh, yes." He opened a door that led to both a walk-in closet and the bathroom. "In here."

She's freshening up! he thought, almost dancing as he neatly hung up his own coat. *There's a girl in my bathroom and she's freshening up!* He cleaned the apartment every Thursday just in case this happened. And now it had. Wiping damp palms against his thighs, he wondered if he should get out the chips and dip. *No,* he decided, trying to settle himself in a nonchalant position on the sofa, *that would be for later. For after.*

Coming out of the bathroom, Coreen had a look around the huge closet. Still no coffin; it looked like she was safe. Norman's clothes were hung neatly by type, shirts together, pants together, a gray polyester suit hanging in solitary splendor. His shoes, a pair of brown loafers and a pair of spotless sneakers, were lined up toes to the wall. Although she didn't quite have the nerve to check his dresser drawers, Coreen figured Norman as the type who'd fold his underwear. Tucked into one corner, looking very out of place, was a hibachi perched across the top of a plastic milk crate. She would have investigated the contents of the crate except the smell behind the smell of plastic roses seemed to originate from that corner and, mixed with the beer, it made her feel a little ill.

Probably some lab project he's working on at home. Her mind produced a vision of Norman in a long white coat attaching wires to the electrodes in the neck of his latest creation and she had to stifle a giggle as she came out into the main room.

She didn't like the look that crossed Norman's face as she perched on the other end of the couch and she began to think she'd made a big mistake coming up here. "Well?" she demanded. "You said you had something to show me, something that would prove the existence of the vampire to the rest of the world." If he wasn't Renfield, she had no idea what he was up to.

Norman frowned. Had he said that? He didn't think he'd said that. "I, I, uh, do have something to show you, but it's not exactly a vampire."

Coreen snorted and stood, heading for the door. "Yeah, I bet." Something to show her indeed. If he showed it to her, she'd cut it off.

"No, really." Norman stood as well, tottering a little on the heels of his cowboy boots. "What I can show you will prove that supernatural forces are at work in this city. It can't be a very big step from that to vampires. Can it?"

"No." In spite of the whiny tone, he really did sound like he knew what he was talking about. "I suppose not."

"So won't you sit down again?"

He took a step toward her and she took three steps back. "No. Thanks. I'll stand." She could feel her grip on her temper slipping. "What do you have to show me?"

Norman drew himself up proudly and, after a little fumbling, managed to slip his thumbs behind his belt loops. This would impress her. "I can call up demons."

"Demons?"

He nodded. She'd be his now and forget all about her dead boyfriend and her stupid vampire theory.

Coreen added a conical hat with stars and a magic wand to her earlier vision of Norman and the monster and this time couldn't stop the giggle from escaping. Nerves, as much as anything, prompted the reaction for despite his reputation she almost believed he spoke the truth and was ready to be convinced.

Norman had no way of knowing that.

She's laughing at me. How dare she laugh at me after I was the only one who didn't laugh at her. How dare she! Incoherent with hurt and anger, Norman dove forward and grabbed Coreen's shoulders, thrusting his mouth at hers with enough force to split his upper lip against her teeth. He didn't even feel that small pain as he began to grind his body, from mouth to hips, down the soft yielding length of her. He'd teach her not to laugh at him!

The next pain forced the breath out of him and sent him staggering backward making small mewling sounds. Tripping on the edge of the trunk, he sat, clutching his crotch and watching the world turn red, and orange, and black.

Coreen jabbed at the elevator button for the lobby, berating herself for being so stupid. "Calling up demons, yeah, right," she snarled, kicking at the stainless steel wall. "And I almost believed him. It was just another pickup line." Except that, just for a moment, as he grabbed her, his face had twisted and for that moment she'd been truly afraid. He almost hadn't looked human. And then the attack became something she had long ago learned to deal with and the moment passed.

"Men are such bastards," she informed the elderly, and somewhat surprised, East Indian gentleman waiting at the ground floor.

At the door, she discovered that one of her new red leather gloves had fallen out of her jacket pocket during the scuffle and was still in Norman's apartment. "Great, just great." She considered going back for it—she knew she could take Norman in a fight—but decided against it. If she got the opportunity to close her hands around his scrawny neck, she'd probably strangle him.

Shoulders hunched against the wind, she stomped out to her car and soothed her lacerated feelings by burning rubber the length of the parking lot.

As the pain receded, the anger grew.

She laughed at me. I shared the secret of the century with some stupid girl who believes in vampires, and she laughed at me. Carefully, not certain his legs would hold him, Norman stood. *Everyone always laughed at me. Last*

*one chosen to play baseball. Never wearing quite the same
clothes as the other kids. They even laughed when I got
perfect marks on tests.* He'd stopped telling them all about
it eventually; about the A plus papers, about the projects
used as study aids by the teachers, about winning the
science fair three years in a row, about reading *War and
Peace* over the weekend. They weren't interested in his
triumphs. They always laughed.

Just like she *laughed.*

The anger burned away the last of the pain.

Knees carefully apart, Norman shoved the trunk up
against the wall, then grabbed the afghan off the sofa and
hung it on the half dozen hooks he'd put over the apartment door. The heavy wool would trap most of the odors
before they could reach the hall. For the rest, he opened
the balcony door about two inches and used one of the
mushroom shaped air fresheners to keep it from slamming closed. Ignoring the sudden stream of cold air and
the increase in noise from above, he pushed the fan up
tight against the crack and turned it on.

Then he went into the closet for the hibachi and the
plastic milk crate.

The tiny barbecue he set up as close as he could to the
fan. He built a pyramid of three charcoal briquets, soaked
them in starter fluid and dropped in a match. The fan and
the high winds around the building took care of almost
all of the smoke and, as he'd disconnected his smoke
detector and the four that covered the ninth floor hallway,
he didn't worry about the small amount of smoke that
remained. He let the fire burn down while he got out the
colored chalks to draw the pentagram.

No-wax tile flooring doesn't hold chalk well, so Norman actually used chalk pastels. It didn't seem to make
a difference. At each of the five corners of the pentagram,
he set two candles; a black one nine inches high, and a
red one six inches high. He'd had to cut them both down
from twelves and eights and had discovered that a few of
the blacks were actually dark purple. That hadn't seemed
to matter either.

Candles lit, he knelt before the now glowing coals and
began the steps to call the demon.

He'd bought six inches of the eighteen karat gold chain at a store in Chinatown. With a pair of nail scissors, he clipped off three or four links and let them fall into the glowing red heart of the charcoal briquettes. Norman knew that the hibachi couldn't possibly deliver enough heat to melt even that little bit of gold but, although he sifted the remaining ash every time, there was never an answering gleam of metal.

The frankincense came from a trendy food store on Bloor Street West. He had no idea what other people used the bright orange flakes for—he couldn't imagine eating them although he supposed they might be a spice. The half handful he threw on the heat ignited slowly, creating a thick, pungent smoke that the fan almost managed to deal with.

Coughing and rubbing the back of one hand across watering eyes, he reached for the last ingredient. The myrrh had come from a shop specializing in essence oils and the creation of personal, signature perfumes. Ounce for ounce it had been more expensive than the gold. Carefully, using the plastic measuring set his mother had given him when he moved out, he dribbled an eighth of a teaspoon over the coals.

The heavy scent of the frankincense grew heavier still and the air in the apartment picked up a bitter taste that coated the inside of Norman's mouth and nose. The first night he'd tried this, he'd almost stopped with the myrrh, had almost been unable to get past the weight of history that came with it. For centuries myrrh had been used to treat the dead, and all those centuries of death were released every time the oil poured over the coals. By the second time, he could shrug aside the dead with the knowledge of worse to come. By this, the seventh calling, it no longer distracted him from the task at hand.

The sterile pins, identical to the ones the Red Cross used to take the initial drops of blood from donors, he'd bought at a surgical supply house. Usually he hated this part, but tonight the anger drew him through it without pause. The small pain spread down from his fingertip until it joined the throbbing between his legs and the sudden sexual tension almost threw him out of the ritual.

His breathing ragged, he somehow managed to maintain control.

Three drops of blood onto the coals and as each drop fell, a word of calling.

The words he'd found in one of the texts used in his Comparative Religions class. He'd created the ritual himself, made it up out of equal parts research and common sense. *Anyone could do it,* he thought smugly. *But only I have.*

The air over the center of the pentagram shivered and changed as though something were forcing it aside from within. Norman stood and waited, scowling, as the smell of the burning spices gave way to a fetid odor of rot and the beat of his neighbor's stereo gave way to a sound that throbbed inaudibly in brain and bone.

The demon, when it came, was man-sized and vaguely man-shaped and all the more hideous for the slight resemblance.

Norman, breathing shallowly through his mouth, stepped to the edge of the pentagram. "I have called you," he declared. "I am your master."

The demon inclined its head and its features shifted with the movement as if it had no skull beneath the moist covering of skin. "You are master," it agreed, although the fleshy hole of a mouth didn't adapt its constant motion to utter the words.

"You must do as I command."

The huge and lidless yellow eyes scanned the perimeters of its prison. "Yes," it admitted at last.

"Someone laughed at me tonight. I don't want her to ever laugh at me again."

The demon waited silently, awaiting further instruction, its color changing from muddy-black to greenish-brown and back again.

"Kill her!" There, he'd said it. He clenched his hands to stop their trembling. He felt ten feet tall, invincible. He'd taken charge at last and accepted the power that was his by right! The throbbing grew more powerful until his whole body vibrated with it.

"Kill who?" the demon asked.

The mildly amused tone dragged him back to earth,

shaking with fury. "DON'T LAUGH AT ME!" He stepped forward and, remembering just in time, twisted his foot at an awkward angle to avoid crossing the pentagram.

The demon's answering lunge brought them almost nose to nose.

"Hah!" Norman spat the word forward even as he retreated back. "You're just like them! You think you're so great and you think I'm shit! Well, just remember you're in there and I'm out here. I called you! I control you! I AM THE MASTER!"

Unmoved by the stream of vitriol, the demon settled back in the center of the pentagram. "You are master," it said placidly. "Kill who?"

The amusement remained in the creature's voice, driving Norman almost incoherent with anger. Through the red haze, he realized that screaming *Kill Coreen!* at the demon would accomplish nothing. He had to think. How to find one person in a city of over three million? He stomped to the far wall and back, caught the heel of his right boot and almost fell. When, after much tottering, he'd regained his balance, he bent and picked up the bit of scarlet leather that had nearly brought him down.

"Here!"

The demon speared the glove out of the air with a six inch talon, the loose folds of skin hanging between its arm and body snapping taut with the motion.

Norman smiled. "Find the glove that matches this one and kill the person who has it. Don't let anyone else see you. Return to the pentagram when you've finished."

The odor of decay lingered in the air after the demon had disappeared, a disgusting aftereffect that only time would remove. Sucking the finger he'd pricked, Norman strutted to the window and looked out at the night.

"No one," he vowed, "is ever going to laugh at me again." No more toys, no more clothes, no more computers; he'd taken up his power tonight and when the demon returned, well-fed on Coreen's blood, he'd send it out after a symbol of that power. Something the world would be forced to respect.

The throbbing beat grew more powerful and Norman rubbed against the windowsill, hips jerking to its rhythm.

* * *

Still seething, Coreen pulled into the MacDonald's parking lot. Norman Birdwell. She couldn't believe she'd even spoken to Norman Birdwell let alone gone back to his apartment with him. He'd sounded so damned believable back in the pub. She shook her head at her own credulity. Of course, she hadn't realized who he was back at the pub, but still. . . .

"I hope you appreciate this, Ian," she said to the night, slamming the car door and locking it. "When I vowed to find your killer, I never counted on having to deal with geek lust." It had gotten colder and she'd reached in her pocket for her gloves before she remembered that she now possessed only glove, singular. Grinding her teeth, she headed inside. Some moods only a large order of fries could deal with.

On her way to the counter, she spotted a familiar face and detoured.

"Hey, Janet. I thought you were all going over to Alison's?"

Janet looked up and shook her head. "Long story," she muttered around a mouthful of burger.

Coreen snorted and tossed her remaining glove down on top of the junk piled on a neighboring seat. Under the fluorescents it looked almost obscenely bright. "Yeah? Well, I've got a longer one. Don't go away."

Sometime later, Janet was staring at Coreen in astonishment, an apple pie poised forgotten halfway to her open mouth.

". . . so I kneed him in the balls and split." She took a long swallow of diet cola. "And I bet I'm never going to see my other glove again either," she added sadly.

Janet closed her mouth with an audible snap. "Norman Birdwell?" she sputtered.

"Yeah, I know." Coreen sighed. She should never have told Janet. Thank God they were heading into a long weekend; it might slow the spread of the story. "Like majorly stupid. It must've been the beer."

"There isn't enough beer in the world—no, in the universe—to make me go anywhere with that creep," Janet declared, rolling her eyes.

Coreen mashed the onions she'd scraped off her burger into a pureed mess. "He said he knew something about the creature that killed Ian," she muttered sheepishly. She *really* shouldn't have told Janet. What could she have been thinking of?

"Right," Janet snorted, "another fearless vampire hunter and you fell for it."

Coreen's eyes narrowed. "Don't make fun of it."

"Fun of it? You're just as likely to find Norman's demon killed Ian as some stupid vampire." She knew the words were a mistake the moment they left her mouth, but by then it was too late.

"Vampires have been documented historically and all the facts fit. . . ."

Twenty-three minutes later—Janet had been timing the lecture with barely concealed glances at her watch—Coreen stopped suddenly and stood. "I have to go to the bathroom," she said. "Wait for me. I'll be right back."

"Not bloody likely," Janet muttered the second Coreen disappeared down the stairs to the basement. Digging her gear free of the pile, she headed for the door, shrugging into her jacket as she went. She liked Coreen, but if she heard one more word about vampires she was going to bite somebody herself. Any vampire Coreen ran into was going to be able to claim self-defense.

At the door, she discovered she'd picked up Coreen's remaining red glove. *Damn! I take it back and it's more of the Count Dracula power hour.* She stood there for a moment, slapping the leather fingers into her palm, torn between doing the right thing and running to save her sanity.

Sanity won.

As the bright lighting turned the top of Coreen's ascending head to flame, Janet shoved the glove into her pocket, spun on her heel, and escaped into the night. *If I run,* she thought and matched the action to it, *I could*

*be clear of the parking lot lights before Coreen looks out
the window.* In the darkness beyond, she'd be safe.

* * *

It came up through the ground. It preferred to travel that
way, for then it need waste no energy on remaining unseen. And until it fed, it had little energy to waste. It
sensed the prey above it, but it waited, following, until
no other lives could be felt.

Then it emerged.

The urge to kill was strong, nearly overpowering. It
had been so commanded by its "master" and its nature
called it to feed. Only fear of what failure would bring
managed to deflect the killing stroke that instinct had
begun so that it struck bone and not soft tissue.

The prey cried out and crumpled, silent now but sill
alive.

It longed to lap at the warm blood that filled the night
with the scent of food but it knew that feeding, once
begun, could not be stopped and that this was not the
place marked for death. Gathering the prey up, it turned
its face to the wind and began to run, using all three of
its free limbs. It could not take the prey to the earth, nor
could it take to the sky with so heavy a burden. It must
trust to speed to keep it unseen.

The prey would die. It would obey its "master" in
that, but it would obey an older master as well and the
prey would die in the pattern.

Unnoticed, the crushed red glove lay just beyond the
edge of the parking lot lights. Beside it was a splash of
darker red, already freezing.

Nine

"And repeating our top story, the strange deaths in the Toronto area continue with the seventh body, found early this morning by police on Foxrun Avenue, just south of the Oakdale Golf and Country Club. Homicide investigators at the site have confirmed only that death occurred after a violent blow to the throat and will not say if this victim had also been drained of blood. Police are withholding the victim's name pending notification of the next of kin.

"Weather for southern Ontario will be colder than the seasonal norm and. . . ."

Vicki stretched out an arm and switched off the radio then lay for a moment on the weight bench, listening to the sounds of the city, convincing herself that the rumble of a distant truck was not the tread of a thousand clawed feet and that a high-pitched keening to the east was only a siren.

"So far, no demonic hordes." She reached down and pressed her palm against the parquet floor. "Touch wood." It looked like she still had time to find the bastard dealing out these deaths and break every bone in. . . .

Cutting off the thought, she stood and went into the living room where she'd taped the map of the city to the wall. Vengeance was all very well, but dwelling on it obscured the more pressing problem: finding the scum.

The first six deaths had occurred on Sunday, Monday and Tuesday nights, a week apart. This Thursday night killing broke the pattern. Squinting at the map, Vicki circled Foxrun Avenue. She had no idea how this fit geographically or if it fit geographically or if it broke that pattern to pieces as well.

She pushed her glasses up her nose and forced her teeth to unclench.

Henry could play connect the dots this evening when he woke; she had other leads to follow.

If Henry was right, and the person calling the demon was receiving stolen goods for each life, those goods had to have been reported missing. Find the goods, find the demon-caller. Find the demon-caller, stop the killing. It was all very simple; she only had to check every occurrence report in the city for the last three weeks and pull out unusual and unexplained thefts.

"Which," she sighed, "should only take me about two years." And at that, two years of searching was infinitely better than another second sitting on her ass, helpless. Trouble was, with eighteen divisions in Metro, where did she start?

She tapped the map with her pencil. The morning reports at 31 Division would have details on the death the radio hadn't released. Details Henry might need to pin down the next site, the next killing. Also, the two lines from the previous six deaths intersected in 31 Division. That might be meaningless now, but it was still a place to begin.

Clutching the bag containing the four doughnuts—two strawberry jelly and two chocolate glazed—in one hand and the bag with the accompanying coffees in the other, Vicki lowered her head and rounded the corner onto Norfinch Drive. With the York-Finch hospital at her back, nothing stood between her and a vicious northwest wind but the police station and a few square miles of industrial wasteland. Squat and solid, 31 Division made a lousy windbreak.

A patrol car rolled out of the station parking lot as she approached and she paused to watch it turn east on Finch Avenue. At 9:20 on Good Friday morning, traffic was sparse and it would be easy to get the mistaken impression that the city had taken this opportunity—a religious holiday observed by only about a third of its population—

to sleep in. The city, as Vicki well knew, never did anything that restful. If traffic complaints were down, then domestic complaints would be up as loving families spent the entire day together. And in the Jane-Finch corridor, the direction the car had been heading, where there were few jobs to take a holiday from and tempers teetered on the edge on the best of days. . . .

Back when she was in uniform, she'd spent almost a year working out of 31. Remembering certain highlights as she continued toward the station, she found she didn't miss police work at all.

"Well, if it isn't "Victory" Nelson, gone but not forgotten. What brings you out to the ass-end of the city?"

"Just the thought of seeing your smiling face, Jimmy." Vicki set the two bags on the counter and pushed her glasses up her nose with frozen fingers. "It's spring and, like the swallows, I'm returning to Capistrano. Is the Sarge around?"

"Yeah, he's in the . . ."

"None of her damned business what he's in!" The bellow would have shaken a less solidly constructed building and following close behind it, Staff-Sergeant Stanley Iljohn rolled into the duty area, past Jimmy, and up to the counter. "You said you'd be here by nine," he accused. "You're late."

Silently, Vicki held up the bag of doughnuts.

"Bribes," the sergeant snorted, the ends of his beautifully curled mustache quivering with the force of the exhalation. "Well, stop standing around with your thumb up your ass. Get in here and sit. And you," he glared down at Jimmy, "get back to work."

Jimmy, who was working, grinned and ignored him. Vicki did as she was told, and as Sergeant Iljohn settled himself at the duty sergeant's desk, she pulled up a chair and sat across from him.

A few moments later, the sergeant meticulously brushed a spray of powdered sugar off his starched shirt front. "Now then, you know and I know that allowing you to read the occurrence reports is strictly against department regs."

"Yes, Sarge." If anyone else had been on duty, she

probably wouldn't have been able to manage it without pulling in favors from higher up.

"And we both know that you're blatantly trading on the reputation you built as a hotshot miracle worker to get around those regs."

"Yes, Sarge." Iljohn had been the first to recommend her for an advanced promotion and had seen her arrest record as proof of his assessment. When she'd left the force, he'd called her, grilled her on her plans, and practically commanded her to make something of her life. He hadn't exactly been supportive, but his brusque goodwill had been something to lean on when Mike Celluci had accused her of running away.

"And if I catch shit over this, I'm going to tell them you used the unarmed combat you private investigators are supposed to be so damned good at to overpower me and you read the reports over my bleeding body."

"Should I slap you around a little?" Although he stood barely over minimum height for the force, rumor had it that Stanley Iljohn had never lost a fight. With anything.

"Don't be a smart ass."

"Sorry, Sarge."

He tapped one square finger against the clipboard lying on his desk and his face grew solemn. "Do you really think you can do something about this?" he asked.

Vicki nodded. "Right now," she told him levelly, "I have a better chance than anyone in the city."

Iljohn stared at her for a long moment. "I can draw lines on a map, too," he said at last. "And when you line up the first six deaths, x marks the spot just north of here. Every cop at this station is watching for something strange, something that'll mark the killer, and you can bet these reports," a short, choppy wave indicated the occurrence reports of the last couple of weeks which were hanging on the wall by the desk, "have been gone through with several fine toothed combs. Gone through by everyone here and by the boys and girls from your old playground."

"But not by me."

He nodded acknowledgment. "Not by you." His palm slapped down on the papers on his desk. "This last death, this was in my territory and I'm taking it personally. If you know something you're not telling, spit it out now.''

There's a demon writing a name in blood across the city. If we don't stop it, it will be only the beginning.

How do you know?

A vampire told me.

She looked him right in the eye, and lied.

''Everything I know, I've told Mike Celluci. He's in charge of the case. I just think it'll help if I look myself.''

Iljohn's eyes narrowed. She could tell he didn't believe her. Not completely.

Slowly, after a moment that stretched into all the time they'd ever worked together, he pushed the clipboard across the desk. ''I want this to be the last death,'' he growled.

Not as much as I do, Vicki thought.

How many deaths in a demon's name?

She bent her head to read.

''Victims one and seven were both students at York University. Not much of a connection to base an investigation on.''

Celluci sighed. ''Vicki, at this point I'd base an investigation on ties a lot more tenuous. Did you call to give me a hard time or did you have something constructive to say?''

Vicki twisted the phone cord around her fingers. Late in the afternoon, arriving at 52 Division, her search had actually turned something up. One of the uniforms coming in off shift change had overheard her talking to the duty sergeant about unusual cases and had filled her in on one he'd taken the call for. Trouble was, she couldn't figure out how to present the information to Celluci. ''So you'll be concentrating the search at York?'' she asked instead.

He sighed again. ''Yeah. For now. Why?''

She took a deep breath. There really wasn't an easy way to do this. ''Don't ask me how I know, because you wouldn't believe me, but there's a very good chance the person you're looking for will be wearing a black leather jacket. A nine hundred dollar black leather jacket.''

"Jesus Christ, Vicki! It's a university. Half the fucking people there will be in black leather jackets."

"Not like this one. I've got a full description for you."

"And where did you get it? Out of a fortune cookie?"

Vicki opened her mouth then closed it again. This was just too complicated. "I can't tell you," she said at last. "I'd be compromising my sources."

"You hold back information on me, Vicki, and I'll compromise sources you never knew you had!"

"Listen, asshole, you can choose to believe me or not, but don't you dare threaten me!" She spit out the description of the jacket and slammed the receiver down. All right. She'd done her duty by telling the police what she knew. Fine. They could act on it or not. And Mike Celluci could go straight to hell.

Except that was what she was desperately trying to prevent.

Grinding her teeth in frustration, she kicked a kitchen chair into the living room and, panting slightly, stood looking down at the twisted piece of furniture.

"Life used to be a lot simpler," she told it, sighed, and went back to the phone. York University was the only connection they had and Coreen Fergus was a student there. She probably wouldn't be able to help—Celluci was right, the irritating s.o.b., finding one leather jacket on campus would be like finding one honest politician— but it certainly couldn't hurt to check.

"Coreen Fergus, please."

"I'm sorry, but Coreen's not in right now. Can I take a message?"

"Do you know when she'll be back?"

" 'Fraid not. She left this morning to stay with friends for a few days."

"Is she all right?" If that child had gotten herself hurt going up to some strange man's apartment. . . .

"Well, she's a little shook; she was like really good friends with the girl whose body they found last night."

Bad enough, coming so soon after Ian, but thank God that was all it was. "When she comes home, could you tell her Vicki Nelson called?"

"Sure thing. That all?"

"That's all."

And that was all, unless Henry had come up with something concrete.

"This one, this one, or this one." Henry looked from the map to the page of symbols.

"Can you find the next point in the pattern?" Vicki bent over the table, as far away as possible from the grimoire. She hesitated to say the ancient book exuded an aura of evil—that sounded *so* horror novel cliché—but she noticed that even Henry touched it as infrequently as possible.

Henry, busy with protractor and ruler, laughed humorlessly. "The next three points in three possible patterns," he pointed out.

"Great." Vicki straightened and shoved her glasses up her nose. "More complications. Where do we do first?"

"Where do I go first," Henry corrected absently. He straightened as well, rubbing his temples. The bright light that Vicki seemed to need to function was giving him a headache. "It had better be this area here." He tapped the map just east of the Humber River between Lawrence and Eglinton Avenues. "This pattern continues the least complicated of the three. Theoretically, it will be the first finished."

"Theoretically?"

Henry shrugged. "This is demon lore. There aren't any cut and dried answers. Experts in the field tend to die young."

Vicki took a deep breath and let it out slowly. There were *never* any cut and dried answers. She should know that by now. "So you've never actually done this sort of thing before."

"Not actually, no. 'This sort of thing' doesn't happen very often."

"Then if you don't mind my asking," she flicked a finger at the grimoire, still carefully keeping her distance, "why do you own one of these?"

Henry looked down at the book although Vicki could tell from his expression he wasn't really seeing it. "I took it from a madman," he said harshly. "And I don't wish to speak of it now."

"All right." Vicki fought the urge to back away from the raw anger in Henry's voice. "You don't have to. It's okay."

With an effort, he put the memory aside and managed what he hoped was a conciliatory smile. "I'm sorry. I didn't mean to frighten you."

She stiffened. "You didn't."

The smile grew more genuine. "Good."

Well aware she was being humored, Vicki cleared her throat and changed the subject. "You said the other night we had no way of knowing if these were all the demonic names."

"That's right." He'd been trying not to think of that.

"So these deaths might be spelling out a name that's not in the book."

"Right again."

"Shit." Arms wrapped around herself, Vicki walked over to the window and rested her forehead against the cool glass. The points of light below, all she could see of the city, looked cold and mocking. A thousand demonic eyes in the darkness. "What are we supposed to do about it?"

"Exactly what we are doing." It could have been a rhetorical question, but sometimes Henry felt even they needed answering and he wanted to give her what comfort he could. "And we hope and we pray and we don't give up."

Vicki's head rose and she turned to face him. "I never give up," she said testily.

He smiled. "I never thought you did."

He really does have a phenomenal smile, Vicki thought, appreciating the way his eyes crinkled at the corners. She felt her own lips begin to curl in answer and gave herself a mental shake, forcing her face to give no indication of a sudden strong wave of desire. *Four hundred and fifty years of practice, a body in its mid-twenties, supernatural prowess. . . .*

Henry heard her heart speed up and his sensitive nose caught a new scent. He hadn't fed for forty-eight hours and he would need to soon. *If she wants me, it would be foolish to deny her. . . .* Having long since outgrown the need to prove himself by forcing the issue—he knew he could take what he wanted—he would allow her to make the first move. *And what of vows to stay uninvolved until after the demon has been dealt with?* Well, some vows were made to be broken.

Her heartbeat began to slow and, while he applauded her control, he didn't bother to hide his disappointment.

"So." The word caught and Vicki cleared her throat. *This is ridiculous. I'm thirty-one years old. I'm not seventeen.* "I learned a few things up at 31 Division that might have some bearing on the case."

"Oh?" Henry raised a red-gold brow and perched on the edge of the table.

Vicki, who would have given her front teeth to be able to raise a single brow without her entire forehead getting involved, frowned at the picture he made. To give him credit, she didn't think he was aware of how the light from the chandelier burnished his hair, and how the position stretched the brown corduroy pants he wore tight over muscular thighs. With an effort, she got her mind back on track. This was *not* the time for that sort of thing; whatever sort of thing it might end up to be later on. "Several people, mostly employees of the local MacDonald's, reported a foul smell lingering around the parking lot at the Jane-Finch Mall. Sulfur and rotting meat. The gas company sent someone around, but they found no leaks."

"The demon?" Henry bent over the map, trying to ignore his growing hunger. It was difficult with her so close and physically, at least, so willing. "But the body was found. . . ."

"There's more. Someone reported a bear running along the shoulder of Jane Street. The police didn't bother investigating because the caller said he'd only caught a glimpse of it as it passed his car doing about a hundred kilometers an hour."

"The demon." This time it wasn't a question.

Vicki nodded. "Odds are good." She returned to the table and the map. "My best guess is that it picked up the body here and carried it over here to kill it. Why? There had to be people closer.''

''Perhaps this time it was told who to kill.''

''I was afraid you were going to say that.''

''It's the only logical answer,'' Henry said, standing. ''But look at the bright side.''

''There is no bright side,'' Vicki snarled. She'd finished her day with the coroner's report.

''At the risk of sounding like a Pollyanna,'' Henry told her dryly, ''there's always a bright side. Or at least a side that's less dark. If the demon was instructed to kill this young woman, perhaps the police can find the link between her and its master.''

''And if it was just indulging in demonic perversity?''

''Then we're no farther behind than we were. Now, if you'll excuse me, with the timetable shattered, I'd better get out to the Humber in case the demon is recalled tonight.''

At the door, Vicki stopped, a sudden horrific thought bleaching the color from her face. ''What's stopping this thing from showing up inside someone's house? Where you can't see it? Where you can't stop it?''

''Demons,'' Henry told her, smiling reassuringly as he secured the belt of his trenchcoat, ''are unable to enter a mortal's home unless expressly invited.''

''I thought that referred to vampires?''

With one hand in the small of her back, Henry moved her firmly out into the hall. ''Mr. Stoker,'' he said, as he locked the door to the condo, ''was indulging in wishful thinking.''

Henry leaned against the cemetery fence and looked out over the small collection of quiet graves. They were old stone slabs for the most part, a uniform size and a uniform age. The few marble monuments looked pretentious and out of place.

To the west, the cemetery butted against the Humber River park system, and the muttering of the swollen river filled the night with sound. To the north lay residential areas. To the east and south, vacant land. He wondered if the cemetery had something to do with the lack of development. Even in an age of science, the dead were often considered bad neighbors. Henry couldn't understand why; the dead never played Twisted Sister at 130 decibels at three in the morning.

He could feel, not the pattern, but the anticipation of it. A current of evil waiting for its chance, waiting for the final death that would anchor it to the world. This feeling, which raised the hair on the back of his neck and made him snarl, was strong enough to convince him that he'd chosen correctly. This name would be the first to finish; this demon lord the first to break free of the darkness and begin the slaughter.

He must stop the lesser demon in the few seconds between its appearance and the killing blow, for once the blood struck the ground he'd have its demonic master to contend with. Unfortunately, the pattern allowed for a wider area than he could watch all at once, so he'd done the only thing he could—walking a pentagram well outside the boundaries the pattern demanded, leaving the last six inches unclosed. When the demon entered, to attack a life within it or carrying a life in from outside, he'd close it. Such an ephemeral prison wouldn't last more than a few seconds but should give him control long enough to get to the demon and . . .

". . . and stop it." Henry sighed and turned up the collar of his coat. "Temporarily." Trouble was, the lesser demons were pretty much interchangeable. If he stopped this one, there was nothing stopping its "master" from calling up another. Fortunately, these demons, like most bullies, weren't fond of pain and he might be able to convince it to talk.

"If it *can* talk." He shoved his hands in his pockets and sagged against the fence. Rumor had it that not all of them could.

There was an added complication he hadn't mentioned to Vicki because he knew she'd scoff. Tonight, all over the world, millions of people were crying that Christ was dead. This century might have lost its ability to see the power in believing, but Henry hadn't. Most religions had marked a day of darkness on the calendar and, given the spread of the Christian church, this was among the most potent. If the demon returned before Christ rose again, it would be stronger, more dangerous, harder to stop.

He checked his watch. 11:40. Bound by centuries of tradition, the demon would be called—if it was called at all tonight—at midnight. According to Vicki, all the previous deaths had occurred between midnight and one o'clock. He wondered how the police had missed such an obvious clue.

The wind snapped his coat around his knees and lifted bright strands of his hair. Like all large predators, he could remain motionless for as long as the hunt required, senses straining for the first sight or sound or scent of prey.

Midnight passed.

Henry felt the heart of darkness go by and the current of evil strengthened momentarily. He tensed. He would have to move between one heartbeat and the next.

Then the current began to fade.

When it had sighed away to a mere possibility, Henry checked his watch again. 1:20. For tonight, for whatever reason, the danger was past.

Relief caused him to sag against the fence, grinning foolishly. He hadn't been looking forward to the battle. He was grateful for the reprieve. He'd head back downtown, maybe drop in on Caroline, get something to eat, spend the hours until sunrise not worrying about being ripped to pieces by the hordes of hell.

"Peaceful, isn't it?"

The white-haired man never knew how close he came to dying. Only the returning surge of the pattern, sensing death, stopped Henry's strike. He forced his lips back over his teeth and shoved his trembling hands in his pockets.

"Did I frighten you?"

"No." The night hid the hunter while Henry struggled to resecure his civilized mask. "Startled me, that's all." The wind from the river had kept him from scenting the blood and the sound of the water had muffled the approach of crepe soled shoes. It was excusable that he'd been taken by surprise. It was also embarrassing.

"You don't live around here?"

"No." As he came closer, Henry revised his original impression of the man's age. No more than fifty, and a trim, athletic fifty at that, with the weathered look of a man who worked outside.

"I thought not, I'd have remembered you." His eyes were pale blue and just beyond the edge of a gray down jacket, a vein pulsed under tanned skin. "I often walk at night when I can't sleep."

Hands hanging loose beside his faded jeans, he waited for Henry's explanation. Ridged knuckles testified to past fights and somehow Henry doubted he'd lost many of them.

"I was waiting for someone." Remaining adrenaline kept him terse although amusement had begun to wash it away. "He didn't show." He answered the older man's slow smile with one of his own, captured the pale blue gaze, and held it. Leading him into the shadows of the cemetery, allowing his hunger to rise, he considered this ending to the few last hours and, stifling slightly hysterical laughter, Henry realized there was truth in something he'd always believed; *The world is not only stranger than you imagine, it's stranger than you can imagine—a vampire, waiting for a demon, gets cruised in a graveyard. Sometimes I love this century.*

* * *

"Detective? I mean, Ms. Nelson?" The young constable blushed at his mistake and cleared his throat. "The, uh, sergeant says you might want to hear about the call I had this morning."

Vicki glanced up from the stack of occurrence reports and pushed her glasses up her nose. She wondered when they'd started allowing children to join the force. Or when twenty had started looking so damned young.

Standing a little straighter, the constable began to read from his notes. "At 8:02 this morning, Saturday, 23rd of March, a Mr. John Rose of 42 Birchmont Avenue reported an item missing from his gun collection. Said collection, including the missing item, was kept in a locked case behind a false wall in Mr. Rose's basement. Neither the wall nor the lock appeared to have been tampered with and Mr. Rose swore that only he and his wife knew the combination. The house itself showed no signs of forced entry. All papers and permits appeared to be in order and . . .''

"Constable?"

"Yes, ma'am?"

"What item was Mr. Rose missing?"

"Ma'am?"

Vicki sighed. She'd had a sleepless night and a long day. "What kind of gun?"

"Oh." The constable blushed again and peered down at his handwriting. "The, uh, missing item was a Russian assault rifle, an AK-47. With ammunition. Ma'am."

"Shit!"

"Yes, ma'am."

* * *

"I don't believe it!" Norman kicked the newspaper box, the toe of his running shoe thudding into the metal with a very satisfactory boom. He'd stopped to read the front page story about the seventh victim and discovered that the stupid demon had killed the wrong girl. What was worse, it had killed the wrong girl Thursday night and here it was Saturday before he found out.

Coreen had been walking around alive for two extra days!

The throbbing, which had not disappeared with the demon as it always had before, grew louder.

He dug his change purse out of his pants' pocket, muttering, "A decent country would have a decent information service." If he'd known about this yesterday, he'd have called the demon back last night instead of spending the time on the net, looking for someone who could tell him how to operate his new equalizer. *Too bad I couldn't take* that *to class. They'd all notice me then.* What really made him angry was that the demon had come back on Thursday and then gone off and gotten him the rifle without ever letting on it had screwed up.

When he saw a Saturday paper cost a dollar twenty-five, he almost changed his mind, but the story was about him, in a way, so, grumbling, he fed coins into the slot. Besides, he needed to know what the demon had done so he could find a way to punish it tonight. As long as he had it trapped in the pentagram, there must be something he could do to hurt it.

Paper tucked under his arm—he'd have taken two, but a single weekend edition was bulky enough on its own—he continued into the small corner store for a bag of briquettes. He had only one left and he needed three for the ritual.

Unfortunately, he was seventy-six cents short.

"What!"

"The charcoal is three dollars and fifty-nine cents plus twenty-five cents tax which is coming to three dollars and eighty-four cents. You have only three dollars and eight cents."

"Look, I'll owe it to you."

The old woman shook her head. "Sorry, no credit."

Norman's eyes narrowed. "I was born in this country. I've got rights." He reached for the bag, but she swept it back behind the counter.

"No credit," she repeated a little more firmly.

He was halfway around the counter after it, when the old woman picked up a broom and started toward him. Scooping up his money, he beat a hasty retreat.

She probably knows kung fu or something. He shifted the paper under his arm and started back to his apartment. On the way past, he kicked the newspaper box again. The closest bank machine closed at six. He'd never make it. He'd have to head into the mall tomorrow to find an open one.

This was all that old lady's fault. After he worked out a suitable punishment for the demon and made sure that Coreen got hers, maybe he'd do something about the immigrant problem.

The throbbing grew louder still.

* * *

"Look at this!"

Scrubbing at her face with her hands, Vicki answered

without looking up. "I've seen it. I brought them over, remember?"

"Is the entire city out of its mind?"

"The entire city is scared, Henry." She put her glasses back on and sighed. Although she had no intention of telling him, she'd slept last night with the bedroom light on and still kept waking, heart in her throat, drenched with sweat, sure that something was climbing up the fire escape toward her window. "You've had since 1536 to come to terms with violent death. The rest of us haven't been so lucky."

As if to make up for the lack of news over Good Friday, all three of the Saturday papers carried the seventh death as a front page story, emphasized that this body, too, had been drained of blood, and all three, the staid national paper finally jumping on the bandwagon, carried articles on vampires, columns on vampires, historical and scientific exploration of vampires—all the while claiming no such creature existed.

"Do you know what the result of all this will be?" Henry slapped the paper he held down on the couch where the pages separated and half of it slithered to the floor.

Vicki swiveled to face him as he moved out of her limited field of vision. "Increased circulation?" she asked, covering a yawn. Her eyes ached from a day spent reading occurrence reports and the news that their demon-caller had turned to more conventional weapons had been all she needed to hear.

Henry, unable to remain still, crossed the room in four angry strides, turned, and came back. Bracing his hands on the top of the couch, he leaned toward her. "You're right, people are afraid. The papers, for whatever reasons, have given that fear a name. Vampire." He straightened and ran one hand back through his hair. "The people writing these stories don't believe in vampires, and most of the people reading these stories don't believe in vampires, but we're talking about a culture where more people know their astrological sign than their blood type. Somewhere out there, somebody is taking all this seriously and spending his spare time sharpening stakes."

Vicki frowned. It made a certain amount of sense and she certainly wasn't going to argue for the better natures of her contemporaries. "One of the local stations is showing *Dracula* tonight."

"Oh, great." Henry threw up both hands and began to pace again. "More fuel on the fire. Vicki, you and I both know there's at least one vampire living in Toronto and, personally, I'd rather not have some peasant, whipped into a frenzy by the media, doing something I'll regret based on the tenuous conclusion that he never sees me in the daytime." He stopped and drew a deep breath. "And the worst of it is, there's not a damned thing I can do about it."

Vicki pulled herself to her feet and went to stand beside him at the window. She understood how he felt. "I doubt it'll do any good, but I have a friend who writes a human interest column at the tabloid. I'll give her a call when I get home and see if she can defuse any of this."

"What will you tell her?"

"Exactly what you told me." She grinned. "Less the part about the vampire actually living in Toronto."

Henry managed a crooked grin in return. "Thank you. She'll likely think you're losing your mind."

Vicki shrugged. "I used to be a cop. She thinks I lost my mind ages ago."

Her eyes on their reflection in the glass, Vicki realized, for the first time, that Henry Fitzroy, born in the sixteenth century, stood four inches shorter she did. At least. An admitted snob concerning height, she was a little surprised to discover that it didn't seem to matter. Her ears as red as the young constable's had been that afternoon, she cleared her throat and asked, "Will you be going back to the Humber tonight?"

Henry's reflection nodded grimly. "And every night until something happens."

* * *

Anicka Hendle had just come off an exhausting shift in emergency. As she parked her car in the lane behind her house and stumbled up the path, all she could think of was bed. She didn't see them until she'd almost reached the porch.

Roger, the elder brother, sat on the top step. Bill, the younger, stood in the frozen garden, leaning against the house. Something—it looked like a hockey stick although the light was too bad to really tell—leaned against the wall beside him. The two of them, and an assortment of "friends," rented the place next door and although Anicka had complained to their landlord on a number of occasions, about the noise, about the filth, she couldn't seem to get rid of them. They'd obviously spent the night drinking. She could smell the beer.

"Morning, *Ms*. Hendle."

Just what she needed, a confrontation with Tweedledee and Tweedledum. "What can I do for you, gentlemen?" They were usually too dense, or too drunk, for sarcasm to have any effect, but she hadn't given up hope.

"Well . . ." Roger's smile was a lighter slash across the gray oval of his face. "You can tell us why we never see you in the daytime."

Anicka sighed; she was too tired to deal with whatever idiot idea they had right now. "I am a night nurse," she said, speaking slowly and enunciating clearly. "Therefore, I work nights."

"Not good enough." Roger took another long pull from the bottle in his left hand. His right hand continued to cradle something in his lap. "No one works nights all the time."

"I do." This was ridiculous. She strode forward. "Now go back where you came from before I call . . ." The hands grabbing her shoulders took her completely by surprise.

"Call who?" Bill asked, jerking her up against his body.

Suddenly frightened, she twisted frantically trying to free herself.

"Us three," Roger's voice seemed to come from a distance, "are just going to stay out here till the sun comes up. Then we'll see."

They were crazy. They were both crazy. Panic gave her the strength she needed, and she yanked herself out of Bill's grip. She stumbled on the porch stairs. This couldn't be happening. She had to get to the house. In the house she'd be safe.

She saw Roger stand. She could get by him. Push him out of the way.

Then she saw the baseball bat in his hand.

The force of the blow knocked her back onto the lawn.

She couldn't suck enough air through the ruin of her mouth and nose to scream.

Her face streaming blood, she scrambled up onto her elbows and knees and tried to crawl back toward the house. *If I can get to the house, I'll be safe.*

"Sun's coming up. She's trying to get inside."

"That's good enough for me."

The hockey stick had been sharpened on one end and with the strength of both men leaning on it, it went through jacket and uniform and bone and flesh and out into the ground.

As the first beam of sunlight came up over the garage, Anicka Hendle kicked once more and was still.

"Now we'll see," Roger panted, retrieving his beer.

The sunlight moved across the yard, touched a white shoe, and gently spread out over the body. The blood against the frozen dirt burned with crimson light.

"Nothing's happening." Bill turned to his brother, eyes wide in a parchment pale face. "She's supposed to turn to dust, Roger!"

Roger took two steps back and was noisily sick.

Ten

"All stand for the word of the Lord. We read today from The Gospel According to St. Mathew, Chapter twenty-eight, Verses one to seven."

"Praised be the word of the Lord."

"In the end of the Sabbath, as it began to dawn toward the first day of the week, came Mary Magdalene and the other Mary to see the sepulchre. And, behold, there was a great earthquake: for the angel of the Lord descended from heaven, and came and rolled back the stone from the door, and sat upon it. His countenance was like lightning, and his raiment white as snow: and for fear of him the keepers did shake, and became as dead men. And the angel answered and said unto the women, Fear not ye: for I know that ye seek Jesus, which was crucified. He is not here: for he is risen, as he said. Come, see the place where the Lord lay. And go quickly, and tell his disciples that he is risen from the dead; and, behold, he goeth before you into Galilee; there shall ye see him: lo, I have told you. Thus endeth the lesson."

The Gloria almost raised the roof off the church and just for that moment the faith in life everlasting as promised by the Christian God was enough to raise a shining wall between the world and the forces of darkness.

Too bad it wouldn't last.

* * *

"Back up, please. Move aside."

Hands cuffed behind them, the brothers were brought out through the police barricade and into the alley. Curious neighbors surged forward, then back, like a living sea breaking against a wall of blue uniforms. Neither man noticed the onlookers. Roger, smelling of vomit, dry retched constantly and William cried silent tears, his eyes almost closed. They were shoved, none too gently, into one of the patrol cars, shutters clicking closed in a half dozen media cameras.

Ignoring the reporters' shouted questions, two of the constables climbed into the car and, siren hiccuping, maneuvered the crowded length of the back lane. The other two added their bulk to the living wall that blocked the view of the yard. *"No one speaks to the media,"* the investigator in charge of the case had told them, his tone leaving no room for dissension.

The body came out next, the bouncing of the gurney moving it in a macabre parody of life within the body bag. A dozen pairs of lungs exhaled, the shutters closed again, and over it all a television reporter droned in on-the-spot coverage. The faint antiseptic smell of the coroner's equipment left an almost visible track through the damp morning air.

"I seen her before the cops stuffed her in the bag," confided a neighbor to an avidly listening audience. She paused, enjoying the feeling of power, and cinched her spring coat more tightly over her plaid flannel nightgown. "Her face was all bashed in and her legs were apart." Nodding sagely, she added, "You know what *that* means."

Listeners echoed her nod.

As the coroner's wagon drove away, the police barricade broke up into individual men and women who hurriedly stepped out of the way as Mike Celluci and his partner came out of the yard.

"Get statements from anyone who saw something or who thinks they saw something," Celluci ordered. At any other time he would have been amused at the reaction that invoked in the crowd as half of them preened and the other half quietly slipped away, but this morning he was far beyond amusement. The very senselessness of this killing wrapped him in a rage so cold he doubted he'd ever be warm again.

The reporters, for whom the *story* had more reality

than what had actually happened, surged forward, demanding some sort of statement from the police. The two homicide investigators pushed through them silently until they got to their car, a rudimentary instinct of self-preservation keeping the reporters from actually blocking their way.

As Celluci opened his door, Dave leaned forward and murmured, "We've got to say something, Mike, or God knows what they'll come up with." Celluci glowered at his partner, but Dave refused to back down. "I'll do it if you'd rather not."

"No." Scowling, he looked out at the pack of jackals. "Anicka Hendle is dead because of the asinine stories you lot have been spreading about vampires. You're as much responsible as those two cretins we took away. Quite the story. I hope you're proud of it."

Sliding in behind the wheel, he slammed his car door closed with enough force to create echos between the neighboring houses.

A single reporter moved out of the stunned mass, microphone raised, but Dave Graham shook his head.

"I wouldn't," he suggested quietly.

Microphone still in the air, the reporter stopped and the whole pack of them watched as the two investigators drove away. The unnatural stillness lasted until the car cleared the end of the alley then a voice behind them prodded the pack back into action.

"I seen her before the cops stuffed her in the bag."

* * *

"You still have that friend at the tab?"

"Celluci?" Vicki settled back into her recliner, lifting the phone onto her lap. "What the hell are you talking about?"

"That Fellows woman, the one who writes for the tabloid, are you still seeing her?"

Vicki frowned. "Well I'm not exactly *seeing* her. . . ."

"For Chrissakes, Vicki, this is no time to be coy! I'm not asking if you sleep with her; do you talk to her or not?"

"Yeah." In fact, she'd been going to call her that very afternoon to see what could be done to ease Henry's fears about peasant hordes with stakes and garlic. What weird serendipity had Celluci thinking about Anne Fellows on the same day? They'd only met once and hadn't hit it off, had spent the entire party circling each other like wary dogs looking for an exposed throat. "Why?"

"Get a pen and paper, I've got some things I want to tell her."

His tone sent Vicki scrabbling in the recliner's side pocket and by the time he started to talk she'd unearthed a ballpoint and a coffee-stained phone pad. When he finished, she swore softly. "Jesus-God, Mike, can I assume the higher-ups don't know you're passing this along?" She heard him sigh wearily and before he could speak, said, "Never mind. Stupid question."

"I don't want this to happen again, Vicki. The papers started it, they can finish it."

Vicki looked down at the details of Anicka Hendle's life and death, scrawled across three sheets of paper in her precisely readable handwriting, and understood Celluci's anger and frustration. An echo of it brushed her spine like a cold finger. "I'll do what I can."

"Let's hope it's enough."

She recognized the finality in that statement, knew he was hanging up, and yelled his name. The seconds she had to wait before she knew he'd heard her were the longest she'd faced in a while.

"What?" he growled.

"I'll be home tonight."

She could hear him breathing so she knew he was still on the line.

"Thanks," he said at last and the click as he put down the receiver was almost gentle.

From where she sat by Druxy's back wall, Vicki could see the door as well as most of Bloor and Yonge through the huge windows. She'd decided this story was too important to chance a possible misunderstanding over the phone and had convinced Anne to meet her here for lunch. Face-to-face, she knew she'd have a better chance

of convincing the columnist that the press had a responsibility to ensure that there wouldn't be another Anicka
Hendle.

She picked at the rolled cardboard edge of her coffee
cup. Henry wanted the press coverage of the "vampire
situation" stopped to protect himself, and Vicki had been
willing to do what she could. She should have realized
that Henry wasn't the only one in danger. The cardboard
ripped and she swore as the hot coffee spilled over her
hand.

"Some detective. I could've smacked you on the head
with a two by four and you'd never even have noticed I
was there."

"How. . . ?"

"I came in the little door in the east corner, O inves-
tigative one." Anne Fellows slid into the seat across from
Vicki and dumped the first of four packages of sugar into
her coffee. "Now, what's so important you had to drag
me out in the rain?"

Prodding at her pickle with a stir stick, Vicki wondered
where to begin. "A woman got killed this morning. . . ."

"I hate to burst your bubble, sweetie, but women get
killed every morning. What's so special about this one
that you've decided to share it with me?"

"This one's different. Have you talked to your paper
today? Or heard the news?"

Anne rolled her eyes over the edge of her corned beef
on a kaiser. "Give me a break, Vicki. It's Easter Sunday
and I'm off. It's bad enough I have to wallow in this shit
all week."

"Well, then, let me tell you about Anicka Hendle."
Vicki glanced down at her notes, more to settle her
thoughts than for information. "It started with the newspapers and their vampire stories. . . ."

"Not you, too! You wouldn't believe the nut cases
that've been calling the paper the last couple of weeks."
Anne took a swallow of coffee, frowned and put in another sugar packet. "Don't tell me—the kids are scared
and you want me to write that there's no such thing as
vampires."

Vicki thought of Henry, hidden away from daylight barely two blocks from the deli, and then of the young woman who'd been impaled with a sharpened hockey stick, the force of the blow not only killing her but nailing her to the ground like a butterfly on a pin. "That's exactly what I want you to write," she said through clenched teeth. She laid out each gruesome detail of Anicka's story as if she were on the witness stand, all emotion leeched from her voice. It was the only way she could get through it without screaming or throwing something.

Anne put down her sandwich early on and never picked it back up again.

"The press started this," Vicki finished. "It's up to the press to end it."

"Why call me? There were reporters at the scene."

"Because you told me once that the difference between a columnist and a reporter is that the columnist has the luxury to not only ask why but to try to answer it."

Anne's eyebrows went up. "You remember that?"

"I don't forget much."

The two women looked down at the notes and Anne snorted softly. "Lucky you." She scooped them up and at Vicki's nod stuffed them in her backpack. "I'll do what I can, but I'm not making any promises. There's screwballs all over this city and not all of them read my stuff. I suppose I can't ask where you got this information?" Much of it had been minutia not normally released to the press. "Never mind." She stood. "I can work around it without mentioning Celluci's name. I hope you realize that you've ruined my Sunday?"

Vicki nodded and crushed her empty cup. "Happy Easter."

"Henry Fitzroy is not able to come to the phone at the moment, but if you leave your name and number and a reason for your call after the tone, he'll get back to you as soon as possible. Thank you. If that's you, Brenda, I'll have it done by deadline. Stop worrying."

As the tone sounded, Vicki wondered who Brenda was and what *it* referred to. Then she remembered Captain

Macho and the young lady with the heaving bosoms. The concept of a vampire with an answering machine continued to amuse her even as she recognized its practicality—creatures of the night, welcome to the twentieth century. "Henry, it's Vicki. Look, there's no point in me coming over tonight. We don't know anything new and I certainly can't help with your stakeout. If something happens, call me. If not, I'll call you tomorrow." She frowned as she hung up. Something about talking to machines made her voice sound like Jack Webb doing narration for old *Dragnet* episodes. "I had a cheese danish," she muttered, pushing her glasses up her nose. "Friday had a cruller."

Grabbing up her jacket and her bag, she headed for the door. When Celluci left the station, he'd be expected at his grandmother's to spend Easter Sunday with assorted aunts, uncles, cousins, and offspring. It happened every holiday and there wasn't an excuse good enough to get him out of it if he wasn't actually working. If he couldn't get what he needed from them, and, given what had happened to Anicka Hendle he doubted he could—however supportive and loving his family was, they didn't, couldn't understand the anger and the frustration—he'd be over no earlier than eight. She had time to go through at least a division's worth of occurrence reports this afternoon.

As she locked the door, the phone began to ring. She paused, staring into the apartment through the six inch gap. It couldn't be Henry. It wouldn't be Celluci. Coreen was still out of town. It was probably her mother. She closed the door. She wasn't up to the guilt.

". . . as well as all cables, a power bar, and a surge suppressor. In short, a complete system." Vicki tapped the occurrence report with the end of her pencil. What she knew about computers could be easily copied onto the head of a pin and still leave room for a couple of angels to tango but, if she read these numbers correctly, the system that had been lifted out of the locked and guarded computer store made her little clone back at the apartment look like an abacus.

"Well, well, well. If it isn't the Winged Victory."

Vicki's lips drew back in a snarl. She shifted the snarl a millimeter at both ends, almost creating a smile. "Staff-Sergeant Gowan, what an unexpected pleasure."

Not bothering to hide his own snarl, Gowan snatched the reports up off the desk and swung his bulk around to face the duty sergeant. "What the fuck is this civilian doing here?" He shook the fistful of papers. "And where did she get the authorization to read these?"

"Well, I . . ." the duty sergeant began.

Gowan cut him off. "Who the fuck are you? This is my station and I say who comes in and who doesn't." He shoved his gut in Vicki's direction and she hurriedly stood, before he moved the desk so far she was trapped behind it. "This *civilian* has no fucking business being anywhere near this building, no matter what kind of a hot-shit investigator she used to be."

"Don't give yourself a coronary, Staff-Sergeant." Vicki shrugged into her jacket and slung her bag over her shoulder. "I'm just leaving."

"Fucking right, you're leaving, and you won't be back either, Nelson, remember that." The veins in his throat bulged and his pale eyes blazed with hatred. "I don't care who you had to blow to get your rank, but you don't have it now. Remember that, too!"

Vicki felt a muscle jump in her jaw with the effort of maintaining control. In her right hand, the pencil snapped, the crack of the splintering wood ringing through the quiet station like a gunshot. The radio operator jumped, but neither she nor the duty sergeant made a sound. They didn't even seem to be breathing. Moving with brittle precision, Vicki dropped both pieces of pencil in the waste basket and took a step forward. Her world centered on the two watery blue circles under silver-gray brows that glared down at her. She took another step, teeth clenched so tightly the force hummed in her ears.

"Go ahead," he sneered. "Take a shot at me. I'll have you cuffed so fast your ass'll be in holding before your head knows what happened."

With tooth and claw, Vicki managed to hold onto her temper. Losing it would accomplish nothing and, as much as she hated to admit it, Gowan was right. Her rank no longer protected her from him nor from the system. Maneuvering somehow through the red haze of her fury, she managed to get out of the station.

On the steps, she began to tremble and had to lean against the brick until it stopped. Behind her, she could hear Gowan's voice raised again. The duty sergeant would be catching the force of his anger and it infuriated her that there was nothing she could do to stop it. Had she known the staff-sergeant would be dropping in at the station on his day off, not even the hordes of hell could've gotten her out there.

Desperate to be a detective, Gowan had never made it out of uniform. Ignoring the fact that in many respects the staff-sergeants ran the force, he wanted to be an inspector so bad he could taste it, but he'd been passed over twice for promotion and knew he'd never make it now. He hated Vicki on both counts and hated her more because she was a woman who'd beaten the boys at their own game and he hated her finally and absolutely for having him reprimanded after having come upon him roughing up a kid in the holding cells.

Vicki returned the sentiment. *Power always attracts those who will abuse it.* She'd never forgotten that line from the orientation lecture at the police academy. Some days, it was easier to remember than others.

Too strung out to take transit, she flagged down a taxi, thinking, and damn the twenty bucks it would probably cost to get her home.

The afternoon hadn't been a total loss. She'd call a friend who knew computers with the information on the stolen system and see if he could pinpoint what a setup like that would be used for. Just about anything, she suspected, but it never hurt to ask and maybe they'd pick up another handle on the demon-caller.

She hunched down into the stale smelling upholstery as the rain splattered against the taxi's grimy windows. *After all, how many hackers with black leather jackets, assault rifles, and their own personal demons can there be in Toronto?*

* * *

Celluci showed up just after nine.

Vicki took one look at his expression and said, "They treated you with kid gloves."

"Like they were walking on eggshells," he agreed, scowling.

"They mean well."

"Don't tell me what they mean." He threw his coat over a chair. "I *know* what they mean!"

The fight that developed left them both limp and wrung out. When it was over, when its inevitable aftermath was over, Vicki pushed damp hair off Celluci's forehead and kissed him gently. He sighed without opening his eyes, but his arms tightened around her. Snagging the duvet with the tip of one finger, she tugged it over them both, then stretched again and flicked off the light.

There was a very good reason a lot of cops turned to substance abuse of one kind or another. Throughout the four years of their relationship, until Vicki had left the force, she'd acted as Mike Celluci's safety valve and he'd done the same for her. Just because the situation had changed, *that* didn't need to. She didn't know what he'd done during the eight months they hadn't been speaking. She didn't want to know either.

Shifting his weight a little, she closed her eyes. Besides, all things considered, she'd just as soon not sleep alone. It would be nice to have someone warm to hold on to when the nightmares came.

* * *

The trees surrounding the graveyard bent almost double in the wind, their silhouettes wild and ragged. Henry shivered. Three nights of waiting had left him edgy and longing for a confrontation of any kind. *Even losing would be better than much more of this.* Demonic lore left large pieces to the imagination and his imagination obligingly kept filling them in.

The path of power, still waiting for an anchor, pulsed sullenly, damped down by Easter Sunday and the symbolic rising of Christ.

Then it changed.

The pulse quickened, the darkness deepening into something other than night.

Somewhere, Henry knew, the pentagram had been drawn, the fire had been lit, and the call had begun. He tensed, senses straining, ready to close his own pentagram at the first sign. This was it. The lesser demon then, if he couldn't stop it, the greater and with it the end of the world. His right hand rose in the sign of the cross. "Lord, lend your strength," he prayed.

The next thing he knew, he was kneeling on the damp ground, tears streaming from light sensitive eyes as afterimages danced in glory on the inside of his lids.

* * *

The third drop of blood hit the coals, and the air over the pentagram shivered and changed. Norman sat back on his heels and waited. This afternoon, he'd found where Coreen lived—the student records at York had been almost insultingly easy to hack into. Tonight, there would be no more mistakes and she'd pay for what she'd done to him.

The throbbing in his head grew until it seemed the entire world thrummed with it.

He frowned as the shimmering grew more pronounced and a hazy outline of the demon appeared. It almost seemed to be fighting against something, lashing out against an invisible opponent. Its mouth opened in a soundless shriek and abruptly the pentagram was clear.

At that same instant, the coals in the hibachi blazed up with such power that Norman had to throw himself backward or be consumed. The throbbing became a high-pitched whine. He clawed at his ears, but it went on and one and on.

After three or four seconds of six-foot flames, the tempered steel of the hibachi melted to slag, the flames disappeared, and a gust of wind from the center of the pentagram not only blew the candles out but threw them against the far wall where they shattered.

"That isn't p–possible," he stammered into the sudden silence. His ears still rang with echoes, but even the throbbing had died, leaving an aching emptiness where it had been. While a part of his mind cowered in fear, another disbelieved the evidence of his eyes. Heat enough to melt the cast iron hibachi should have taken the entire apartment building with it.

He reached out a trembling hand and touched the pool of metal, all that remained of the tiny barbecue. His fingertips sizzled and a heartbeat later he felt the pain.

It hurt too much to scream.

* * *

When his sight finally returned, Henry dragged himself to his feet. He hadn't been hit that hard in centuries. Why he hadn't assumed it was the Demon Lord breaking through he had no idea, but he hadn't, not even during that first panicked instant of blindness.

"So what was it?" he asked, sagging against a concrete angel and brushing mud off his knees. He could just barely feel the power signature of the naming. It had retreated as far as it could without returning to hell altogether. "Any ideas, mister, miss . . ." he asked, turning to read the name off the headstone. Carved into the stone at the angel's feet was the answer.

CHRISTUS RESURREXIT! *Christ is risen.*

Henry Fitzroy, vampire, raised a good Catholic, dropped back to his knees and said a Hail Mary—just in case.

Eleven

Coreen slipped through the double doors moments before the class was about to begin and made her way across the lecture hall to a cluster of her friends. Her eyes had the fragile, translucent look of little sleep and much crying. Even the bright red tangle of her hair seemed dimmed.

The cluster opened and let her in, seating her in the safety of their circle, offering expressions of shock and sympathy. Although Janet had been a friend to all of them, Coreen had seen her last and that gave her grief an immediacy theirs couldn't have.

None of them, Coreen least of all, was aware of the expression of hatred that crossed Norman Birdwell's face every time he glanced in their direction.

How dare she still live when I said she was to die.

The throbbing had returned sometime during the night, each pulse reassuring Norman that the power was still his, each pulse demanding that Coreen pay.

Coreen had become the symbol for everyone who had ever laughed at him. For every slut who'd spread her legs for the football team but not for him. For every jock who pushed him aside as if he wasn't there. Well, he was there, and he'd prove it. He'd turn his demon loose on the lot of them—but first Coreen had to die.

Very carefully, he moved his bandaged hand from his lap to the arm of the chair. After spending a virtually sleepless night, he'd stopped by the student medical center before class. If that's what his student funds paid for, he wasn't impressed. First, they'd made him wait until two people who'd arrived before him went in—even though he was obviously in more pain—and then the stupid cow had hurt him when she'd taped down the gauze. They hadn't even wanted to hear the story he'd made up about how he did it.

Briefcase awkwardly balanced on his knees, he pulled out the little black book he'd bought in high school to keep girls' phone numbers in. The first four or five pages had been raggedly torn out and on the first remaining page, under the word Coreen, he wrote, *the Student Medical Center.*

From here on, Norman Birdwell was going to get even.

He didn't understand what had gone wrong the night before. He'd performed the ritual flawlessly. Something had interfered, had stopped the demon, had stopped *his* demon. Norman frowned. Obviously, there were things around stronger than the creature he called to do his bidding. He didn't like that. He didn't like that at all. How dare something be able to interfere with him.

He could see only one solution. He'd have to get a stronger demon.

After the lecture, he made his way to the front of the class and planted himself between the professor and the door. Over the years he'd learned that the best way to get answers was to block the possibility of escape.

"Professor Leigh? I need to talk to you."

Resignedly, the professor set his heavy briefcase back by the lectern. He tried to be available when his students needed him, recognizing that a few moments of answering questions could occasionally clarify an entire semester's work, but Norman Birdwell would corner him for no better reason than to prove how clever he was. "What is it, Norman?"

What was it? The throbbing had grown so loud again it had become difficult to think. With an effort, he managed to blurt out, "It's about my seminar topic. You said earlier that as well as a host of lesser demons there were also Demon Lords. Can I assume that the Demon Lords are the more powerful?"

"Yes, Norman, you can." He wondered briefly what the younger man had done to his fingers. *Probably got them caught in a metaphorical cookie jar. . . .*

"Well, how can you tell what you're going to get? I

mean if you call up a demon, how can you ensure that you're going to get a Demon Lord?''

Professor Leigh's brows rose. This sounded like it was going to be one hell of a seminar. So to speak. ''The rituals for calling up one of the demon kind are very complicated, Norman. . . .''

Norman hid a sneer. The rituals were nonspecific but hardly complicated. Of course, he'd never be able to convince the professor that. Professor Leigh thought *he* knew everything. ''How do they differ for a Demon Lord?''

''Well, just for starters, you need a name.''

''Where do I find one?''

''I am not going to do your research for you, Norman.'' The professor picked up his briefcase and headed for the door, expecting Norman to move out of his way. Norman stayed right where he was. Faced with a shoving match or surrender, Professor Leigh sighed and surrendered. ''I suggest you have a word with Dr. Sagara at the University of Toronto's Rare Book Room. She might have something that can help.''

Norman weighed the worth of that information for a moment then nodded, stepping back against the blackboard. It was less than he wanted, but it was a beginning and he still had ten hours until midnight.

''Fine. I'll call Dr. Sagara and tell her you'll be coming down.'' Once safely out in the corridor, the professor grinned. He almost wished he could be there to see the irresistible force come up against the immovable object. Almost.

A few flakes of snow slapped wetly against his face as Norman stood waiting for the bus. He shifted his weight from foot to foot, glad he'd worn his sneakers—cowboy boots, he'd discovered, had next to no insulation against the cold. The black leather jacket kept him reasonably warm, although the fringe kept flapping up and whipping him in the back of the neck.

When he saw the bus approaching, he moved to the curb, only to be engulfed by the waiting pack of students and pushed back almost to the end of the line. All his efforts to regain his place met with failure and finally he gave in, shuffling forward with the line and fuming.

Just wait. . . . Norman shifted his grip on his briefcase, ignoring the way it cracked against the shins of the person next to him. *When I have my Demon Lord, there'll be no more lines, no more buses, no more sharp elbows.* He glared at the back of the tall skinny young man attached to the elbow in question. As soon as he got a chance, that guy was going on the list.

* * *

Vicki allowed herself to be caught up in the rush of students and carried with them out through the back doors of the bus. Intensive eavesdropping during the long trip had taught her two things; that nothing had changed much since she'd gone to university and that the verb "says" seemed to have disappeared from common usage.

". . . so then my dad goes, if you're going to take the car out I gotta know where you're going like and . . ."

And what's really depressing is that she's probably an English major. Out on the sidewalk at last, Vicki fastened her jacket and took a quick look back at the bus. The doors were just closing behind the last of the students fleeing the campus and, as she watched, the heavily loaded vehicle lumbered away. Well, that was that, then; no changing her mind for another forty minutes.

She felt a little foolish, but this was the best idea she could come up with. With any luck, the head of the computer science department would be able—and willing—to tell her who'd be likely to own and use the stolen computer system. Coreen might have had information that could help sort the living needle out of the haystack, after all, she was a student out here, but when Vicki'd called her apartment at about 8:30 there'd been no answer.

Pushing her glasses up her nose, she started across the parking lot, watching for black leather jackets. As Celluci had pointed out, there were a number of them on males and females both. Vicki knew full well that physical characteristics had nothing to do with the ability to commit crime, but she looked anyway. Surely a demon-caller must show some outward manifestation of that kind of evil.

* * *

Norman pushed into the first available seat. His injured hand should've entitled him to one the moment he got on the bus but not one of his selfish, self-centered fellow students would get up although he'd glared at all and sundry. Still sulking, he fished his calculator out of his shirt pocket, and began to work out the time he'd need to spend downtown. He was, at that very moment, missing an analytical geometry class. It was the first class he'd ever skipped. His parents would have fits. He didn't care. As much as he'd hoarded every A and A plus—he had a complete record of every mark he'd ever received—he'd realized in the last couple of days that some things were more important.

Things like getting even.

When the bus finally wheezed into the subway station, Norman was deep in a pleasant fantasy of rearranging the world so that jocks and their sort were put where they belonged and he got the recognition and the women he deserved. Chin up, he strutted down to the trains, oblivious to the raised brows and the snickers that followed him. A Norman Birdwell run world would be set up to acknowledge the value of Norman Birdwell.

"Dr. Sagara?"

"What?"

Norman was a little surprised at the vehemence in the old lady's voice; he hadn't even asked her for anything yet. "Professor Leigh said I should talk to you."

"What about?" She glared up at him over the edge of her glasses.

"I'm doing a project on demons. . . ."

"The ones on the Board of Directors?" She sniggered, then shook her head at his complete lack of reaction. "That was a joke."

"Oh." Norman peered down at her, annoyed at the lack of light. Bad enough that the Rare Book Room itself was so dark—a few banks of fluorescents would be a decent start until the whole smelly mess could be transcribed onto a mainframe—but it really was unnecessary to carry the conceit over into the offices. The brass lamp threw a pool of gold onto the desk, but Dr. Sagara's face itself was in shadow. He looked around for a wall switch but couldn't see one.

"Well?" Dr. Sagara tapped the fingers of one hand against her desk blotter. "What does Professor Leigh think your project has to do with me? He was singularly nonspecific on the phone."

"I need to find out about Demon Lords." His voice picked up the rhythm of the throbbing.

"Then you need a grimoire."

"A what?"

"I said," she spoke very slowly and distinctly as though to an idiot, "you need a grimoire; an ancient practically mythological book of demon lore."

Norman bent forward, squinting a little as he came within the sphere of the desk lamp. "Do you have one?"

"Well, your Professor Leigh seems to think I do."

Grinding his teeth, Norman wished U of T paid more attention to its retirement regulations. The old lady was obviously senile. "Do you?"

"No." She laced her fingers together and leaned back in her chair. "But if you really want one, I suggest you contact a young man by the name of Henry Fitzroy. He came to visit me when he first moved to Toronto. Spitting image of his father as a young man. His father had a great love of antiquities, books in particular. Donated a number of the books we have in our collection here. God knows what young Henry inherited."

"This Henry Fitzroy has a grimoire?"

"Do I look like God? *I* don't know what he has, but he's your best bet in the city."

Norman pulled his electronic address book out of his briefcase. "Do you have his number?"

"Yes. But I'm not going to give it to you. You have his name, look it up. If he's not in the phone book, he obviously doesn't want to be bothered."

Norman stared at her in astonishment. She couldn't

just not tell him, could she? The throbbing became a kettledrum between his ears.

Yes, she could.

"Good afternoon, young man."

Norman continued to stare.

Dr. Sagara sighed. "Good afternoon," she repeated more firmly.

"You have to tell me. . . ."

"I don't have to tell you anything." Whining topped her rather considerable list of character traits she couldn't abide. "Get out."

"You can't talk to me like that!"Norman protested.

"I can talk to you anyway I like, I have tenure. Now are you going to leave or am I going to call library security?"

Breathing heavily through his nose, he whirled and stamped toward the door.

Dr. Sagara watched him go, brows drawn down and two vertical lines cutting into her forehead. Professor Leigh would be hearing from her about this. Obviously, he still bore a grudge for that C minus.

She'll be sorry. Norman charged through the dim quiet of the Rare Book Room and careened off the entrance turnstile. *They'll all be sorry!* The exit was on the other side of the guard's desk. *If anyone laughs at me, they're dead.*

He slammed into the exit bar and got his briefcase caught between it and the desk. The grinding noise brought a startled exclamation from the guard.

"No, I don't need your help!" Norman snarled. Bandaged hand waving, he yanked at the case and jammed it more tightly. "This is all your fault," he growled as the guard came around to see what could be done. "If you built these things properly, there'd be room!"

"If you were more careful going through them. . . ." the guard muttered, jiggling the mechanism and hoping he wasn't going to have to call building maintenance.

"You can't talk to me like that. It wasn't *my* fault." In spite of his awkward position, Norman drew himself up and looked the guard right in the eye. "Who's your supervisor?"

"Wha. . . ." The guard, who had never considered himself an imaginative man, had the strangest feeling that something not the least human studied him from behind the furious gaze of the young man. The muscles in his legs felt suddenly weak and he wanted desperately to look away.

"Your supervisor, who is he? I'm going to register a complaint and you'll lose your job."

"And I'll what?"

"You heard me." With a final heave, the briefcase came free, deeply scored down one side. "You just wait!" Norman backed out the door, almost running down two students trying to enter. He scowled at the confused guard. "You'll see!"

He felt better by the time he'd walked to Bloor Street. With every step, he imagined pulling one of those stupid so-called rare books off the shelves, throwing it on the sidewalk in front of him, and kicking it out into traffic. Still breathing a little heavily, he went into the phone booth at the gas station and looked up the name the crazy old woman had given him.

Henry Fitzroy had no listed number.

Letting the phone book fall, Norman almost laughed. If they thought a minor detail like *that* could stop him. . . .

On the way back to his apartment, he added Dr. Sagara, the library guard, and a surly TTC official to his black book. He didn't worry much about the lack of names; surely a Demon Lord would be powerful enough to work without them.

Once home, he added his upstairs neighbor. On principle more than anything else, for the heavy metal beat pounding through his ceiling only seemed to enhance the beat pulsing in his head.

Breaking into the phone system took him less time than he'd anticipated, even considering that he had to type one-handed.

The only Henry Fitzroy listed lived at 278 Bloor Street East, unit 1407. Given the proximity to Yonge and Bloor,

Norman suspected the building consisted of expensive condominiums. He glanced around at his own tiny apartment. As soon as he called the Demon Lord, *he'd* have that kind of address and be living in the style he deserved.

But first, he'd have to get the grimoire he was certain Henry Fitzroy had—that wacko old lady was obviously just being coy.

Of course, Henry Fitzroy wouldn't lend it to him, no point in even asking. People who lived in those kinds of buildings were too smug about what they owned. Just because they had lots of money, the world was below their notice and a perfectly reasonable request to borrow a book would be denied.

"He probably doesn't even know what he has, thinks it's just some old book worth money. *I* know how to use it. That makes it mine by right." It wouldn't be stealing to take a book that by rights should be his.

Norman turned and looked down at the pool of metal that had been the hibachi. There was only one way to get his property out of a high security building.

* * *

"Anything much happen today?" Greg asked sliding into the recently vacated chair. He should've waited a little longer. It was still warm. He hated sitting in a chair warmed by someone else's butt.

"Mr. Post from 1620 stalled his car goin' up the ramp again." Tim chuckled and scratched at his beard. "Every time he tried to put it in gear he'd roll backward, panic, and stall again. Finally let it roll all the way down till it rested on the door and started from there. I almost split a gut laughing."

"Some men," Greg observed, "are not meant to drive standards." He bent over and picked up a package from the floor by the desk. "What's this?"

The day guard paused, half into his hockey jacket, his uniform blazer left hanging on the hook in its place. "Oh that—it came this afternoon, UPS from New York. For that writer up on fourteen. I rang his apartment and left a message on his machine.''

Greg put the package back on the floor. ''Guess Mr. Fitzroy'll be down for it later.''

''Guess so.'' Tim paused on the other side of the desk. ''Greg, I've been thinking.''

The older guard snorted. ''Dangerous that.''

''No, this is serious. I've been thinking about Mr. Fitzroy. I've been here four months now and I've never seen him. Never seen him come down for his mail. Never seen him take his car out.'' He waved a hand in the general direction of the package. ''I've never even been able to get him on the phone, I *always* talk to his machine.''

''I see him most nights,'' Greg pointed out, leaning back in his chair.

''Yeah, that's my point. You see him nights. I bet you never see him before the sun sets.''

Greg frowned. ''What are you getting at?''

''Those killings where the blood was sucked out; I think Mr. Fitzroy did it. I think he's a vampire.''

''I think you're out of your mind,'' Greg told him dryly, allowing the front legs of his chair to come to ground with a thud. ''Henry Fitzroy is a writer. You can't expect him to act like a normal person. And about those vampires. . . .'' He reached down and pulled a copy of the day's tabloid out of his old leather briefcase. ''I think you better read this.''

With the Leafs actually winning the division playoffs after the full seven games, the front page was dedicated to hockey. Anicka Hendle had to settle for page two.

Tim read the article, brows drawn down over some of the larger words. When he finished, Greg raised a hand to cut off his reaction and turned the page. Anne Fellows' column didn't attempt to appeal to the reason of her readers, she played Anicka Hendle's death for every ounce of emotion it held. She placed the blame squarely in the arms of the media, admitting her own involvement, and demanding that the scare tactics stop. *Are there not enough real terrors on our streets without creating new ones?*

''They made up all that stuff about vampires?''

"Looks that way, doesn't it?"

"Just to sell papers." Tim shook his head in disgust. He pushed the tabloid back across the desk, tapping the picture on the front page. "You think the Leafs are going to go all the way this year?"

Greg snorted. "I think there's a better chance that Henry Fitzroy's a vampire." He waved the younger guard out of the building then came around the desk to hold the door open for Mrs. Hughes and her mastiff.

"Get down, Owen! He doesn't want your kisses!"

Wiping his face, Greg watched as the huge dog bounded into the elevator, dragging Mrs. Hughes behind him. The lobby always seemed a little smaller after Owen had passed through. He checked that the lock on the inner door had caught—it was a little stiff, he'd have to have a word with maintenance—before returning to the desk and picking up his paper.

Then he paused, memory jogged by the smell of the ink or the feel of the newsprint, suddenly recalling the first night the vampire story had made the paper. He remembered Henry Fitzroy's reaction to the headline and he realized that Tim was right. He'd never seen the man before sunset.

"Still," he shook himself, "man's got a right to work what hours he chooses and sleep what hours he chooses." But he couldn't shake the memory of the bestial fury that had shone for a heartbeat in the young man's eyes. Nor could he shake a feeling of disquiet that caressed the back of his neck with icy fingers.

* * *

As the light released its hold on the city, Henry stirred. He became aware of the sheet lying across his naked body, each thread drawing a separate line against his skin. He became aware of the slight air current that brushed his cheek like a baby's breath. He became aware of three million people living their lives around him and the cacophony nearly deafened him until he managed to push through it and into the silence once again. Lastly, he became aware of self. His eyes snapped open and he stared up into the darkness.

He hated the way he woke, hated the extended vulnerability. When they finally came for him, this was when it would happen; not during the hours of oblivion, but during the shadow time between the light and dark when he would feel the stake and know his death and be able to do nothing about it.

As he grew older, it happened earlier—creeping closer to the day a few seconds at a time—but it never happened faster. He woke the way he had when he was mortal— slowly.

Centuries ago, he'd asked Christina how it was for her.

"Like waking out of a deep sleep—one moment I'm not there, the next I am."

"Do you dream?"

She rolled over on her side. "No. We don't. None of us do."

"I think I miss that most of all."

Smiling, she scraped a fingernail along his inner thigh. "We learn to dream while we wake. Shall I show you how?"

Occasionally, in the seconds just after he woke, he thought he heard voices from his past, friends, lovers, enemies, his father once, bellowing for him to get a move on or they'd be late. In over four hundred years, that was as close as he'd come to what the mortal world called dreaming.

He sat up and paused in mid-stretch, suddenly uneasy. In absolute silence he moved off the bed and across the carpet to the bedroom door. If there was a life in the apartment, he'd sense it.

The apartment was empty, but the disquiet remained.

He showered and dressed, becoming more and more certain that something was wrong—worrying at the feeling, poking and prodding at it, trying to force an understanding. When he went down to the desk to pick up his package, the feeling grew. The civilized mask managed to exchange pleasantries with Greg and flirt a little with old Mrs. McKensie while the rest of him sorted through a myriad of sensations, searching for the danger.

Heading back to the elevator, he felt the security guard's eyes on him so he turned and half smiled as the doors opened and he stepped inside. The closing slabs of stainless steel cut off Greg's answering expression. Whatever was bothering the old man, he'd have to deal with later.

* * *

"Private Investigations. Nelson." As she had no way of knowing what callers were potential clients, she'd decided to assume they all were. Her mother objected, but then her mother objected to a number of things she had no intention of changing.

"Vicki, it's Henry. Look, I think you should come over here tonight."

"Why? Have you turned up something new we should talk about before you head out?"

"I'm not heading out."

"What?" She swung her feet down off her desk and glared at the phone. "You better have a good reason for staying home."

She heard him sigh. "No, not exactly. I've just got this feeling."

Vicki snorted. "Vampire intuition?"

"If you like."

"So you're just going to stay home tonight because you're got a *feeling*?"

"Essentially, yes."

"Just letting demons run loose all over the city while you ride a hunch?"

"I don't think there'll be any demons tonight."

"What? Why not?"

"Because of what happened last night. When the power of God reached out and said, 'No.'"

"Say what?"

"I don't really understand myself. . . ."

"What happened last night, Fitzroy?" She growled out the question through clenched teeth. She'd interviewed hostile witnesses who'd been more generous with details.

"Look, I'll tell you when you get here." He did not want to explain a religious experience to a woman raised in the twentieth century over the phone. He'd have enough trouble convincing her of what had happened face-to-face.

"Does this *feeling* have anything to do with what happened last night?"

"No."

"Then why. . . ."

"Listen, Vicki, over time I've learned to trust my feelings. And surely you've ridden a few hunches in the past?"

Vicki pushed her glasses up her nose. She didn't have much choice when it came right down to it—she had to believe he knew what he was doing. Believing in vampires had been easier. "Okay, I've got a few things to take care of here, but I'll be over as soon as I can."

"All right."

He sounded so different than he had on other occasions that she frowned. "Henry, is something wrong?"

"Yes. . . . No. . . ." He sighed again. "Just come over when you can."

"Listen, I have a . . . damn him!" Vicki stared at the receiver, the loud buzz of the dial tone informing her that Henry Fitzroy didn't care what she had. And yet she was supposed to drop everything and hurry over there because he had a feeling. "That's just what I need," she muttered, digging around in her bag, "a depressed vampire."

The list the computer science professor had finally given her held twenty-three names, students he figured would actually be able to make use of the potential of the stolen computer system. Although, as he'd pointed out, the most sophisticated of home systems were often used for no better purpose than games. *"And even you could run one under those parameters,"* he'd added. He had no idea which ones of the twenty-three wore black leather jackets. It just wasn't the sort of thing he paid attention to.

"Have any of them been acting strangely lately?"

He'd smiled wearily. "Ms. Nelson, this lot doesn't act any way but strangely."

Vicki checked her watch. 9:27. How had it gotten so damned late? On the off chance that Celluci might finally be at his desk—he hadn't been in since she'd started trying to reach him around four in the afternoon—she called headquarters. He still wasn't there. Nor was he at home.

Leaving yet another message, she hung up. "Well, he can't say I didn't *try* to pass on all relevant information." She tacked the list to the small bulletin board over the desk. Actually, she had no idea how relevant the names were. It was the slimmest of chances they'd mean anything at all, but so far it was the only chance they had and these twenty-three names at least gave her a place to start.

9:46. She'd better get over to Henry's and find out just what exactly *had* happened the night before.

"The hand of God. Right."

Demons and Armageddon aside, she couldn't even begin to guess at what would make such an impression on a four hundred and fifty year old vampire.

"Demons and Armageddon aside. . . ." She reached for the phone to call a cab. "You're getting awfully blasé about the end of the world."

Her hand was actually on the plastic when the phone rang and her heart leapt up into her throat at the sudden shrill sound.

"Okay." She took a deep breath. "Maybe not so blasé after all." By the third ring she figured she'd regained enough control to answer it.

"Hi, honey, have I called at a bad time?"

"I was just on my way out, Mom." Another five minutes and she'd have been gone. Her mother had a sixth sense about these things.

"At this hour?"

"It isn't even ten yet."

"I know that, dear, but it's dark and with your eyes. . . ."

"Mom, my eyes are fine. I'll be staying on well lighted streets and I promise I'll be careful. Now, I really have to go."

"Are you going alone?"

"I'm meeting someone."

"Not Michael Celluci?"

"No, Mom."

"Oh." Vicki could practically hear her mother's ears perk up. "What's his name?"

"Henry Fitzroy." Why not? Short of hanging up, there was no way she was going to get her mother off the phone, curiosity unsatisfied.

"What does he do?"

"He's a writer." As long as she stuck to answering her mother's questions, the truth would serve. Her mother was not likely to ask, *"Is he a member of the bloodsucking undead?"*

"How does Michael feel about this?"

"How should he feel? You know very well that Mike and I don't have that kind of relationship."

"If you say so, dear. Is this Henry Fitzroy good looking?"

She thought about that for a moment. "Yes, he is. And he has a certain presence. . . ." Her voice trailed off into speculation and her mother laughed.

"It sounds serious."

That brought her back to the matter at hand. "It is, Mom, very serious, and that's why I have to go now."

"Very well. I was just hoping that, as you couldn't make it home for Easter, you might have a little time to spend with me now. I had such a quiet holiday, watched a bit of television, had supper alone, went to bed early."

It didn't help that Vicki was fully aware she was being manipulated. It never had. "Okay, Mom. I can spare a few moments."

"I don't want to put you out, dear."

"Mother. . . ."

Almost an hour later, Vicki replaced the receiver, looked at her watch, and groaned. She'd never met anyone as capable as her mother at filling time with nothing at all. "At least the world didn't end during the interim," she muttered, squinting at Henry's number up on the corkboard and dialing.

"Henry Fitzroy is not able to come to the phone at the moment. . . ."

"Of all the nerve!" She hung up in the middle of the

message. "First he asks me to come over and then he buggers off." It wasn't too likely he'd met an untimely end while her mother had held her captive on the phone. She doubted that even vampires had the presence of mind to switch on their answering machines while being dismembered.

She shrugged into her jacket, grabbed up her bag, and headed out of the apartment, switching her own machine on before she left. Moving cautiously, she made it down the dark path to the sidewalk, then pointed herself at the brighter lights that marked College Street half a block away. She'd been going to call for a taxi, but if Henry wasn't even at home, she'd walk.

Her mother attempting to call attention to her disability had nothing to do with the decision. Nothing.

* * *

Henry grabbed for the phone, then ground his teeth when the caller hung up before the message had even finished. There were few things he hated more and that was the third time it had happened this evening. He'd turned the machine on when he sat down to write, more out of habit then anything, with every intention of picking up the receiver if Vicki chanced to call. Of course, he couldn't tell who was calling if they didn't speak. He looked at his watch. Ten past eleven. Had something gone wrong? He dialed her number and listened to her complete message before hanging up. It told him nothing at all.

Where was she?

He considered going to her apartment and trying to pick up some kind of a trail but discarded the idea almost immediately. The feeling that he should stay in the condo was stronger than ever, keeping him in a perpetual sort of twitchy unease.

As long as he had to hang around anyway, he'd been attempting to use that feeling in his writing.

Smith stepped backward, sapphire eyes wide, and snatched the captain's straight razor off his small shaving stand. "Come one step closer," she warned, an intriguing little catch in her voice, "and I'll cut you!"

It wasn't going well. He sighed, saved, and turned off the computer. What was taking Vicki so long?

Unable to remain still, he walked into the living room and peered down at the city. For the first time since he'd bought the condo, the lights failed to enthrall him. He could only think of them going dark and the darkness spreading until the world became lost in it.

He moved to the stereo, turned it on, pulled out a CD, put it back, and turned the stereo off. Then he began to pace the length of the living room. Back and forth, back and forth, back. . . .

Even through the glass doors of the bookcase he could feel the presence of the grimoire but, unlike Vicki, he named it evil without hesitation. A little over a hundred years ago it had been one of the last three true grimoires remaining in the world, or so he'd been told, and he had no reason to doubt the man who'd told him—not then, not now.

* * *

"So you're Henry Fitzroy." Dr. O'Mara gripped Henry's hand, his large pale eyes gleaming. "I've heard so much about you from Alfred here, I feel that I already know you."

"And I you," Henry replied, stripping off his evening gloves and carefully returning exactly the amount of pressure applied. The hair on the back of his neck had risen and he had a feeling that appearing stronger than this man would be just as dangerous as appearing weaker. "Alfred admires you a great deal."

Releasing Henry, Dr. O'Mara clapped Alfred on the shoulder. "Does he now?"

The words held an edge and the Honorable Alfred Waverly hastened to fill the silence that followed, his shoulder dipping slightly under the white knuckled grip. "It's not that I've told him anything, Doctor, it's just that. . . ."

"That he quotes you constantly," Henry finished with his most disarming grin.

"Quotes me?" The grim expression eased. "Well, I suppose one can't object to that."

Alfred beamed, eyes bright above slightly flushed cheeks, the expression of terror that had caused Henry to intervene gone as though it had never existed.

"If you will excuse me, Mr. Fitzroy, I have a number of things I must attend to." The doctor waved an expansive hand. "Alfred will introduce you to the other guests."

Henry inclined his head and watched his host leave the room through narrowed eyes.

The ten other guests were all young men, much like the Honorable Alfred, wealthy, idle, and bored. Three of them, Henry already knew. The others were strangers.

"Well, what do you think?" Alfred asked, accepting a whiskey from a blank-faced footman after introductions had been made, the proper things said, and they were standing alone again.

"I think you've grossly misled me," Henry told him, refusing a drink. "This is hardly a den of iniquity."

Alfred's smile jerked up nervously at the corners, his face paler than usual under the flickering gaslight. "Dash it, Henry, I never said it was." He ran his finger around the edge of his whiskey glass. "You're lucky to be here, you know. There's only ever twelve invited and Dr. O'Mara wanted you specifically after Charles . . . uh, had his accident."

Accident; Charles was dead, but Alfred's Victorian sensibilities wouldn't let him say the word. "I've been meaning to ask you, why did Dr. O'Mara want me?"

Alfred flushed. "Because I told him all about you."

"*All* about me?" Given the laws against homosexuality and Alfred's preferences, Henry doubted it, but to his surprise the young man nodded.

"I couldn't help myself. Dr. O'Mara, well, he's the kind of person you tell things to."

"I'm sure he is," Henry muttered, thanking God and all the Saints that Alfred had no idea of what he actually was. "Do you sleep with him, too?"

"I say, Henry!"

The bastard son of Henry VIII, having little patience

with social conventions, merely asked the question again. "Are you sleeping with him?"

"No."

"But you would. . . ."

Managing to look both miserable and elated, Alfred nodded. "He's magnificent."

Overpowering was closer to the word Henry would have used. The doctor's personality was like a tidal wave, sweeping all lesser personalties before it. Henry had no intention of being swept, but he could see how he might be if he were the idle young man he appeared to be; could see how the others in the room had been, and he didn't like it.

Just after eleven, the doctor disappeared and a gong sounded somewhere in the depths of the house.

"It's time," Alfred whispered, clutching at Henry's arm. "Come on."

To Henry's surprise, the group of them, a dozen young men in impeccable evening dress, trooped down into the basement. The huge central room had been outfitted with torches and at one end stood what appeared to be a stone block about waist high, needing only a knight lying in effigy on its top to complete the resemblance to a crypt. Around him, his companions began stripping off their clothes.

"Get undressed," Alfred urged, thrusting a loose black robe in Henry's direction. "And put this on."

Suddenly understanding, Henry had to bite back the urge to laugh. He'd been brought in as the twelfth member of a coven; a group of juvenile aristocrats dressing up in black bedsheets and capering around in a smoky basement. He allowed Alfred to help him change and he remained amused until Dr. O'Mara appeared behind the altar.

The Doctor's robe was red, the color of fresh blood. In his right hand he carried a human skull, in his left an ancient book. He should have looked as foolish as his sycophants. He didn't. His pale eyes burned and his personality, carefully leashed in the drawing room, blazed forth, igniting the chamber. He used his voice to whip the young men to a frenzy, one moment filling the room with thunder, the next dropping it low, wrapping it about them, and drawing them close.

Henry's disgust rose with the hysteria. He stood in the deepest shadows, well away from the torches, and watched. A sense of danger kept him there, a pricking up and down his spine that told him no matter how ludicrous this looked, the doctor, at least, played no game and the evil that spread from the altar was very real.

At midnight, two of the anonymous, black clad bodies held a struggling cat upon the stone while a third wielded the knife.

"Blood. Blood! BLOOD! BLOOD!"

Henry felt his own need rise as the blood scent mixed with the smell of smoke and sweat. The chant grew in volume and intensity, pulsing like a heartbeat and pounding against him. Robes began to fall, exposing flesh and, surging just below the surface, blood . . . and blood . . . and blood. His lips drew back off his teeth and he stepped forward.

Then, over the mass of writhing bodies between them, he met the doctor's eyes.

He knows.

Terror broke through the blood lust and drove him from the house. Clad only in the robe, and more frightened than he'd been in three hundred and fifty years, he made his way back to his sanctuary, gaining it just before dawn, falling into the day with the memory of the doctor's face before him.

The next night, as little as he wanted to, he went back. The danger had to be faced. And eliminated.

"I knew you'd return." Without rising from behind his desk, Dr. O'Mara waved Henry to a chair. "Please, sit down."

Senses straining, Henry moved slowly into the room. Except for the sleeping servants on the third floor the doctor was the only life in the house. He could kill him and be gone with no one the wiser. He sat instead, curiosity staying his hand. How did this mortal know him and what did he want?

"You blend quite well, vampire." The doctor beamed

genially at him. "Had I not been aware already of the existence of your kind, I would have disregarded young Alfred's babblings. You made quite an impression on him. And on me. The moment I realized what you were, I had to have you with me."

"You killed Charles to make room for me."

"Of course, I did. There can never be more than twelve." At Henry's utterance of disgust, he only laughed. "I saw your face, vampire. You wanted it. All those lives, all that blood. Fresh young throats to rip. And they'd have given themselves joyously to your teeth if I commanded it." He leaned forward, pale eyes like cold flames. "I can give you this, each and every night."

"And what do I give you?"

"Eternal life." Hands became fists and the words rang like a bell. "You will make me as you are."

That was enough. More than enough. Henry threw himself out of the chair and at the doctor's throat.

Only to slam up against an invisible barrier that held him like a fly in a web. He could thrash about where he stood, but he could move neither forward nor back. For a moment he fought against it with all his strength and then he hung, panting, lips drawn back, a soundless growl twisting his face.

"I rather suspected you would refuse to cooperate." The doctor came around the desk, standing so close Henry could feel his breath as he spoke. "You thought I was a posturing fool, didn't you, vampire? You never thought I would hold real power; power brought out of dark places by unspeakable means, gained by deeds even you would quail to hear. That power holds you now and will continue to hold you until you are mine."

"You cannot force me to change you." Raw fury kept the fear from his voice.

"Perhaps not. You are physically very strong and mentally almost my match. Nor can I bleed you and drink, for a touch would release the bonds." Turning, the doctor scooped a book up off the desk and held it up to Henry's face. "But if I cannot force you, I have access to those who can."

The book covered in greasy red leather, was the same

one he'd held the night before during the ceremony. At such close quarters, the evil that radiated from it struck Henry with almost a physical blow and he rocked back against the unseen chains that held him.

"This," said Dr. O'Mara, caressing it lovingly, "is one of the last true grimoires left. I have heard there are only two others in the world. All the rest are but pale copies of these three. The man who wrote it sold his soul for the information it contains, but the Prince of Lies collected before he could use the knowledge so dearly bought. If we had the time, dear vampire, I would tell you what I had to do to make it mine, but we do not— you must be mine as well before dawn."

The naked desire in his eyes was so consuming that Henry felt sick. He began to struggle, fighting harder when he heard the doctor laugh again and move away.

"From months of ceremonies, I have drawn what I need to control the demon," the doctor remarked conversationally, rolling up the carpet before the fire. "The demon can give me anything save life eternal. You can give me that so the demon will give me you." He looked up from the pentagram cut into the floor. "Can you stand against a Lord of Hell, vampire? I think not."

His mouth dry and his breath coming in labored gasps, Henry threw all his strength against the binding. Muscles straining and joints popping, he fought for his life. Just as it seemed he could no longer contain a wail of despair, his right arm moved.

The candles lit and a foul powder burning on the fire, Dr. O'Mara opened the book and began to read.

His right arm moved again. And then his left.

A shimmering began in the center of the pentagram.

Power fed into the calling bled power away from the bindings, Henry realized. They were weakening. Weakening. . . .

The shimmer began to coalesce, falling into itself and forming. . . .

With a howl of rage, Henry tore free and flung himself across the room. Before the doctor could react, Henry grabbed him, lifted him, and threw him with all his remaining strength against the far wall.

The doctor's head struck the wooden wainscoting and the wood proved stronger. The thing in the pentagram faded until only a foul smell and a memory of terror remained.

Weak and trembling, Henry stood over the body. The light in the pale eyes had gone out, leaving them only a muddy gray. Blood pooled at the base of the wall, hot and red and Henry, who desperately needed to feed, thanked God that dead blood held no call. He'd have starved before he'd have fed from that man.

His skin crawling at the touch, he picked the grimoire up from the floor and staggered into the night.

* * *

"I should have destroyed it." Palms flat against the glass doors of the bookcase, Henry stared at the grimoire. He never asked himself why he hadn't. He doubted he wanted to hear the answer.

* * *

"Yo, Victory!"

Vicki turned slowly in the open phone booth, her heart doing a pretty fair impersonation of a jackhammer.

Tony grinned. "My, but we're jumpy. I thought I heard you didn't work nights no more."

"Any more," Vicki corrected absently, while her heart slowed to a more normal rhythm. "And do I look like I'm working?"

"You always look like you're working."

Vicki sighed and checked him out. Physically, he'd didn't look good. The patina of dirt he wore told her he'd been sleeping rough, and his face had the pinched look that said meals had been infrequent of late. "You don't look so great."

"Things have been better," he admitted. "Could use a burger and some fries."

"Why not." Henry's answering machine insisted he still wasn't available. "You can tell me what you've been doing lately."

He rolled his eyes. "Do I look like I'm crazy?"

* * *

The three coals burned in the bottom of a cast iron frying pan his mother had bought him. It was the first time he'd ever used it. The gold, the frankincense, the myrrh, had all been added. The three drops of blood sizzled in the heat and Norman backed quickly away, just in case.

Something had stopped the demon from materializing last night but, as that was the first and only time it had occurred, statistically, tonight, the demon should be able to get through. Norman believed strongly in statistics.

The air in the center of the pentagram shivered. Norman's bandaged fingers began to burn and he wondered if it was going to happen again. It shouldn't. Statistically, it shouldn't.

It didn't.

"I have called you," he declared, bouncing forward when the demon had fully formed. "I am your master."

"You are master," the demon agreed. It seemed somewhat subdued and kept turning to look behind it.

Norman sneered at this pitiful tool. After tonight he would command a real demon and nothing could stop him then.

Twelve

"Do you know what a grimoire is?"

"Yes, master." It hunched down in the exact center of the pentagram, still leery after the pain that had flung it back from the last calling.

"Good. You will go here."

The master showed it a building marked on a map. It translated the information to its own image of the city, a much more complex and less limited view.

"You will go to this building by the most direct route. You will get the grimoire from unit 1407 and you will bring it immediately back to the pentagram using the same route. Do not allow people to see you."

"Must feed," it reminded the master sullenly.

"Yeah, okay, then feed on the way. I want that grimoire as soon as possible. Do you understand?"

"Yes, master." In time it would feed on this one who called it. It had been promised.

It could feel the Demon Lord it served waiting. Could feel the rage growing as it moved farther from the path of the name. Knew it would feel that rage more closely still when it returned from the world.

There were lives in plenty on its route and as it had so many from which to pick and choose, it fed at last where the life would end to mark the name of another Demon Lord. The name would take another four deaths to finish, but perhaps this second Lord would protect if from the first on the chance that it would control the gate.

It did not know hope, for hope was foreign to the demonkind, but it did know opportunity and so it did what it could.

It fed quickly, though, and traveled warily lest it attract

the attention of the power that had broken the calling the night before. The demonkind had battled this power in the past and it had no desire to do so now, on its own.

It could feel the grimoire as it approached the building the master had indicated. Wings spread, it drifted lower, a shadow against the stars, and settled on the balcony. The call of the book grew stronger, the dark power reacting to one of the demonkind.

It sensed a life close by but did not recognize it; too slow to be mortal, too fast to be demon. It did not understand, but then, understanding was not necessary.

Sniffing the metal around the glass, it was not impressed. A soft metal, a mortal metal.

Do not be seen.

If it could not see the street, then the lives on the street could not see it. It sank its claws into the frame and pulled the glass from its setting.

* * *

Captain Roxborough stepped closer, his hands out from his sides, his gray eyes never leaving the blade. "Surely, you don't think . . ." he began. Only lightning reflexes saved him as the razor arced forward and he jumped back. A billowing fold of his shirt had been neatly sliced, but the skin beneath had not been touched. With an effort, he held his temper. "I am beginning to lose patience with you, Smith."

Henry froze, fingers bent over the keyboard. He'd heard something on the balcony. Not a loud sound—more like the rustle of dead leaves in the wind—but a sound that didn't belong.

He reached the living room in less than seconds, the overpowering smell of rotting meat warning him of what he'd face. Two hundred years of habit dropped his hand to his hip although he had not carried a sword since the early 1800s. The only weapon he owned, his service revolver, was wrapped in oilcloth and packed away in the basement of the building. *And I don't think I have time to go get it.*

The creature stood, silhouetted against the night, holding the glass door between its claws. It almost filled the tiny solarium that linked the dining room to the balcony.

Woven like a red cord through the stench was the odor of fresh blood, telling Henry the demon had just fed and reminding him how long it had been since he had done the same. He drew in a long, shuddering breath. *I was a fool not to have protected the apartment!* An open pentagram like the trap he'd prepared by the Humber. . . . *I should have known.* Now, it all came down to this.

"Hold, demon, you have not been asked to enter!"

Huge, lidless, yellow eyes turned in his direction, features reshaping to accommodate the movement. "Ordered," it said, and threw the door.

Henry dove forward and the glass crashed harmlessly to the floor where he had been. He twisted past talons, leapt, and slammed both clenched fists into the demon's head. The surface collapsed upon itself like wet cork, absorbing the blow and reforming. The demon's backswing caught him on the way down and flung him crashing through the coffee table. He rolled, narrowly avoiding a killing blow, and scrambled to his feet with a metal strut in his hand, the broken end bright and sharp.

The demon opened Henry's arm below the elbow.

Biting back a scream, Henry staggered, almost fell, and jabbed the strut into its hip.

A flap of wing almost held him then, but panic lent him strength and he kicked his way free, feeling tissue give beneath his heels. His shoulder took the blow meant for his throat. He dropped with it, grabbed above a misshapen foot, and pulled with all he had left. The back of the demon's head proved more resilient than Henry's television, but only just.

* * *

"Down, Owen! Be quiet!" Mrs. Hughes leaned back against the leash, barely managing to snag her door and close it before Owen, barking hysterically, lunged forward and dragged her down the hall. "Owen, shut up!" She could hardly hear herself think, the dog was so loud. The sound echoed, louder even than it had been in the confines of her apartment, and no matter how extensive the soundproofing between units, noise always seemed to carry in from the hall. She had to get Owen out of the building before he got them thrown out by the residents' committee.

A door opened at the end of the corridor and a neighbor she knew slightly emerged. He was a retired military man and had two small dogs of his own, both of whom she could hear barking through the open door—no doubt in response to Owen's frenzy.

"What's wrong with him?" he yelled when he was close enough to make himself heard.

"I don't know." She stumbled and almost lost her footing when Owen suddenly threw his powerful body up against Henry Fitzroy's door, scrabbling with his claws around the edges and when that didn't work, trying to dig his way under. Mrs. Hughes attempted to pull him away without much success. She wished she knew what her Owen had against Mr. Fitzroy—of course, at the moment she'd settle for knowing they weren't going to be evicted for disturbing the peace. "Owen! Sit!" Owen ignored her.

"He's never acted like this before," she explained. "All of a sudden he just started barking, like he'd been possessed. I thought if I got him outside. . . ."

"It'd be quieter, anyway," he agreed. "Can I give you a hand?"

"Please." Her voice had become a little desperate.

Between the two of them, they dragged the still barking mastiff into the elevator.

"I don't understand this," she panted. "He usually wouldn't hurt a fly."

"Well, he hasn't hurt anything but a few eardrums," he reassured her, moving his blocking knee out of the way as the doors closed. "Good luck!"

He could hear Owen's deep chested bark still sounding up the elevator shaft, could hear the frenzied barking of his own two. Then, as suddenly as it began, it stopped. He paused, frowning, heard one final whimper, and then complete and utter silence. Shaking his head, he went inside.

* * *

Dribbling viscous yellow fluid from a number of wounds, it snatched up the grimoire and limped out onto the balcony. The names and incantations made the book of demon lore an uncomfortable weight, by far the heaviest item it had yet retrieved. And it hurt. The not-mortal it had fought had hurt it. Much of its surface changed sluggishly back and forth from gray mottled black to black mottled gray and its right wing membrane had been torn.

It must return the grimoire to the master, but first it needed to feed. The injured membrane could carry it from this high dwelling to the ground and once there it must quickly find a life to heal it. There were many lives around. It did not think it would have difficulty finding one to take.

It dropped off into the night, yellow fluid glistening where it had been standing.

* * *

Mrs. Hughes smiled as she listened to Owen bounding around in the bushes. To her intense relief, he'd calmed down in the elevator and had been a perfect lamb ever since. As if aware of her thought, he backed out into a clearing, checked to see where she was, wuffled happily, and bounded off again.

She knew she was supposed to keep him on the leash, even in the ravine, but when they came down at night with no one else around she always let him run—both for his enjoyment and for hers. Neither one of them was happy moving at the other's pace.

Tucking her hands into her pockets, she hunched her shoulders against a sudden chill wind. Spring. She was certain, had arrived before Easter when she was a girl and they'd never had to wear gloves sixteen days into April. The wind made a second pass and Mrs. Hughes wrinkled her nose in distaste. It smelled very much like something at least the size of a raccoon had died over to the east and was now in an advanced stage of decay.

What was worse, from the way the bushes were rustling, Owen had already found it and was no doubt preparing to roll.

"Owen!" She advanced a couple of steps, readying the leash. "Owen!" The fetid smell of rotting meat grew stronger and she sighed. First the hysteria and now this— she'd be spending the rest of the night bathing the dog. "Ow. . . ."

The demon ripped the second half of the word from her throat, caught the falling body in its other hand, and pulled the wound up to the gaping circle of its mouth. Sucking noisily, it began to ingest the blood it needed to heal. It staggered and almost dropped its meal as a heavy weight slammed into it from the back and claws dragged lines of pain from shoulders to hip. Snarling, drooling red, it turned.

Owen's lips were drawn back, his ears were flat against his skull, and his own snarl was more a howl as he threw himself forward again. He twisted in midair, spun around by a glancing blow, and landed heavily on three legs, blood staining his tan shoulder almost black. Maddened by the demon's proximity, he snarled again and struck at the dangling bit of wing, crushing it in his powerful jaws.

Before the dog could bring his massive neck and shoulder muscles into play, the demon kicked out. One long talon drove through a rib and dragged six inches deep through the length of the mastiff's body, spilling a glistening pile of intestines into the dirt.

With one last, feeble toss of his head, Owen managed to tear the already injured wing membrane further, then the light blazing in his eyes slowly dimmed and with a final hate-filled growl, he died.

Even in death, his jaws kept their hold and the demon had to rip them apart before it could be free.

Ten minutes later, a pair of teenagers, searching for a secluded corner, came down into the ravine. The path had a number of steep and rocky spots and with eyes not yet adjusted to the darkness it was doubly treacherous. The young man walked a little out in front, trailing her behind him at the end of their linked hands—not from any chivalrous need to test the path, he was just the more anxious to get where they were going.

When he began to fall, other arm windmilling, she cast the hand she held away lest she be dragged down, too. He hit the ground with a peculiar, damp sound and lay there for a moment, staring into shadows she couldn't penetrate.

"Pat?"

His answer was almost a whimper and he scrambled backward and onto his feet. Both his hands and knees were dark as though he'd fallen into mud. She wrinkled her nose at a smell she could almost but not quite identify.

"Pat?"

His eyes were wide, whites gleaming all around, and although his mouth worked, no sound emerged.

She frowned and, after taking two very careful steps forward, squatted. The ground under her fingertips was damp and slightly sticky. The smell had grown stronger. Gradually her eyes adjusted and, not bound by any social expectations of machismo, she screamed. And continued to scream for some time.

*   *   *

Vicki squinted, trying desperately to bring the distant blur of lights into focus. She knew the bright white beam pouring down into the ravine had to be the searchlight of a police car, although she couldn't actually see the car. She could hear an excited babble of voices but not make out the crowd they had to be coming from. It was late. She should be at Henry's. But there might be something she could do to help. . . . Keeping one hand on the concrete wall surrounding the ManuLife head office, she turned onto St. Paul's Square and aimed herself at the light.

It never failed to amaze her how quickly an accident of any kind could draw a crowd—even at past midnight on a Monday. Didn't any of these people have to be at work in the morning? Two more police cars screamed past and a couple of young men running up the street to watch nearly knocked her down. She barely noticed either of them. Past midnight. . . .

Fingers skimming along the concrete, she began to move faster until one of the voices rising out of the babble stopped her in her tracks.

". . . her throat gone just like the others."

Henry had been wrong. The demon had killed again tonight. Although why here, practically at the heart of the city, miles from any of the possible names? Henry, and the *feeling* that kept him at his apartment tonight. . . .

"Damn!" Trusting her feet to find their own path, Vicki turned and started to run, thrusting her way through the steadily arriving stream of the curious. She stumbled over a curb she couldn't see, clipped her shoulder against an ill-defined blur that might have been a pole, and careened off at least three people too slow to move out of her way. She had to get to Henry.

As she reached his building, an ambulance raced by and a group of people surged up the circular drive and after it, trailing along behind like a group of ghoulish goslings as it squealed around the corner onto St. Paul's Square. The security guard must've been among them for when Vicki pushed through the doors and into the lobby, his desk was empty.

"God *double* damn!"

She reached over and found the switch that opened the inner door but, as she'd feared, he'd locked it down and taken the key with him. Too furious and too worried even to swear, she gave the door a vicious yank. To her surprise it swung open, the lock protesting as a metal tongue that hadn't quite caught pulled free. She dashed through, took a second to shut it carefully behind her—old habits die hard—raced across the inner lobby and jabbed at the elevator buttons.

She knew full well that continued jabbing would do no good, but she did it anyway.

The ride up to the fourteenth floor seemed to take days, months even, and adrenaline had her bouncing off the walls. Henry's door was locked. So certain was she that Henry was in trouble, it never even occurred to her to knock. Scrambling in her bag, she pulled out her lock picks and took a few deep breaths to steady her hands. Although fear still screamed *Hurry!* she forced herself to slowly insert the proper probe and more slowly still work on the delicate manipulations that would replace the key.

After an agonizingly stretched few moments during which she thought the expensive lock was beyond her skill, just about when she was wishing Dirty Harry would show up and blow the door off its hinges, the last of the tumblers dropped. Breathing again, thanking God the builders hadn't gone with electronics, she threw the picks into her bag and yanked open the door.

The wind whistling in from the balcony had blown away much of the stench, but a miasma of rot lingered. Again she thought of the old woman they had found six weeks dead in high summer, but this time her imagination gave the body Henry's face. She knew the odor came from the demon, but her gut kept insisting otherwise.

"Henry?"

Reaching behind her, she tugged the door closed and groped for a light switch. She couldn't see a damned thing. Henry could be dead at her feet and she'd never. . . .

He wasn't quite at her feet. He lay sprawled over the tipped couch, half covered in torn upholstery. And he wasn't dead. The dead have a posture the living are unable to imitate.

Impossible to avoid, glass glittered in the carpet like an indoor ice field. The balcony door, the coffee table, the television—the part of Vicki trained to observe in the midst of disaster inventoried the different colored shards as she moved. Henry appeared to be in little better shape than his apartment.

She wrestled the solarium door closed, forcing it through drying, sticky puddles of yellow fluid, then dropped to one knee by the couch and pressed her fingers against the damp skin of Henry's throat. His pulse was so slow that each continuing beat came almost as an afterthought.

"Is that normal? How the hell am I supposed to tell what's normal for you?"

As gently as possible, she untangled him from the upholstery and discovered that, miraculously, no bones seemed broken. His bones were very heavy, she noticed, as she carefully straightened arms and legs and she wondered wildly if he'd gotten them from the vampirism or from a more mortal heredity—not that it mattered much now. He'd been cut and gouged in a number of places, both by the shards of glass and by what she had to assume were the demon's talons.

The wounds, even the deepest, bled sluggishly if at all.

His skin was cool and damp, his eyes had rolled back, and he was completely unresponsive. He was in shock. And whatever the validity of the vampire legends, Vicki knew they were wrong about one thing. Henry Fitzroy was no more undead than she was; he was dying now.

"Damn. Damn! DAMN!"

With one hand guiding Henry's body so that it slid down onto the torn cushions, she heaved the couch back upright, knelt again beside it and reached for her bag. The small blade of her Swiss Army knife was sharpest— she used it less frequently—so she set its edge against the skin of her wrist. The skin dimpled and she paused, sending up a silent prayer that this would work, that whatever the legends were wrong about, they'd be right about this.

It didn't hurt as much as she expected. She pressed the cut to his lips and waited. A crimson drop rolled out the corner of his mouth, drawing a line in red across his cheek.

Then his throat moved, a small convulsive swallow. She felt his lips mold themselves to her wrist and his tongue lap once, twice at the flowing blood. The hair on the back of her neck rose and, almost involuntarily, she pressed the wound harder against his mouth.

He began to feed, sucking frantically at first, then more calmly when something in him realized he wasn't going to be denied.

Will he know when to stop? Her breathing grew ragged as the sensations traveling up her arm caused answering sensations in other parts of her body. *Will I be able to stop him if he doesn't?*

Two minutes, three, she watched him feed and during that time it was all he was—hunger, nothing more. It reminded her of an infant at the breast and under jacket, sweater, and bra, she felt her nipples harden at the thought. She could see why so many stories of vampires tied the blood to sex—this was one of the most intimate actions she'd ever been a part of.

* * *

First there was pain and then there was blood. There was nothing but blood. The world was the blood.

* * *

She watched as consciousness began returning and his hand came up to grasp hers, applying a pressure against that of his mouth.

* * *

He could feel the life that supplied the blood now. Smell it, hear it, recognize it, and he fought the red haze that said that life should be his. So easy to give in to the hunger.

* * *

She could see the struggle as he swallowed one last time and then pushed her wrist away. She didn't understand. She could feel his need, feel herself drawn to it. She raised her wrist back toward his mouth, crimson drops welling out from the cut.

He threw it away from him with a strength that surprised her, the marks of his fingers printed white on her arm. Unfortunately, it was all the strength he had, his body going limp again, head lolling against her shoulder.

The pain of his grip helped chase the fog away, although it was still desperately difficult to think. She shifted position. The room slid in and out of focus and she realized as she swam up out of the darkness why he'd forced himself to stop. She couldn't give him all the blood he needed, not without giving herself in the process.

"Shit, shit, shit!" It wasn't very creative, but it made her feel better.

Settling him back onto the couch, she patted him down and pulled his keys from his pants' pocket—if she was to save Henry's life she had no more time to waste on picking locks. *He needs more blood. I have to find Tony.*

The sudden rise to her feet turned out to be a bad idea, the world slipped sideways and her run for the door became more of a stumble. *How could he have taken so much in such a short time?* Breathing heavily, she moved out into the hall and jogged for the elevator.

* * *

"Good lord, that's Owen!"

Owen? Greg pushed his way through to the front of the crowd. If Owen had been hurt, Mrs. Hughes might need his help.

Owen had been more than hurt. Owen's jaws had been forced so far apart his head had split.

And Mrs. Hughes was beyond any help he could give.

* * *

She had to get to Yonge and Bloor but her body was not cooperating. The dizziness grew worse instead of better and she careened from one solid object to another, stubbornly refusing to surrender to it. By Church Street, surrender became a moot point.

"Yo, Victory."

Strong hands grabbed her as she fell and she clutched at Tony's jean jacket until the sidewalk stopped threatening to rise up and smack her in the face.

"You okay, Victory? You look like shit."

She pushed away from him, changing her grip from his jacket to his arm. *"How the hell am I supposed to put this?"* "Tony, I need your help."

Tony studied her face for a moment, pale eyes narrowed. "Someone been beating on you?"

Vicki shook her head and wished she hadn't. "No, that's not it. I. . . ."

"You been doing drugs?"

"Of course not!" The involuntary indignation drew her up straighter.

"Then what the fuck happened to you? Twenty minutes ago you were fine."

She squinted down at him, the glare from the street light adding to her difficulty in focusing. He looked more angry than concerned. "I'll explain on the way."

"Who says I'm going anywhere?"

"Tony, please. . . ."

The moment he took to make up his mind was the longest she'd known for a long time.

"Well, I guess I don't got anything better to do." He let her drag him forward. "But the explanation better be good."

* * *

Wide-eyed, Greg stared over the shoulder of the burly police constable. All he could see of Mrs. Hughes was running shoe, the upturned sole stained red, and a bit of sweatpant-covered leg—the coroner blocked his view of the actual body. Poor Mrs. Hughes. Poor Owen.

"No doubt about it." The coroner stood and motioned for the ambulance attendants to take care of the body. "The same as the others."

An awed murmur rippled through the crowd. The same as the others. Vampire!

At the sound, one of the police investigators turned and glared up the hill. "What the hell are these people doing down here? Get them back behind the cars! Now!"

Greg moved with the others, but he paid no attention to the speculations that buzzed around him, caught up in his own thoughts. In spite of the hour, he recognized a number of tenants from his building in the crowd. Henry Fitzroy wasn't among them. Neither were a great many others, he acknowledged, but Mr. Fitzroy's absence had suddenly become important.

Owen, who had liked everyone, had never liked Henry Fitzroy.

Unable to forget the expression that had surfaced in the young man's eyes or the terror it had evoked, Greg had no doubt Mr. Fitzroy could kill. The question became, had he?

Weaving his way through to the edge of the crowd, Greg hurried back to Bloor Street. It was time for some answers.

⁎ ⁎ ⁎

Vampires. Demons. Tony flicked his thumbnail against his teeth and studied Vicki's face, his expression warily neutral. "Why tell *me* this kind of a secret?"

Vicki sagged against the elevator wall and rubbed at her temples. Why, indeed? "Because you were closest. Because you owe me. Because I trust you not to betray it."

He looked startled, then pleased. It had been a long time since someone had trusted him. Really trusted him. He smiled and suddenly appeared years younger. "This is for real, isn't it? No shit?"

"No shit," Vicki agreed wearily.

Picking his way carefully through the glass, Tony walked over to the couch and stared down at Henry, his eyes wide. "He doesn't look much like a vampire."

"What were you expecting? A tuxedo and a coffin?" There'd been no change while she'd been gone and if he looked no better, at least he looked no worse.

"Hey, chill out, Victory. This is all kind of weird, you know."

She sighed and brushed a lock of red-gold hair back off Henry's forehead. "I know. I'm sorry. I'm worried."

"S'okay." Tony patted her arm as he came around the couch. "I understand worried." He took a deep breath and rubbed his palms against his jeans. "What do I have to do?"

She showed him where to kneel, then put the point of her knife against his wrist.

"Maybe I'd better do it myself," he suggested when she hesitated.

"Maybe you had."

His blood looked very red against the pale skin and Vicki felt his hand tremble as she guided the cut to Henry's mouth.

What the hell am I doing? she wondered as he began to suck and Tony's expression became almost beatific. *I'm pimping for a vampire.*

* * *

Blood again but this time the need was not as great and it took much less to become aware of the world beyond it.

* * *

"He's really doing it. He's really. . . ."

"A vampire. Yeah."

"It's, uh, interesting." He shifted a little, tugging at the leg of his jeans.

Remembering the feeling, and thankful Tony couldn't see her blush, she shrugged out of her jacket and headed for the bathroom, wondering if the modern vampire kept anything useful in his medicine cabinet. The extent of Henry's wounds were beyond the tiny first aid kit she carried in her bag although she'd improvise if she had to.

To her surprise, the modern vampire owned both gauze and adhesive tape. Gathering it up, along with two damp washcloths, a towel, and the terry cloth dressing gown she'd found hanging on the door, she hurried back to the living room, leaning on walls and furniture whenever possible.

She'd take care of the one deep cut on Henry's arm, and then she'd rest. Maybe for a couple of days.

* * *

Fumbling a little with his keys, Greg opened the locker in the recreation room and pulled the croquet stake out of its box.

"It's just a precaution," he told himself, studying the point. "Just a sensible precaution."

* * *

Trying not to think of the depth or the damage, she washed out the wound and, pressing the edges of torn skin and muscle as close together as they'd go, bound them in place with the gauze. Henry's arm trembled, but he made no attempt to pull away.

Tony carefully kept his eyes averted. ·

* * *

With awareness of self came confusion. Who was he feeding from? Vicki's scent was unmistakable, but he didn't know the young male.

He could feel his strength returning, could feel his body begin to heal as the blood he took was no longer necessary for the mere sustaining of life. Now all he needed was time.

* * *

"I think he's finished."

"Has he stopped, then?"

Tony held up his wrist. "That's usually what finished means." The cut gaped a little, but only one tiny drop of blood rolled down under the grimy sleeve of the jean jacket.

Vicki leaned forward. "Henry?"

"Half a mo, Victory." Tony rocked back on his heels and stood. "If you're going to wake him, I'm out of here."

"What?"

"He doesn't know me and I don't think I oughta be here while you convince him I ain't going to tell."

A second's reflection convinced Vicki that might not be such a bad idea. She had no concept of how Henry was going to take the betrayal of his secret to a complete stranger. In his place, she'd be furious.

She followed Tony to the door. "How do you feel?"

"Horny. And a little dizzy," he added before she could say anything. "I don't think he took as much from me as he did from you. Course, I'm younger."

"And mouthier." She reached out and grasped his shoulder, shaking it gently. "Thanks."

"Hey, I wouldn't have missed it." For a second his face was open, vulnerable, then the cocky grin returned. "I wanna hear how this all comes out."

"You'll hear." She pulled a handful of crumpled bills out of her pocket and pressed it into his hand. "Drink lots of liquids over the next little while. And Tony, try not to let the guard see you on the way out."

"Teach granny to suck eggs, Victory."

* * *

In the elevator, Greg slapped the two and a half foot length against his leg. He didn't really believe Henry Fitzroy was a vampire, not really, but then, he didn't really believe Mrs. Hughes was dead and she undeniably was. Belief, he had come to realize over the course of a long life, had little to do with reality.

At the fourteenth floor, he squared his shoulders and stepped out into the corridor, determined to do his duty. He didn't consider himself to be a particularly brave man but he did have a responsibility to the tenants in his building. He hadn't faltered against the Nazis, he hadn't faltered in Korea, he wouldn't falter now.

At Henry Fitzroy's door, he checked to be sure his pant leg covered the stake—he wouldn't use it if he didn't have to—and knocked.

* * *

"Damn!" Vicki glanced from Henry to the door. It didn't sound like the police—a police knock was unmistakable—but ignoring it might still be the worst thing to do. If someone on the street had seen the demon on Henry's balcony. . . .

The fisheye showed her a distorted view of the old security guard from the front desk. As she watched, he raised his hand and knocked again. She didn't know what he wanted, she didn't really care. He couldn't talk to Henry and she had to get rid of him without allowing him to see the battlefield in the living room. If the guard had suspicions—and from his expression he certainly wasn't happy about something—she had to leave him no doubt as to what Henry'd spent the last couple of hours doing. And if the guard had no suspicions, it was important he not acquire any.

* * *

This is crazy, Greg realized suddenly. *I should be here after sunrise, when he's sleeping*. His fingers moved nervously up and down the ridges on the croquet mallet. *I can get the passkey, and be sure, one way or another and. . . .*

The door opened and his mouth with it as he stared at the tousle-haired woman who gazed sleepily out at him, a man's bathrobe more or less clutched around her.

Vicki had turned off all the lights except the one directly behind her in the front hall, hoping its dazzle would block anything her body didn't. She filled the space between the door and the molding, leaning on both, and just to be on the safe side, let the upper edge of the bathrobe slide a little lower. She wasn't intending to blind the guard with her beauty, but if she read the elderly man correctly this was exactly the kind of situation that would embarrass him most.

So maybe it was a stupid idea. It was also the only thing she could come up with.

"Can I help you?" she asked, covering a not entirely faked yawn.

"Um, no, I, that is, Is Mr. Fitzroy home?"

"He is." Vicki smiled and pushed her glasses up her nose. The robe shifted a little further of its own volition. "But he's sleeping. He's kind of . . ." She paused just long enough for the guard's ears to finish turning scarlet. ". . . exhausted."

"Oh." Greg cleared his throat and wondered how he could gracefully get out of this. It was obvious that Henry Fitzroy hadn't been out of his apartment in the last few hours. It was equally obvious he hadn't been driving fangs into this young woman's neck, or most other parts of her anatomy. Which Greg wasn't looking at. "I just, uh, that is, there was an *incident* in the ravine and I just thought he might have seen something, or heard something as he's usually up at night. I mean, I know his windows don't face that way. . . ."

"I don't think he noticed anything. He was . . ." Again the pause. Again the blush rose on the guard's face. ". . . busy."

"Look, I'm real sorry I bothered you. I'll talk to Mr. Fitzroy another time."

He looked so depressed, Vicki impulsively put out a hand. "This incident, did it happen to someone you knew?"

Greg nodded, responding to the sympathy in her voice. "Mrs. Hughes and Owen. Owen was her dog. They lived just down at the end of the hall." He pointed and Vicki's breath caught in her throat when she saw what was in his hand.

He followed her gaze and grew even redder. The brightly painted stripes on the top of the croquet stake seemed to mock him. He'd forgotten he was carrying it. "Kids," he hurriedly explained. "They leave stuff lying around all over. I'm just taking this back where it goes."

"Oh." With an effort she forced her gaze away from the stake. Showing too much interest in it would ruin everything and ripping it out of his hand and throwing it down the elevator shaft—which is what she wanted to do—could probably be considered showing too much interest. "I'm sorry about the woman and her dog," she managed.

He nodded again. "So am I." Then he straightened and Vicki could practically see duty and responsibility settling back onto his shoulders. "I've got to get back to my post. I'm sorry I bothered you. Good night, ma'am."

"Good night."

He waited until he heard her turn the lock and then he headed back to the elevator. As the doors slid closed behind him, he looked down at the stake and shook his head. The last time he'd been so embarrassed he'd been nineteen, it was World War II, and he'd wandered into the WRENS' bathroom by mistake. "Vampires, ha! I must be getting senile."

Vicki sagged against the inside of the door, reaction weakening her knees. That had been too close. Flipping the living room light back on, she picked her way carefully back to Henry.

His eyes were open and he had flung one arm up to shield them from the glare.

"Feeling better?" she asked.

"That depends . . . better than what?" He swung his legs off the couch and dragged himself up into a sitting position. He hadn't felt this bad in a very long time.

Vicki reached out and steadied him when he almost toppled. "Apparently Mr. Stoker didn't exaggerate when he mentioned the recuperative powers of vampires."

Henry tried a smile. It wasn't particularly successful. "Mr. Stoker was a hack." He rotated his shoulders and stretched out both legs. Everything seemed to work, although not well and not without pain. "Who was the boy?"

"His name's Tony. He's been on the street since he was a kid. He's very good at accepting people for what they are."

"Even vampires?"

She studied his face. He didn't look angry. "Even vampires. And he knows what it's like to want to be left alone."

"You trust him?"

"Implicitly. Or I'd have thought of something else. Someone else." Although what or who she had no idea. She hadn't even thought of Celluci. Not once. *Which only goes to prove that even half-conscious, I'm smarter than I look.* Celluci's reaction would not have been supportive. *I suppose I could've robbed the Red Cross.* "You needed more, but you wouldn't . . ."

"Couldn't," he interrupted quietly. "If I'd taken more, I'd have taken it all." His eyes below the purple and green bruise that marked his forehead were somber. "Too much blood from one person, and we risk losing control. I could feel your life, and I could feel the desire rising to take it."

She smiled then, she couldn't help it.

"What?" Henry saw nothing to smile about. They'd both come very close to death this night.

"A line from a children's book just popped into my head, *it's not like he's a tame lion.* You're not at all tame, are you? For all you look so civilized."

He thought about it for a moment. "No, I guess by your standards I'm not. Does that frighten you?"

Both brows went up and fell again almost immediately. She was just too tired to maintain the expression. "Oh, please."

He smiled then and lifted her hand, turning the wrist to the light. "Thank you," he said, one finger softly tracing the line of the vein.

Every hair on Vicki's body stood on end and she had to swallow before she could speak. "You're welcome. I'd have done the same for anyone."

Still holding her hand, his smile grew slightly puzzled. "You're wearing my dressing gown."

Pushing her glasses up her nose, Vicki tried not to glance at the pile of clothing dumped on the dining room table. "It's a long story." She let him pull her down beside him and nervously wet her lips. Her skin throbbed under his hand. *And he's not even touching anything interesting.*

Then his expression changed and she twisted to see what had caused such a look of horrified disbelief. One door of the wall unit, glass still surprisingly intact, swung open.

"The demon," Henry told her, his voice echoing his expression, "has the grimoire."

Thirteen

Henry lurched to his feet and stood swaying. "I must. . . ."

Vicki reached up and guided him down onto the couch as he fell. "Must what? You're in no shape to go anywhere."

"I must get the grimoire back before the Demon Lord is called." He shook off her hands and stood again, shoulders set. "If I begin now, I might be able to track the demon, In order to carry the grimoire it must maintain a physical form."

"Track it how?"

"Scent."

Vicki glanced at the balcony and back to Henry. "Forget it. It has wings. It'll be flying. I don't care what you are, you can't track something if there's nothing for it to leave its scent *on.*"

"But . . ."

"But nothing. If you weren't what you were, you'd be dead. Trust me. I may not have seen the centuries of death you have, but I've seen enough to tell."

She was right. Henry walked to the window and rested his forehead gently against the glass. Cool and smooth, it helped to ease the ache in his head. Everything worked, but everything hurt. He couldn't remember the last time he'd felt this weak or in this much pain and his body, now that the initial rush of energy that came with feeding had passed, was insisting he rest and allow it to heal. "You saved my life," he admitted.

"Then don't throw it away." Vicki felt a faint echo of warmth surging up from the cut on her wrist. She ignored it. Maybe they'd get a chance to continue where they'd left off, but this certainly was not the time. *And anything more energetic than heavy petting would probably kill both of us.* Scooping up her clothes, she moved into the kitchen and pulled one of the louvered doors closed. "You did what you could, now let someone else take over."

"You."

"You see anyone else around?"

Henry managed half a smile. "No." She was right about that as well. He'd had his chance and failed.

"Fine." She zipped up her jeans and shrugged out of the bathrobe. "You can join me after sunset if you're mobile by then."

"Give me a day of rest and I should be back to normal. Okay, not quite normal," he amended at Vicki's snort of disbelief, "but well enough to function."

"That'll do. I'll leave a message on your machine as soon as I know where I'm likely to be."

"You've got less than twenty-four hours to find the person with the grimoire in a city of three million people. You may have been a good cop, Vicki. . . ."

"I was the best," she informed him, carefully stretching the neck of her sweatshirt around her glasses.

"All right. You were the best. But you weren't *that* good. No one is."

"Maybe not," her tone argued the point even if her words didn't, "but while you were spending your nights waiting for the demon to strike, I haven't been spending my days just sitting on my butt." Carefully picking her way through the glass, she came back to the couch and sat down to put on her shoes. "One of the items the demon picked up was a state of the art computer system. Apparently, they don't make them smarter or faster than this particular machine. I went out to York University today—enough bits and pieces have pointed in that direction to convince me there's a connection—and spoke to the head of the Computer Science Department. He gave me a list of twenty-three names, students who could really make a system like that sing." She straightened and pushed her glasses up her nose. "So instead of one in three million, I've got one in twenty-three in about twenty thousand.''

"Terrific." Henry tore off the ruin of his shirt as he walked back across the room. Dropping carefully onto the couch, he tossed the ball of fabric at the destroyed face of the television. "One in twenty-three in twenty thousand."

"Those aren't impossible odds. What's more I won't have to deal with all twenty thousand. The men and women on the list are part of a pretty narrowly defined group. If I can't find them, I think I can flush them out."

"In a day? Because if that grimoire is used tomorrow night, that's all the time you have before the slaughter begins."

Her chin rose and her brows drew down. "So what do you suggest? I give up because you don't think it can be done? You thought you could defeat the lesser demon, remember?" Her eyes swept over his injuries. "You're not exactly infallible where this stuff is concerned."

Henry closed his eyes. Her words cut deeper than any other blow he'd taken tonight. She was right. It was his fault the grimoire had been taken, his fault the world faced pain and death on a scale few mortal minds could imagine.

"Henry, I'm sorry. That was uncalled for."

"But true." She'd moved closer. He could feel her heartbeat tremble the air between them. Her hand closed lightly around his, and he waited for the platitudes that would do nothing to ease his guilt.

"Yes," she agreed.

His eyes snapped open.

"But you wouldn't have lived as long as you have if you hadn't figured out how to learn from your mistakes. When I find this person, I'm going to need you for backup."

"Well, thank you very much." Just what he needed, being patronized by someone whose ancestors had no doubt been grubbing out a living on a peasant's plot when he'd been riding beside a king. He pulled his hand out from under hers and tried not to wince when the motion twisted the wound in his arm.

''Before you get snooty, Your Royal Highness, perhaps you should consider who the hell else I can use? Trust me on this one, suspicion of demon-calling is not likely to impress the police. I don't even think it's a crime.''

''What about young Tony?''

''Tony goes his own way. Besides, this isn't the sort of thing he can help me with.''

''So I'm the only game in town?''

''We're the only game in town.''

They locked eyes for a moment and Vicki suddenly realized that was a stupid thing to do—all the stories, all the movies about vampires warned against it. For a moment, she felt herself teetering on the edge of an abyss and she fought against the urge to throw herself into the depths. Then the moment passed, the abyss replaced with a pair of tired hazel eyes and she realized, her heart beating a little more quickly, that it had been the man, not the vampire she'd been reacting to. Or perhaps the man as vampire. Or the vampire as man. Or something. *Wonderful. The city—the world even—is about to go up in flames and I'm thinking with my crotch.*

''I'm going to need an early start. I'd better get going.''

''Perhaps you had.''

There were several dozen things left unsaid.

He watched her shrug into her jacket, the sound of her heartbeat nearly overpowering. Had he taken even a little more blood from her, he wouldn't have been able to stop himself from taking her life as well. That feeding was the sweetest of all to his kind and acquiring a taste for it had brought down many a vampire. Bringing him the boy had saved them both. She truly was a remarkable woman, few other mortals would have had the strength to resist the pull of his need.

He wanted more. More of her. If they survived the next twenty-four hours. . . .

She paused on her way to the door, one hand clutching a chair back for support. ''I just remembered, where were you earlier? I kept calling and getting your machine.''

''That was why you came so late?''

''Well, no point in coming over if you weren't here.''

"I was here. I turned on the machine to screen calls."
His brows went up as hers went down. "You don't do that?"

"If I'm home, I answer the phone."

"If I had, and you'd been here when the demon arrived. . . ."

"We'd both be dead," she finished.

He nodded. "Vicki?"

Her hand on the knob, she turned back to face him.

"You do realize that there's a very good chance we'll fail? That you may come up blank or nothing we can do will stop the Demon Lord?"

She smiled at him and Henry discovered with a slight shock that he wasn't the only predator in the room.

"No," she said, "I don't realize any such thing. Get some rest." Then she was gone.

* * *

The city streets ran with blood and all of the wailing people who dragged themselves through it looked to her for their salvation. She raised her hands to help them and saw that the blood poured out through great ragged gashes in her wrists.

"He's coming, Vicki." Henry Fitzroy dropped to his knees before her and let the blood pour over him, his mouth open to catch the flow.

She tried to step back and found she couldn't move, that hardened concrete covered her feet to the ankles.

"He's coming, Vicki," Henry said again. He leaned forward and began to lap at the blood dribbling down her arms.

A cold wind blew suddenly on her back and she could hear the sound of claws on stone as something huge dragged itself toward her. She couldn't turn to face it; Henry's hands and the concrete held her in place. She could only fight against her bonds and listen to it coming closer, closer. The smell of rot grew more intense and when she looked down, it wasn't Henry but the old woman's decomposing corpse whose mouth had clamped onto her wrist. Behind her stood what was left of Mike Celluci.

"Why didn't you tell me?" he asked through the ruin of his mouth. "Why didn't you tell me?"

* * *

Vicki groped for the light switch and sat panting in the sudden glare, her heart drumming painfully. The dream that wakened her had been only the latest in a series. Fortunately, she remembered none of the others in detail.

Hands trembling, she pushed the arms of her glasses over her ears and peered at the clock. 5:47. Almost three hours sleep.

She turned off the useless alarm—she'd set it for 6:30—and swung her legs out of bed. If the demon-caller followed the established pattern, the Demon Lord would show up at midnight. That gave her eighteen hours to find him or her and stuff the grimoire down his or her throat one page at a time. The dreams had terrified her and nothing made her more angry than fear she could do nothing about.

Slowly, carefully, she stood. The liter of orange juice and the two iron supplements she'd taken after arriving home might have helped to offset the blood loss, but she knew she wasn't going to be in top condition. Not today. Not for some time. The cut on her wrist appeared to have almost healed although the skin around it was slightly bruised and a little tender. The memory of the actual feeding had become tangled up with the memory of the dream, so she set them both aside to be sorted out later. There were more important things to worry about at the moment.

She'd have stayed in the shower longer, trying to wash the dream away, but she couldn't shake the feeling that something was behind her. With sight and sound blocked by the spray, she felt too vulnerable and exposed to linger.

With the coffee maker on, and another liter of orange juice in her hand, she stood for a moment staring out at the street. One or two other windows were lit and as she watched, young Edmond Ng came yawning out onto his porch and started down to the corner to pick up his route's copies of the morning paper, completely unaware this might be his last trip. In eighteen short hours, the hordes of hell could be ripping the city and its people apart.

"And the only thing in the way is one half-blind ex-cop and the bastard son of Henry VIII." She took a long pull at the jug of juice and pushed her glasses back up her nose. "Kind of makes you think, doesn't it?" Except she didn't like what it made her think about.

Find one in twenty-three in twenty thousand. Actually, as far as a lot of police work was concerned, the odds weren't all that bad. Even if she could get the students' addresses out of the administration of the university—and frankly, without a badge she doubted she could—talking with the students themselves would likely get her further. The top of the heap usually knew who shared the view with them and if one of the twenty-three was the person she was looking for, then at least one of the others should be able to point the finger.

Of course, the possibility existed that she'd assembled all the bits and pieces into the wrong picture. That she was not not only barking up the wrong tree but searching in the wrong forest entirely.

Sweat prickled along her spine and she resisted the urge to turn. She knew the apartment was empty, that nothing stood behind her, and she wasn't going to give in to phantoms—there were enough real terrors to spend fear on.

There was time for breakfast before she headed up to York; no point in arriving empty at an empty campus. At 6:35, scrambled eggs eaten and a second cup of coffee nearly gone, she phoned Mike Celluci, let it ring three times, and hung up. What was she going to tell him? That she thought she knew who the killer was? She'd known that since the night out at Woodbine when she'd met Henry. That one of twenty-three computer geniuses out at York University was calling up demons in his or her spare time and that if not stopped was going to call up more than he or she could handle and destroy the world? He'd think she'd flipped.

"Everything comes back to the demon. Everything. Shit." The computer that pointed, however tenuously, to one of those twenty-three students had no tie to the murders Celucci worked on except through the demon. "And how do I know about the demon? A vampire told me." She drained the mug and set it down on the table with more force than was absolutely necessary. The handle broke off in her hand. With a quick jerk of her arm, she threw the piece across the room and listened with satisfaction as it smashed into still smaller pieces against the wall.

The satisfaction faded a heartbeat later.

"One half-blind ex-cop and the bastard son of Henry VIII," she repeated, as it sank in, really sank in, that she wasn't a cop anymore. In spite of everything—her eyes, her resignation—for the last eight months she'd still thought of herself as a police officer. She wasn't. There'd be no backup, no support. Until sunset she was completely on her own and if anyone needed to have complete information, it wasn't Mike Celluci, it was Henry Fitzroy.

"Damn." She rubbed her sleeve across her eyes and slammed her glasses back down on her nose. It didn't make her feel any better to know that she couldn't have gotten this far if she'd still been on the force, that rules and regulations—even as flexible as the top brass tried to be—would have tied her hands. Nor could she have gotten this far if she'd *never* been on the force, the information just wouldn't have been available to her. "I seem to be exactly what the situation calls for—a one-woman chance of stopping Armageddon."

She took a deep breath and her jaw went out. "So, let's get on with it." The eggs sat like a lump of lead in her stomach and her throat had closed up into an aching pillar that bore little relation to flesh. That was okay. She could work around it. With luck, there'd be time to sort her feelings out later.

She should've taken a copy of the list to Henry's the night before. She didn't want to take the time now—not to copy it, not to drop it off.

"Henry, it's Vicki." Fortunately, his machine took an

unlimited message because the list of names and her plans for the day used over five minutes of tape. "When I know more, I'll get back to you."

Five to seven. Seventeen hours. Vicki threw the list into her bag, grabbed her jacket, and headed for the door. An hour to get out to York would leave her only sixteen hours to search.

She was already at the door, fumbling with its lock, when the phone rang. Curious about who'd be calling so early, she waited while her message ran through and the tone sounded.

"Hi, Ms. Nelson? It's Coreen. Look, if you've been trying to reach me, I'm sorry I wasn't around, but I've been staying with some friends."

The lock slipped into place. She'd talk with Coreen later. One way or another, by midnight the case would be closed.

"It's just I was pretty upset because the girl who got killed, Janet, was a good friend of mine. I can't help but think that if I hadn't been so stupid about Norman Birdwell she'd have waited for me to give her a ride home."

"Shit!" The lock proved as difficult to reopen as it had been to close. Norman Birdwell was one of the names on the list.

"I guess if you find the vampire that killed Ian you'll find the one that killed Janet, too, won't you? I want it found now more than ever."

She paused and her sigh was almost drowned out in the rattle of the chain falling free.

"Uh, I'll be at home all day if you want to call. . . ."

"Coreen? Don't hang up, it's me, Vicki Nelson."

"Oh. Hi." She sounded a little embarrassed, caught talking to a machine. "Did I wake you up? Look, I'm sorry I'm calling so early, but I've got an exam today and I want to get over to the library to study."

"It's no problem, trust me. I need you to tell me about Norman Birdwell."

"Why? He's a geek."

"It's important."

Vicki could almost hear the shrug. "Okay. What do you want to know?"

"How well do you know him?"

"Puh-leese, I said he was a geek. He's in my Comparative Religions Class. That's all."

"How were you stupid about him?"

"What?"

"You said earlier if you hadn't been so stupid about Norman Birdwell, Janet might have waited for a ride home."

"Yeah, well. . . . I wouldn't have gone with him if I hadn't had the beers, but he said he could prove that vampires existed and that he knew who killed Ian. Well, I guess he didn't really say that . . . but something like that. Anyway, I went up to his apartment with him, but all he wanted to do was score. He had nothing to do with vampires."

"Did you happen to notice if he had a computer system? A fairly large and complicated setup."

"He had a system. I don't know how complicated it was. I was busy trying not to get squeezed and being fed some bull about calling up demons."

The world stopped for a moment.

"Ms. Nelson? You still there?"

"Trust me, I'm not going anywhere." Vicki fell into her desk chair and rummaged for a pen. "This is very important, Coreen, where does Norman live."

"Uh, west of the campus somewhere."

"Can you give me his exact address."

"No."

"NO?" Vicki took a deep breath and tried to remember that yelling wouldn't help. Tucking the receiver under her chin, she heaved the white pages up off the floor by the desk. Bird . . . Birddal . . . Bird of Paradise. . . .

"But if it's so important I could probably take you there. Like, I drove that night so I could probably find it again. Probably."

"Probably's good enough." There was no Birdwell listed in the phone book. It made sense, he'd probably moved into his apartment in the fall, at the beginning of the school year, and new numbers were listed around the end of May. "I'll be right there. Where can you meet me?"

"Well, I can't meet you until five. Like I said, I've got an exam today."

"Coreen, this is important!"

"So is my exam." Her tone showed no willingness to compromise.

"Before the exam. . . ."

"I *really* have to study."

Okay, 5:00, was still early enough. A little over two hours until sunset and still seven hours until midnight. They had a positive identification and seven hours would be plenty of time. And besides, yelling wouldn't help. "5:00, then. Where?"

"Do you know where Burton Auditorium is?"

"I can find it."

"Meet me outside the north doors."

"All right. 5:00 pm, at the north doors of Burton Auditorium, I'll see you then."

Vicki hung up the phone and sat for a moment just staring at it. Of all the possible situations that could have developed, up to and including one last desperate confrontation with the Demon Lord itself, this had not occurred to her—that someone would just drop the answer in her lap. She pushed her glasses up her nose and shook her head. It shouldn't, she supposed, come as much of a surprise; once the right questions were dredged up out of the abyss the right answers usually followed.

Doodling on the cover of the phone book, she dialed directory assistance—just in case. "Hi, I'm looking for a new listing for a Norman Birdwell. I don't have an address, but he's somewhere up by York University."

"One moment, please. We have a new listing for an N. Birdwell. . . ."

Vicki scribbled the number across the cover artist's conception of a telephone operator. "Could I possibly trouble you for the address as well?"

"I'm sorry, but we're not permitted to give out that information."

"You'll be sorrier if the world comes to an end," Vicki muttered, cutting the connection with her thumb. That it was the anticipated answer made it no less annoying.

At the Birdwell number, an open modem screamed on the line and Vicki hurriedly cut if off.

"Looks like we're back to Coreen."

8:17. She yawned. She could spend the rest of the day trying to get through to N. Birdwell—who might or might not be Norman—but what she really needed was another four or five hours sleep. The blood loss combined with the late night—she'd always been more of an early to bed early to rise type—had really knocked her on her ass. She should probably still go out to York, still speak to the others on the list, but now that the opportunity to catch up on sleep had been dumped in her lap, her body seemed to be making an independent decision to take advantage of it.

Staggering into the bedroom, she tossed her clothes on the floor and managed to stay awake only long enough to reset her alarm for one o'clock. Her eyes closed almost before her head hit the pillow. Coreen's call had banished the uncertainty, defined the threat, and with it Vicki had a weapon to fight the nightmares if they came again.

"Sometimes we win with greater firepower, through sheer numbers or more powerful weapons, but for the most part it's knowledge that defines our victories. Know something and it has lost its power over you."

Vicki woke with the words of one of her cadet instructors ringing in her head. He'd been much given to purple prose and almost Shakespearean speeches, but what had redeemed him in the eyes of the cadets was not only that he'd believed strongly in everything he said but that most of the time, he was right.

The monster had a name. Norman Birdwell. Now, it could be beaten.

After a bowl of soup, a toasted tomato sandwich, and another iron supplement, she called Henry.

". . . so the moment Coreen gets me to some kind of an address, I'll call and let you know. From the sound of it, he's not going to be that difficult to take care of if there's no demon around. I'll have Coreen take me back to York and I'll wait for you there."

With her finger on the disconnect, she sat listening to the dial tone, staring off into the distance, trying to make

up her mind. Finally she decided. "Well, it can't hurt."
Whether he believed her or not, it was still information
he should have.

"Mike Celluci, please. Yes, I'll hold."

He wasn't in the building and the young man on the
other end of the phone was significantly unhelpful.

"If you could let him know that Vicki Nelson called."

"Yes ma'am. Is that all?" The young man obviously
had never heard of her and he wasn't impressed.

Vicki's tone changed. She hadn't reached her rank at
her age without acquiring the ability to handle snot-nosed
young men. The words came out parade ground clipped.
"Tell him he should check out a student at York University, name of Norman Birdwell. I'll tell him more when
I know more."

"Yes, sir! I mean, ma'am."

She grinned a little sadly as she hung up. "Okay, so
I'm not a cop anymore," she told an old photo of herself
in uniform that hung over the desk. "That's no reason to
throw the baby out with the bath water. Maybe it's time
to forge a whole new relationship with the police department."

As she had the time, and nothing much else to do with
it, Vicki took transit up to York. A childhood spent
pinching pennies kept her out of taxis as much as possible and although she bitched and complained about the
TTC along with most everyone else in Toronto, she had
to admit that if you weren't in a screaming rush or too
particular about who you spent time crammed up against,
it got you where you needed to go more or less when you
needed to get there.

During the long ride up to the university, she pulled
everything she knew into one long, point-form report.
By the time she'd reached her final transfer, she'd also
reached a final question. When they had Norman Bird-
wel, what did they do with him?

*So we take the grimoire away and get rid of the im-
mediate threat.* She stared out the window at a gray
stretch of single-story industrial buildings. *What then?
The most he can be charged with is possession of stolen
property and keeping a prohibited weapon. A slap on the*

wrist and a few hours of community service work—if they don't throw the whole thing out of court on a technicality—and he'll be back calling up demons again. He had, after all, managed to kill seven people before even getting his hands on the grimoire. There had to be an answer beyond the only permanent—and completely out of the question—solution she could think of. *Maybe if he tells the court where he got the computer and the jacket and the various and sundry, he'll be ruled insane.*

Find him.

Get the grimoire.

Let the police deal with the rest.

She grinned at her translucent reflection. Let the police deal with it—it had a certain attraction from where she now sat.

Coreen was waiting outside the main doors of Burton Auditorium, red hair a blazing beacon in yet another drizzly, overcast spring afternoon. "I finished the exam faster than I thought I would," she called as Vicki approached. "Good thing you're early; I would have been bored spitless out here much longer. My car's parked in the back." As Vicki fell into step beside her, she pushed a curl back off her face with a clash of day-glo plastic bangles and sighed. "I'm never sure whether finishing in the minimum time is a good thing or not. Like it means you either knew everything cold, or you didn't know squat and you just thought you knew everything cold."

She didn't appear to need a response, so Vicki kept silent, thinking, *I was never that young.*

"Personally, I think I aced it. Ian always said, there was no point in thinking you'd failed when it was too late to do anything about it." She sobered suddenly, remembering Ian, and said nothing more until they were in the car and out on Shoreham Drive.

"Norman's really doing it, isn't he?"

Vicki glanced over at the younger woman whose knuckles were white on the steering wheel. "Doing what?" she asked, more to stall for time than because she didn't know what Coreen meant.

"Calling up demons, just like he said. I was thinking about it after I talked to you. There's no reason that it couldn't have been a demon instead of a vampire that killed Ian and Janet. That's why you're out here, isn't it?''

Considering her options, Vicki decided that the truth would have to serve. Coreen was obviously not going to think she'd flipped, and all things considered, that was of dubious comfort. ''Yes,'' she said quietly, ''he's really doing it.''

Coreen turned the car north onto Hullmar Drive, tires squealing faintly against the pavement. ''And you're here to stop him.''

It wasn't a question, but Vicki answered it anyway. ''No, I'm just here to find him.''

''But I know where he—four, five, six—is.'' She pulled into the parking lot of a four building apartment complex. ''That's his building right there.'' She stopped the car about three lengths from the door and Vicki jotted the number down.

''Do you remember his apartment number?'' she asked, peering toward the smoked glass of the entrance.

''Nine something.'' Coreen shrugged. ''Nine's a powerful number. It probably helped him in his incantations.''

''Right.'' Vicki got out of the car and Coreen followed.

'I say we should take him out right now.''

Stopped in mid-stride, Vicki stared down at her companion. ''I beg your pardon?''

Coreen stared defiantly back. ''You and me. We should take him out right now.''

''Don't be ridiculous, Coreen. This man is very dangerous.''

''Norman? Dangerous?'' She snorted derisively. ''His demon might be dangerous, but Norman is a geek. I can take him out myself if you're not interested.'' When she started walking again, Vicki stepped in front of her.

''Hold it right there, this is no time for amateur heroics.''

''Amateur heroics?'' Coreen's voice rose an octave. 'You're fired, Ms. Nelson!'' Turning on one heel, she circumvented Vicki's block and stomped toward the building.

Sighing, Vicki followed. She'd save actual physical restraint as a last resort. *After all, she can't even get into the building.*

The inner door to the lobby was ajar and Coreen barged through it like Elliot Ness going after Capone. On her heels, Vicki reached out to stop her.

"Coreen, I. . . ."

"Freeze, both of you."

The young man who emerged from behind the potted palm was unprepossessing in the extreme. Tall and thin, he carried himself as though parts of his body were on loan from someone else. A plastic pocket protector bulged with pens and his polyester pants stopped roughly two inches above his ankles.

Coreen rolled her eyes and headed directly for him. "Norman, don't be such a. . . ."

"Coreen," Vicki's hand on her shoulder rocked her to a halt. "Perhaps we'd better consider doing as Mr. Birdwell suggests."

Grinning broadly, Norman raised the stolen AK-47.

Vicki had no intention of betting anyone's life on the very visible magazine being empty, not when the police report had included missing ammunition.

One of the building's four elevators was in the lobby, doors open. Norman motioned the two women into it.

"I was looking out my window and I saw you in the parking lot," he told them. "I knew you were here to stop me."

"Well, you're right . . ." Coreen began but fell silent as Vicki's grip on her arm tightened.

Vicki had very little doubt that she could get the gun away from Norman without anyone—except possibly Norman—getting hurt, but she sure as hell wasn't going to do it in an elevator with what appeared to be stainless steel walls. Forget the initial burst—the ricochets would rip all three of them to shreds. She kept her grip on Coreen's arm as they walked down the hallway to Norman's apartment, the barrel of the Russian assault rifle waving between them like some sort of crazed indicator switch.

Don't let anyone open their door, she prayed. *I can handle this if everyone just stays calm.* As she couldn't count on neighbors not diving suddenly into the line of fire, she'd have to wait until they were actually in the apartment before making her move.

Norman's place was unlocked. Vicki pushed Coreen in ahead of her. *The moment he closes the door. . . .* She heard the click, dropped Coreen's arm, spun around, and was pushed to one side as Coreen charged past her and threw herself at their captor.

"Damnit!"

She ducked a wildly swinging elbow and tried to shove Coreen down out of the line of fire. The dark, almost blue metal of the barrel scraped across her glasses. She caught one quick glimpse of Norman's fingers white around the pistol grip. Coreen clutched at her shoulder. She didn't see the steel reinforced butt arc around outside her limited periphery. It missed the thinner bone of her temple by a hair—smashing into her skull, slamming her up against the wall, plummeting her down into darkness.

* * *

Brows drawn down into a deep vee, Celluci fanned the phone messages stacked on his desk, checking who they were from. Two reporters, an uncle, Vicki, the dry cleaners, one of the reporters again . . . and again. Growling wordlessly, he crumpled them up and shoved them into his pocket. He didn't have time for this kind of crap.

He'd spent the day combing the area where the latest victim and her dog had been found. He'd talked to the two kids who'd found the body and most of the people who lived in a four block radius. The site had held a number of half obliterated footprints that suggested the man they were looking for went barefoot, had three toes, and very long toenails. No one had seen anything although a drunk camped out farther down in the ravine had heard a sound like a sail luffing and had smelled rotten eggs. The police lab had just informed him that between the mastiff's teeth were particles identical to the bit of whatever-it-was that DeVerne Jones had been holding in his hand. And he was no closer to finding an answer.

Or at least no closer to finding an answer he could deal with.

More things in heaven and earth. . . .

He slammed out of the squad room and stomped down the hall. The new headquarters building seemed to deaden sound, but he made as much as he could anyway.

This place needs some doors you can slam. And Shakespeare should have minded his own goddamned business!

As he passed the desk, the cadet on duty leaned forward. "Uh, Detective, a Vicki Nelson called for you earlier. She seemed quite insistent that you check out. . . ."

Celluci's raised hand cut him off. "Did you write it down?"

"Yes, sir. I left a message on your desk."

"Then you've done your job."

"Yes, sir, but. . . ."

"Don't tell me how to do mine."

The cadet swallowed nervously, Adam's apple bobbing above his tight uniform collar. "No, sir."

Scowling, Celluci continued stomping out of the building. He needed to be alone to do some thinking. The last thing he needed right now was Vicki.

Fourteen

Henry stepped out of the shower and frowned at his reflection in the full-length mirror. The lesser cuts and abrasions he'd taken the night before had healed, the greater were healing and would give him no trouble. He unwrapped the plastic bag from around the dressing on his arm and poked gently at the gauze. It hurt and would, he suspected, continue to hurt for some time, but he could use the arm if he was careful. It had been so many years since he'd taken a serious wound that his biggest problem would be remembering it before he caused himself more pain.

He turned a little sideways and shook his head. Great green splotches of fading bruises still covered most of his body.

"Looks familiar, actually. . . ."

* * *

The lance tip caught him under the right arm, lifting him up and out of the saddle. For a heartbeat, he hung in the air, then as the roar of the watching crowd rose to a crescendo, he crashed down to the ground. The sound of his armor slamming against the packed earth of the lists rattled around inside his head much as his head rattled around inside his helmet. He almost wouldn't mind the falls if only they weren't so thrice-damned loud.

He closed his eyes. *Just until all the noise stops. . . .*

When he opened them again, he was looking up into the face of Sir Gilbert Talboys, his mother's husband. *Where the devil did he come from?* he wondered. *Where did my helmet go?* He liked Sir Gilbert, so he tried to smile. His face didn't seem to be functioning.

"Can you rise, Henry? His Grace, the King, is approaching."

There was an urgency in Sir Gilbert's voice that penetrated the ringing in Henry's ears. Could he rise? He wasn't exactly sure. Everything hurt but nothing seemed broken. The king, who would not be pleased that he had been unseated, would be even less pleased if he continued to lie in the dirt. Teeth clenched, he allowed Sir Gilbert to lift him into a sitting position then, with help, heave him to his feet.

Henry swayed but somehow managed to stay standing even after all supporting hands had been removed. His vision blurred, then refocused on the king, resplendent in red velvet and cloth of gold, advancing from the tournament stand. Desperately, he tried to gather his scattered wits. He had not been in his father's favor since he had unwisely let it be known that he considered Queen Catherine the one true and only Queen of England. This would be the first time his father had spoken to him since he had taken up with that Lutheran slut. Even three years later, the French Court still buzzed with stories of her older sister, Mary, and Henry could not believe that his father had actually put Anne Boleyn on the throne.

Unfortunately, King Henry VIII had done exactly that.

Thanking God that his armor prevented him from falling to one knee—he doubted he'd be able to rise or, for that matter, control the fall—Henry bowed as well as he was able and waited for the king to speak.

"You carry your shield too far from your body. Carry it close and a man cannot get his point behind it." Royal hands flashing with gold and gems lifted his arm and tucked it up against his side. "Carry it here."

Henry couldn't help but wince as the edge of his couter dug into a particularly tender bruise.

"You're hurting, are you?"

"No, Sire." Admitting to pain would not help his case.

"Well, if you aren't now, you will be later." The king chuckled low in his throat, then red-gold brows drew down over deep set and tiny eyes. "We were not pleased to see you on the ground."

This would be the answer that counted. Henry wet his lips; at least the bluff King Hal persona was the easiest to deal with. "I am sorry, Sire, and I wish it been you in my place."

The heavy face reddened dangerously. "You wished to see your Sovereign unseated?"

The immediate area fell completely silent, courtiers holding their breath.

"No, Sire, for if it had been you in my saddle, it would have been Sir John on the ground."

King Henry turned and stared down the lists at Sir John Gage, a man ten years his junior and at the peak of his strength and stamina. He began to laugh. "Aye, true enough, lad. But the bridegroom does not joust for fear he break his lance."

Staggering under a jocular slap on the back, Henry would have fallen but for Sir Gilbert's covert assistance. He laughed with the others, for the king had made a joke, but although he was thankful to be back in favor all he could really think of was soaking his bruises in a hot bath.

* * *

Henry lifted an arm. "A little thinner perhaps but definitely the same shade." Rolling his shoulder muscles, he winced as one of the half-healed abrasions pulled. Injuries that had once taken weeks, or sometimes months, to heal now disappeared in days. "Still, a good set of tournament armor would've come in handy last night."

Last night. . . . He had taken more blood from Vicki and her young friend than he usually took in a month of feedings. She had saved his life, almost at the expense of her own and he was grateful, but it did open up a whole new range of complications. New complications that would just have to wait until the old ones had been dealt with.

He strapped on his watch. 8:10. Maybe Vicki had called back while he was in the shower.

She hadn't.

"Great. Norman Birdwell, York University, and I'll call you back. So call already." He glared at the phone. The waiting was the worst part of knowing that the grimoire was out there and likely to be used.

He dressed. 8:20. Still no call.

His phone books were buried in the hall closet. He dug them out, just in case. No Norman Birdwell. No Birdwell of any kind.

Her message tied him to the apartment. She expected him to be there when she called. He couldn't go out and search on his own. Pointless in any case when she was so close.

8:56. He had most of the glass picked up. The phone rang.

"Vicki?"

"Please do not hang up. You are talking to a compu . . ."

Henry slammed the receiver down hard enough to crack the plastic. "Damn." He tried a quick call out, listened to Vicki's message—for the third time since sunset, and it told him absolutely nothing new—and hung up a little more gently. Nothing appeared to be damaged except for the casing.

9:17. The scrap metal that had once been a television and a coffee table frame were piled in the entryway, ready to go down to the garbage room. He wasn't sure what he was going to do about the couch. Frankly, he didn't care about the couch. Why didn't she call?

9:29. There were stains in the carpet and the balcony still had no door—though he'd blocked the opening with plywood—but essentially all signs of the battle had been erased from the condo. No mindless task remained to keep him from thinking. And somehow he couldn't stop thinking of a woman's broken body hanging from a rusted hook.

"Damn it, Vicki, call!"

The empty space on the bookshelf drew his gaze and the guilt he'd been successfully holding at bay stormed the barricades. The grimoire was his. The responsibility was his. If he'd been stronger. If he'd been faster. If he'd been smarter. Surely with four hundred and fifty years of experience he should be able to outthink one lone mortal with not even a tenth of that.

He looked down at the city regretfully. "I should have. . . ." He let his voice trail off. There was nothing he *could* have done differently. Even had he continued to believe the killer an abandoned child of his kind, even had Vicki not stumbled onto him bending over that corpse, even had he not decided to trust her, it wouldn't have changed last night's battle with the demon, his loss, and the loss of the grimoire. The only thing that could have prevented that would have been his destruction of the grimoire back when he first acquired it in the 1800s, and, frankly, he wasn't sure he could have destroyed it, then or now.

"Although," he acknowledged, right hand wrapped lightly around left forearm, skin even paler than usual against the stark white of the gauze, "had Vicki not worked her way into the equation, I would have died." And there would have been no one to stop the Demon Lord from rising. His lips drew up off his teeth. "Not that *I* seem to be doing much to prevent it."

Why didn't she call?

He began to pace, back and forth, back and forth, before the window.

She'd lost a lot of blood the night before. Had she run into trouble she was too weak to handle?

He remembered the feel of Ginevra's dead flesh under his hands as he cut her down. She'd been so alive. Like Vicki was so alive. . . .

Why didn't she call?

* * *

She'd been conscious now for some time and had been lying quietly, eyes closed, waiting for the pounding at her temples to stop echoing between her ears. Time was of the essence, yes, but sudden movement would have her puking her guts out and she couldn't see where that would help. Better to wait, to gather information, and to move when she might actually have some effect.

She licked her lips and tasted blood, could feel the warm moisture dribbling down from her nose.

Her feet were tied at the ankles. Her arms lashed together almost from wrists to elbows; the binding around her wrists fabric not rope. She'd been dumped on her side, knees drawn up, left cheek down on a hard, sticky surface—probably the floor. Someone had removed her jacket. Her glasses were not on her nose. She fought back the surge of panic that realization brought.

She could hear—or maybe feel—footsteps puttering about behind her and adenoidal breathing coming from the same direction. Norman. From the opposite direction, she could hear short sharp breaths, each exhalation an indignant snort. And Coreen.

So she's still alive. Good. And she sounds angry, not hurt. Even better. Vicki suspected that Coreen was also tied or she wouldn't be so still. *Which, all things considered, is a good thing. Few people get dead faster than amateur heroes. Not,* she added as a flaming spike slammed through the back of her head, *that the professionals are doing so hot.*

She lay there for a moment, playing *if Coreen hadn't interfered* until the new pain faded into the background with the old pain.

The residual stench of the demon was very strong—only in a building used to students could Norman have gotten away with it—overlaid with burning charcoal, candles, air freshener, and toast.

"You know, you could offer me some. I'm starving."

"You'll eat after."

Vicki wasn't surprised to hear that Norman talked with his mouth full. *He probably picks his nose and wears socks with sandals, too. An all-around great guy.*

"After what?"

"After the Demon Lord makes you mine."

"Get real, Birdwell! Demons don't come that powerful!"

Norman laughed.

Cold fingers traced a pattern up and down Vicki's spine, and she fought to keep herself from flipping over so that the thing Norman Birdwell had become was no longer at her exposed back. She'd heard a man laugh like that once before. The SWAT team had needed seven hours to take him out and they'd still lost two of the hostages.

"You'll see," his voice matter-of-fact around the toast. "First I was just going to have you ripped into little pieces, real slow. Then I was going to use you as part of the incantation to call the Demon Lord. Did I tell you it needed a life? Until you showed up I was going to grab the kid down the hall." His voice drew closer and Vicki felt a pointed toe prodding her in the back. "Now I've decided to use her and keep you for myself."

"You're disgusting, Birdwell!"

"DON'T SAY THAT!"

Concussion or not, Vicki opened her eyes in time to see Norman dart forward and slap Coreen across the face. Without her glasses details were a blur, but from the sound of it, it hadn't been much of a blow.

"Did I hurt you?" he asked, the rage gone as suddenly as it had appeared.

The bright mass of Coreen's hair swept up and back as she tossed her head. "No," she told him, chin rising. Fear had crept into her voice but it was still vastly outweighed by anger.

"Oh." Norman finished his toast and wiped his fingers on his jeans. "Well, I will."

Vicki could understand and approve of Coreen's anger. She was furious herself—at Norman, at the situation, at her helplessness. Although she would have preferred to rant and bellow, she held her rage carefully in check. Releasing it now, when she was bound, would do neither her, nor Coreen, nor the city any good. She drew in a deep breath and slowly exhaled. Her head felt as though it were balanced precariously on the edge of the world and one false move would sent it tumbling into infinity.

"Excuse me." She hadn't intended to whisper, but it was all she could manage.

Norman turned. "Yes?"

"I was wondering . . ." *Swallow. Ride the pain. Continue.* ". . . if I could have my glasses." *Breathe, two, three, while Norman waits patiently. He isn't going anywhere, after all.* "Without them, I can't see what you're doing."

"Oh." She could almost hear his brow furrow even though she couldn't see it. "It only seems fair you should get to see this."

He trotted out of her line of sight and she closed her eyes for a moment to rest them. *Only seems fair? Well, I suppose I should be happy he doesn't want to waste front row seats.*

"Here." He squatted down and very carefully slid the plastic arms back over her ears, settling the bridge gently on her nose. "Better?"

Vicki blinked as the intricate stitching on his black cowboy boot came suddenly into focus. "Much. Thank you." Up close, and considering the features without the expression, he wasn't an unattractive young man. A bit on the thin and gawky side perhaps, but time would take care of both. Time that none of them had, thanks to Norman Birdwell.

"Good." He patted her cheek and the touch, light as it was sent ripples of pain through her head. "I'll tell you what I told her. If you scream, or make any loud noise, I'll kill you both."

"I'm going to go do my teeth now," he continued, straightening up. "I brush after everything I eat." He pulled what looked to be a thick pen out of the pocket protector and unscrewed the cap. It turned out to be a portable toothbrush, with paste in the handle. "You should get one of these," he told her, demonstrating how it worked, his tone self-righteously smug. *"I've* never had a filling."

Fortunately, he didn't wait for a reply.

Some lucky providence had put Coreen directly across the small room, making it thankfully unnecessary for Vicki to move her head. She studied the younger woman for a few seconds, noting the red patch on one pale cheek. Even with her glasses, she seemed to be having trouble focusing. "Are you all right?" she called quietly.

"What do you think?" Coreen didn't bother to modulate her voice. "I'm tied to one of Norman Birdwell's kitchen chairs—with socks!"

Vicki dropped her gaze. At least six socks per leg tied Coreen to the chrome legs of the kitchen chair. Gray and black and brown nylon socks, stretched to their limit and impossible to break. Intrigued, in spite of everything, she gave her own bonds an experimental tug; they didn't respond like socks. As it seemed safer than moving her head, she slid her arms up along the floor until she could see them. Ties. At least four, maybe five—the swirling leaps of paisley and the jarring clashes of color made it difficult to tell for sure—and while it might have had more to do with her own weakness than Norman's skill, for she doubted he'd ever been a boy scout, he certainly seemed to know his knots.

"You were about to jump him, weren't you?"

"What?" Vicki looked up and wished she hadn't as her body protested with alternating waves of dizziness and nausea.

"When we came into the apartment and I . . . I mean. . . . Well, I'm sorry."

It sounded more like a challenge than an apology. "Don't worry about it now." Vicki swallowed, trying not to add to the puddle of drool collecting under her cheek. "Let's just try . . . to get out of this mess."

"What do you think I've been trying to do?" Coreen gave a frantic heave that only resulted in bouncing the chair backward less than half an inch. "I don't believe this! I really don't believe this!"

Hearing the tones of incipient panic, Vicki, in the driest voice she was capable of, said, "It *is* a little like . . . Alfred Hitchcock does *Revenge of the Nerds.*"

Coreen stared at her in astonishment, sniffed, and grinned somewhat shakily. "Or David Cronneberg does *I Dream of Genie,*" she offered in return.

Good girl. It took all the energy Vicki had left to smile approvingly. While there were dangers in Coreen not taking Norman seriously, the dangers were greater if the girl fell apart.

Struggling did more damage to her than to the ties. She kept struggling anyway. If the world had to end, she'd be damned if she let it go down under the ridiculously high, cowboy booted heel of Norman Birdwell, adding insult to injury.

* * *

"Enough!" Henry spun away from the window and hurled himself toward the door. He had a name, he had a place, it was time he joined the hunt. "I should never have waited this long."

At the door, he slowed, grabbed his coat, and managed to appear within the parameters of normality as he exited into the hall. He slid the key into the lock, then headed for the stairs, hating the charade that kept him to a mortal's pace.

In the dim light of the stairwell, he let all pretense drop and moved as quickly as aching muscles would allow.

There were slightly less than two hours until midnight.

He completely forgot that the stairwell was part of the building's random monitoring system.

* * *

Vicki drifted up into consciousness thinking, *This has got to stop*. Every time she tried to move, every time she tried to raise her head, she drifted back down into the pit. Occasionally, the blackness claimed her when she was doing nothing more than lying quietly, trying to conserve her strength for another attempt at getting free. *I'm going to have to think of something else*.

All her intermittent struggling had accomplished was to exacerbate her physical condition and to uncover her watch.

Seven minutes after ten. Henry's probably throwing fits. Oh my God, Henry! Her involuntary jerk brought another flash of pain. She ignored it, lost it in sudden horror. *I forgot to warn him about that security guard. . . .*

* * *

Although he recognized the necessity of the surveillance cameras, Greg had never liked them. They always made him feel a bit like a peeping Tom. Two or three guards on constant patrol with one manning a central position at the desk, that's the kind of job he'd prefer to work. A camera just couldn't replace a trained man on the scene. But trained men had to be paid and cameras didn't so he was stuck with them.

As the attractive young lady in the whirlpool stepped out and reached for her towel, he politely averted his eyes. Maybe he was just getting old, but those two scraps of fabric were not what he'd call a bathing suit. When he looked back again, that monitor showed only orderly rows of cars in the underground garage.

He sat back in his chair and adjusted the black armband he wore in honor of Mrs. Hughes and Owen. The building would be different without them. As the night went on, he kept expecting to see them heading out for their last walk before bed and had to keep reminding himself that he'd never see them again. The young man he'd relieved had raised an eyebrow at the armband and another at the explanation. Young people today had no real concept of respect; not for the dead, not for authority, not for themselves. Henry Fitzroy was one of the few young people he'd met in the last ten years who understood.

Henry Fitzroy. Greg pulled at his lower lip. Last night he'd done a very, very foolish thing. He was embarrassed by it and sorry for it, but not entirely certain he was wrong. As an old sergeant of his used to say, *"If it walks like a duck, and it talks like a duck, and it acts like a duck, odds are good it's a duck."* The sergeant had been referring to Nazis, but Greg figured it applied to vampires as well. While he had his doubts that a young man of Mr. Fitzroy's quality could have committed such an insane murder—there'd been nothing crazy about the look Greg had seen in Mr. Fitzroy's eyes so many weeks ago, it had, in fact, been frighteningly sane—he couldn't believe that a man of Mr. Fitzroy's quality would allow a young lady visiting him to answer the door *a deshabille*. He'd have gotten up and done it himself. When he'd calmed down enough to think about it, Greg realized that she had to be hiding something.

But what?

A movement in one of the monitors caught his eye and Greg turned toward it. He frowned. Something black had flickered past the fire door leading to the seventh floor too quickly for him to recognize it. He reached for the override and began activating the cameras in the stairwell.

Seconds later, the fifth floor camera picked up Henry Fitzroy running down the stairs two at a time and scowling. He looked like any other young man in reasonable shape—and a bad mood—who'd decided not to waste his time waiting for an elevator. While Greg himself wouldn't have walked from the fourteenth floor, he realized there was nothing supernatural about Henry Fitzroy doing it. Nor in the way he was doing it.

Sighing, he turned the controls back to their random sequencing.

"And what if it doesn't act like a duck all the time?" he wondered aloud.

* * *

Henry had reached the sixth floor when the abuse his body had taken the night before caught up with him and he had to slow to something more closely approximating a mortal's pace. He snarled as he swung his weight around on the banister, frustrated by the refusal of muscles to respond as they should. Rather than touching down only once on every half flight, he actually had to use every other step.

He was in a *bad* mood when he reached his car and he took the exit ramp from the underground garage much faster than he should have, his exhaust pipe screaming along concrete. The sound forced him to calm. He wouldn't get there any faster if he destroyed his car or attracted the attention of the police.

At the curb, while he waited impatiently for the light to change, he caught a familiar scent.

"A BMW? You've got to be kidding." Tony leaned his forearms through the open window and clicked his tongue. "If that watch is a Rolex," he added softly, "I want my blood back."

Henry knew he owed the boy a great deal, so he tried bury the rage he was feeling. He felt his lips pull back off his teeth and realized he hadn't been significantly successful.

If Tony had doubted his memory of what had happened

the night before, Henry's expression would have convinced him for there was very little humanity in it. Had the anger been directed at him, he would've run and not stopped until sunrise and safety. As it was, he pulled his arms back outside the car, just in case. "I thought you might want to talk. . . ."

"Later." If the world survived the night, they'd talk. It wasn't of immediate concern.

"Yeah. Right. Later's good. Say. . . ." Tony frowned. "Is Victory okay?"

"I don't . . ." The light changed. He slammed the car into gear. ". . . know."

Tony stood watching the car speed away, lips pursed, hands shoved deep in his pockets. He rolled a quarter over and over between his fingers.

"This is my home number." Vicki handed him the card *and turned it over so he could see the other number handwritten on the back.* *"And this is who you call if you're in trouble and you can't get to me."*

"Mike Celluci?" Tony shook his head. *"He don't like me much, Victory."*

"Tough."

"I don't like him much."

"Do I look like I care? Call him anyway."

He pulled the quarter from his pocket and headed to the pay phone on the corner. Four years in a variety of pockets had turned the card limp but the number on the back was still legible. He'd already called the number on the front and wasted a quarter on a stupid machine. Everybody knew Victory never turned the machine on if she was home.

"I gotta talk to Mike Celluci."

"Speaking."

"Victory's in trouble." He was as sure of it as he'd ever been sure of anything in his life.

"Who?"

Tony rolled his eyes at the receiver. And they called them the city's finest. What a dork. "Vicki Nelson. You remember—tall, blonde, pushy, used to be a cop."

"What kind of trouble?"

Good. Celluci sounded worried. "I don't know."

"Where?"

"I don't know." Tony could hear teeth grinding on the other end of the line. If this wasn't so serious, he'd be enjoying himself. "You're the cop, you figure it out."

He hung up before the explosion. He'd done what he could.

Mike Celluci stared at the phone and swore long and loudly in Italian. Upon reflection, he'd recognized the voice as Vicki's little street person and that lent just enough credibility to the message that it couldn't be completely ignored. He dumped a pocket load of little pink slips on the kitchen table and began sorting through them.

"Norman Birdwell. York University." He held it up to the light in a completely futile gesture then tossed it back with the others.

Vicki had never been a grandstander. She'd always played by the rules, made them work for her. She'd never go in to pick up a suspected mass murderer—a suspected psychotic mass murderer—without backup. *But then, she doesn't have backup anymore, does she? And she just might feel like she's got something to prove. . . .*

He'd hit the memory dial to headquarters before he finished the thought.

"This is Celluci. Darrel, I need the number for someone in Administration at York University. I know it's the middle of the night, I want a home number. I *know* I'm off duty. You're not paying my overtime, what the hell are you complaining about?" He balanced the phone under his chin and pulled his shoulder holster up off the back of the chair, shrugging into it as he waited. "So call me at home when you find it. And Darrel, give it top priority. I want that number yesterday."

He reached for his jacket and laid it beside the pnone. He hated waiting. He'd always hated waiting. He dug the pink slip back out of the pile.

Norman Birdwell.

"I don't know what hat you pulled this name out of, Nelson," he growled. "But if I ride to the rescue and you're not in deep shit, bad eyes and insecurity are going to be the least of your problems."

* * *

Norman was talking to the grimoire and had been for some time. His low mumble had become a constant background noise as Vicki drifted in and out of consciousness. Occasionally she heard words, mostly having to do with how the world would now treat Norman the way he deserved. Vicki was all for that.

"Hey, Norman!"

The mumbling stopped. Vicki tried to focus on Coreen. The younger woman looked . . . embarrassed?

Grimoire clutched to his chest, Norman came into her line of sight. She shuddered at the thought of holding that book that closely. The one time she'd touched it back in Henry's apartment had made her skin crawl and the memory still left an unpleasant feeling in her mind.

"Look, Norman, I have really got to go to the bathroom." Coreen's voice was low and intense and left no doubt as to her sincerity and Vicki suddenly found herself wishing she hadn't said that.

"Uh. . . ." Norman obviously had no idea of how to deal with the problem.

Coreen sighed audibly. "Look, if you untie me, I'll walk quietly to the bathroom and then come right back to my chair so you can tie me up again. You can keep me covered with your silly gun the entire time. I *really* have to go."

"Uh. . . ."

"Your Demon Lord isn't going to be too impressed if he shows up and I've peed on his pentagram."

Norman stared at Coreen for a long moment, his hands stroking up and down the dark leather cover of the grimoire. "You wouldn't," he said at last.

"Try me."

It might have been the smile, it might have been the tone of voice, but Norman decided not to risk it.

Vicki drifted off during the untying and came to again as Coreen, once more secured in her chair, said, "What about her?"

Norman shifted his grip slightly on the gun. "She doesn't matter, she'll be dead soon anyway."

Vicki was beginning to be very afraid that he was right. She simply had no reserves left to call on and every time she fought her way up out of the blackness, the world seemed a little further away. *Okay, if I'm dead anyway and I scream and he shoots me, the neighbors will call the police—that thing doesn't have a silencer on it. Of course, he may just whack me on the head again.* That was the last thing she needed. *If I have Coreen scream as well, that may push him over the edge enough that he shoots one of us.*

Coreen, for all the girl believed in vampires and demons and who knew what else, didn't really understand what was about to happen. *Mind you, that's not her fault. I didn't tell her.*

She balanced Coreen's life against the life of the city. It wasn't a decision she had any right to make. She made it anyway. *I'm sorry, Coreen.*

She wet her lips and drew in as deep a breath as she was capable of. "Cor . . ." The butt of the rifle hit the floor inches from her nose, the metal plate slamming against the tiles. The noise and the vibration drove the remainder of her carefully hoarded breath out in an almost silent cry of pain. *Thank God, he had the safety on. . . .*

"Shut up," Norman told her genially.

She didn't really have much choice but to obey as darkness rolled over her once again.

Norman looked around his apartment, exceedingly pleased with himself. Soon all those people who thought him a nobody, a nothing, would pay. He reached out one hand to stroke the book. The book said so.

10:43. Time to start painting the pentagram. It was much more complicated than the form he usually used and he wanted to be sure he got it right.

This was going to be the greatest night of his life.

Fifteen

She knew better than to go near strange men in cars. She'd been raised on horror stories of abduction and rape and young women found weeks later decomposing in irrigation ditches. She answered the summons anyway, her mother's warnings having lost their power from the moment she met the stranger's eyes.

"The administration offices, where are they?"

She knew where the admin offices were, at least, she thought she knew—actually, she wasn't sure what she thought anymore. She wet her lips and offered, "The Ross Building?" She'd seen an office in Ross, maybe more than one.

"Which is where?"

She half turned and pointed. A moment later, she wondered why she was standing in the middle of St. Lawrence Boulevard staring at a set of taillights driving onto the campus—and why she felt a vague sense of disappointment.

Henry scanned the directory board and frowned. Only one office listed might have what he needed: The Office of Student Programs, S302. He sensed a scattering of lives in the building, but he would deal with them as he had to.

11:22. He was running out of time.

The dim lighting was a boon and had anyone been watching they'd have seen only a deeper shadow flickering down the length of the shadowed hall.

The first flight of stairs he found only took him to the second floor. He found another, found the third floor, and began following the numbers stenciled on the doors.

322, 313, 316 . . . 340? He turned and glared at the fire
door he'd just passed through. Surely there had to be a
pattern. No one, not even in the twentieth century, num-
bered a building completely at random.

"I haven't got time for this," he growled.

340, 342, 344, 375a. . . .

A cross corridor carried the numbers off in two directions. Henry paused, there were voices and they were
saying things he couldn't ignore.

"Well, what do you expect when you call out the name
of a Demon Lord in his consort's temple?"

Temple? Consort? Were there now other groups involved in calling demons or had his assumption that only
one person was involved been wrong from the beginning? He didn't have time to check this out. He couldn't
afford not to.

Down the cross corridor, around a corner, and the door
at the end of the hall showed light behind it. There appeared to be several people talking at once.

"I suppose this means the demon has Elias?"

"Good guess. What are you going to do?"

"What can we do? We wait."

"You can wait," a third voice rose out of the tumult,
"but Lexi boots the statue and screams, *'Ashwarn, Ashwarn, Ashwarn, you give him back!'* at the top of her
lungs."

Henry paused, hand on the door. There were six lives
in the room and no feel of a demonic presence. What
was going on?

"Nothing happens."

"What do you mean, nothing?"

"Just what I said, nothing." The young woman sitting
at the head of the table spotted Henry standing, blinking
on the threshold and smiled. "Hi. You look lost."

They were playing a game. That much was obvious
from the piles of brightly colored dice. But a game that
called on demons? "I'm looking for student records. . . ."

"Boy are you in the wrong place." A tall young man
scratched at dark stubble. "You need the WOB." At

Henry's blank look, he grinned and continued. "The West Office Building, WOB, that's where all that shit is."

"Yeah, but the WOB closes down at five." Carefully placing the little lead figure she'd been holding on the table, one of the other players checked her watch. "It's eight minutes after eleven. There won't be anyone there."

Eight after eleven. More time wasted on fruitless searching.

"Hey, don't look so upset, man, maybe we can help?"

"Maybe we can play?" muttered one of the others. The rest ignored her.

Why not? After all, he was looking for a man who called up demons. The connection was there, however tenuous. "I'm looking for Norman Birdwell."

The young woman at the head of the table curled her lip. "Why?" she asked. "Does he owe you money."

"You know him?"

"Unfortunately." The group drawled out the word in unison.

They would have laughed, but Henry was at the table before the first sound escaped. They looked at one another in nervous silence instead and Henry could see memories of nine bodies, throats ripped out, rising in their expressions. He couldn't compel a group this large, he could only hope they were still young enough to respond to authority.

"I need his address."

"We, uh, played at his place once. Grace, didn't you write it down?"

They all watched while Grace, the young woman at the head of the table, searched through her papers. She appeared to have written everything down. Henry fought the urge to help her search.

"Is Norman in trouble?"

Henry kept his eyes on the papers, willing the one he needed to be found. "Yes."

The players closest to him edged away, recognizing the hunter. A second later, with the arrogance of youth, they decided they couldn't possibly be the prey and edged back.

"We, uh, stopped gaming with him 'cause he took the whole thing too seriously."

"Yeah, he started acting like all this stuff was real. Like he was bumping into wizards and warriors and long legged beasties on every street corner."

"He's such a dork."

"It's just a game."

"It's a game we're not playing," someone pointed out.

"Is Norman in bad trouble?"

"Yes."

They stopped talking after that. They didn't have the concepts to deal with the tone of Henry's voice.

Grace handed him the paper tentatively, although not entirely certain she'd keep her fingers in the deal.

"Wait a minute," the tall young man protested. "I don't like Norman either, but should we be giving out his. . . ." Henry turned to look full at him. He paled and closed his eyes.

As he slammed his car into gear and burned rubber the length of the parking lot, Henry checked his watch. 11:36. So little time.

". . . and one final join here." Norman straightened up and beamed proudly down at his apartment floor. The white outline of the pentagram had almost been obscured by the red and yellow symbols surrounding it. He caressed the open page of the grimoire, tracing with his fingertips the diagram he'd just finished reproducing. "Soon," he told it. "Soon."

The smell of the acrylic paint so close to Vicki's face added to the nausea and made her eyes sting and itch. She no longer had the strength to ignore it, so she endured it instead. Scrubbing out a bit of the pentagram before it dried had seemed like a good idea until she realized that it would only release the Demon Lord to the slaughter that much sooner. But there had to be something she could do. She would not, could not, admit Norman Birdwell had won.

Coreen stared from the pentagram to Norman and back to the drying paint. It was real, all of it, and while she'd always believed, now she began to *believe*. Her mouth suddenly dry and her heart beating so loud she felt sure the skinny geek should be able to hear it, she tried harder to free her right leg. When Norman had tied her back up after taking her to the bathroom, she'd worked a bit of slack into the socks. Ever since, while he'd puttered about doing who knew what, she'd been working them looser, stretching them little by little. Sooner or later, she'd have her leg free. For now, her mind refused to deal with anything beyond that point.

The five candles Norman placed around the pentagram were new. Red and yellow spirals had been much easier to find than black candles of any description. He kept the grimoire with him, tucked under an arm when he needed his hands free, clutched close to his chest when he didn't. He had begun to feel incomplete without it, as if it had become a part of him, even taking it to Canadian Tire that afternoon when he bought the new hibachi. Holding it, he knew that his wildest dreams were about to come true.

The throbbing in his head had become louder, wilder, and more compelling. Its tone varied with his actions . . . or possibly his actions varied with the tones— Norman was no longer entirely sure.

As he pulled the tiny barbecue out of its box and set it up by the balcony door, he checked to see if his audience was impressed. The older woman had closed her eyes again, her glasses having slipped down far enough for him to see over them, but she was still breathing and that was really all that counted. He'd be pissed if she died before he killed her 'cause then he'd have to use Coreen and he had other plans for her. Coreen didn't look impressed either, but she looked scared and that would do for now.

"You're not laughing." He prodded her in the back with the grimoire, noting with pleasure the way she flinched away from its touch, then squatted to set up the three charcoal briquettes.

"There's nothing to laugh at, Norman." Coreen twisted around in her chair. He was a little behind her and to one side and she hated not being able to see what he was doing. Although she wanted to shriek, she tried to keep her voice from rising too high. You should talk softly to crazy people—she'd read that in a book. "Look, this has gone far enough. Ms. Nelson needs a doctor." A little pleading wouldn't hurt. "Please, Norman, you let us go and we'll forget we ever saw you."

"Let you go?" It was Norman's turn to laugh at her. He didn't think the Demon Lord could give him anything he'd enjoy so much. He laughed at her the way everyone, all his life, had laughed at him. It grew and grew and she shrank back under the weight of it. He felt it echo in the grimoire, felt his body begin to reverberate with the sound, felt it wrap in and around the pulsing in his head.

"Norman!" It wasn't very loud, but it was enough to cut the laughter off. *All right, so maybe there is power in a name. I've been wrong about other things lately.* Vicki tried to focus on the young man's face, couldn't manage it, and gave up. The insane hysteria of the laughter had stopped. That was the result she'd spent her strength for and she'd have to be content with the victory she'd won.

His brows drawn down into a deep vee, Norman scowled at the woman on the floor. He was glad she was going to die. She'd chased the laughter away. Still scowling, he lit the candles and flicked off the overhead light. Not even Coreen's quick intake of breath at the sudden twilight was enough to put him in a better mood. Not until he got the briquettes burning and the air in the room grew blue with the smoke from a handful of frankincense, did his expression lighten.

Only one thing left to do.

When Vicki next opened her eyes she came closer to panic than she had at any time that night.

When did it get so dark?

She could see five flickering points of light. The rest of the room, Coreen, Norman—gone. And the air . . . it smelled strange, heavy, it hurt to breathe.

Dear God, am I dying?

She tried to move, to fight, to live. Her arms and legs were still bound. That reassured her, slowed her heart and slowed her breathing. If she was tied, she wasn't dead. Not yet.

The lights were candles, could be nothing else, and the air reeked of incense. It must have begun.

She didn't see Norman approach, didn't even realize he was there until he gently pushed her glasses up her nose. His fingers were warm as he wrestled with her arms and pushed the ties back to expose her left wrist. She thought she could see the faint line where Henry had fed the night before and knew she was imagining it. In this light, at this time, she couldn't have seen the wound if her entire hand had been chopped off.

She felt the cold edge of a blade against her skin and its kiss as it opened a vein. And then another. Not the safe horizontal cuts she and Tony had made but vertical cuts that left her wrist awash in darkness and a warm puddle filling the hollow of her palm.

"You have to stay alive through the invocation," Norman told her, pulling her arms away from her body, making them part of the symbols surrounding the pentagram. "So I'm only going to do one wrist. Don't die too fast." She heard the knife clatter down on the floor behind her, and his footsteps move away.

Fucking right I won't. . . . The anger tired her so she let it go. *Essentials only now, never say die.* Especially not when die meant bleeding to death on a dirty floor and delivering her city, not to mention the world, into Armageddon. Sagged over onto her left side, her heart could be no more than four inches off the floor. By concentrating everything she had remaining on her right arm, she managed to get it under her left, elevating the bleeding wrist as high as possible. Maybe not four inches, but it would help to retard the flow.

Pressure'll be low. . . . I could hold on for . . . hours.

It might only be a matter of time, but as much as possible she'd make it her time, not his.

Through her ear pressed against the floor by the weight of her head, all she could hear was a soft rhythmic hissing, like the sound of the ocean in a shell. She lay listening to that, ignoring the chanting rising around her.

* * *

He could have identified the specific building in the complex even without the address. The power surrounding it, the expectation of evil, caused every hair on Henry's body to rise. He was out of the car before it had completely skidded to a stop and through the locked door into the lobby a moment later. The reinforced glass was not thick enough to stop the concrete planter he heaved through it.

* * *

Norman spat the last discordant word into the air and let his left hand fall down to the open grimoire balanced on his right. His throat hurt, his eyes stung, and he was trembling with excitement, waiting for the telltale shimmer of air that would signify his demon was arriving.

It never came.

One second the pentagram was empty and the throbbing beat out a glorious rhythm inside his head. A second later, with no warning, it was full, and only echoes remained in the silence.

Norman cried out and fell to his knees, the grimoire forgotten as he raised both hands to cover his face.

Coreen whimpered and sagged against her bonds, consciousness fleeing what it couldn't accept.

Vicki attempted to breathe shallowly through her teeth, glad for the first time she couldn't really *see*. Every fear she'd ever held, every nightmare, every terror from childhood to yesterday came with the ill-defined shape in the pentagram. She clamped her teeth down on the urge to wail and used her physical condition—the pain, the weakness—to insulate her from the Demon Lord. *I hurt too much now to be hurt any further.*

The thing in the pentagram seemed amused by that.

Colors ran together in ways that colors could not, creating shades that seared the heart and shades that froze the soul, and they built a creature with blond curls and blue eyes and very, very white teeth. Slender and hermaphroditic, it laid no claim to either sex while claiming both of them.

"Enough," said the Demon Lord, and the terror damped down to a bearable level. It checked the boundaries of its prison and then the lives around it. Coreen, it ignored, but by Vicki's side of the pentagram it squatted and smiled approvingly at the patterns of blood on the floor.

"So, you are the life that opens the way for my power." It smiled and Vicki gave thanks she could see only a shadowy outline of the expression. "But you're not being very cooperative, are you?"

Only the nonresponsiveness of her muscles gave her time to fight the compulsion that she lower her bleeding wrist back to the floor. A sudden shock of recognition lent her strength. "I . . . know you." Not the face, not this creature specifically, but the essence, oh, the essence she knew.

"I know you, too." Something writhed for a second in the Demon Lord's eyes. "And this time, I've won. It's over, Victoria."

She really hated that name. "Not till . . . fat lady sings."

"A joke? In your position? I think that your strength might be better spent pleading for mercy." It stood and dusted its hands against its thighs. "A pity I can't allow you to live. I'd get such pleasure from your reactions to my plans."

All Vicki wanted at that moment was enough saliva left to spit.

It turned to Norman, still cowering by the hibachi. "Stand!"

Scooping up the grimoire, holding the book like a talisman, Norman rose shakily to his feet.

"Release me!"

Norman's lower lip went out and his expression grew decidedly mulish. "No. I called you. I am your master." He had the power, not this thing. He did.

The Demon Lord's laughter blew the windows out of the apartment.

As though there were strings attached to his shoulders and the Demon Lord was the puppeteer, Norman began to jerk toward the pentagram. "No," he whined. "I am the master."

He's fighting, Vicki realized. She would have expected his will to be swept aside like so many matchsticks. Conceit and self-interest made a stronger defense than she thought.

* * *

As Henry stepped out of the elevator onto the ninth floor, the smell of blood almost overwhelmed him. It rose over the pervasive demon-taint and drew him to the door he needed. The door was locked.

The metal held. The wood of the doorjamb splintered and gave.

* * *

Vicki heard the noise as though it came from a great distance away. She recognized it, understood its significance, but just couldn't seem to care much.

The Demon Lord heard the noise as well but ignored it. It kept its attention on Norman who stood inches from the edge of the pentagram, sweating and shaking and losing the battle.

The word seemed mostly consonants and it tore at the ears as it tore at the throat.

The Demon Lord snarled and turned, its patina of humanity slipping as it moved. When it saw Henry, its features settled and it smiled. "You call my name, Nightchild, are you the champion here? Have you come to save the mortal world from my domination?"

Henry felt it stroke at his mind and swatted the touch away, his own snarl barely less demonic as he answered. "Go back to the pit, spawn of Satan! This world is not yours!"

"Spawn of Satan?" The Demon Lord shook its head. "You are showing your age, Henry Fitzroy. This world does not believe in the Dark Lord. I will enjoy teaching it differently and you cannot stop me from doing exactly as I wish."

"I will not allow you to destroy this world without a fight." He didn't dare take his eyes from the Demon

Lord's to look for Vicki although he knew it was her blood scent that filled the room.

"Fight all you wish." It bowed graciously. "You will lose."

"NO!" Norman stood, splay legged, grimoire tucked under his arm, clutching the AK-47 with enough force to turn his fingers white. "*I* called your name! I AM THE MASTER! YOU WILL NOT IGNORE ME! YOU WON'T! YOU WON'T! YOU WON'T!"

The short burst sprayed across the pentagram, almost cutting the Demon Lord in half. Howling with rage, it lost control of its form, becoming again the maelstrom of darkness it had been at the beginning.

Firearm violation, Vicki though muzzily, as the slugs tore up the kitchen cabinets behind her.

The noise startled Coreen into full consciousness. With panicked strength she began to fight against her bonds, throwing herself violently from side to side, bouncing the chair legs inches off the floor at a time.

Like night falling in on itself, the Demon Lord reformed and the temperature in the apartment plunged. It smiled, showing great curved teeth it hadn't had before. Once again, Norman began jerking toward it.

The lights came on, throwing the scene into sharp relief, and a voice yelled, "Freeze! Police!"

The first instant of frozen expressions was almost funny, then Henry raised a hand to shield his eyes, the Demon Lord spun about to face a new adversary, and Norman raced toward the door, screaming, "No, it's mine! You can't stop me! It's mine!"

Coreen's leg came free of the socks at last. As Norman passed, she kicked out.

He fought for balance, arms flailing. The grimoire dropped to the floor. A second later, Norman fell into the pentagram.

Then Norman wasn't anymore, but his scream lingered for a heartbeat or two.

Mike Celluci stood at the light switch, his .38 in one hand, the other, under no conscious volition, making the sign of the cross. "Jesus H. Christ," he breathed into the sudden silence. "What the hell is going on in here?"

The Demon Lord turned to face him. "But that's it exactly, Detective. *Hell* is going on in here."

This was worse than anything Celluci could have imagined. He hadn't seen the punk with the assault rifle disappear into thin air. He didn't see the thing standing in the middle of the room smiling.

But he had. And he did.

Then he caught sight of Vicki and all the strangeness became of secondary importance.

"Who did this?" he demanded, moving to her side and dropping to one knee. "What is going on in here!" The question came out sounding more than a bit desperate the second time around. While he felt her throat for a pulse, he kept the Demon Lord covered—the direction of the threat obvious after what he'd seen as he came in.

"Pretty much exactly what it looks like," Henry told him. Clearly the stalwart officer of the law was a friend of Vicki's. What he thought he was doing here could be settled later. "That is a Demon Lord. He just destroyed the . . . person who called him and we're in a great deal of trouble."

"Trouble?" Celluci asked, not bothering at the moment with whether he believed all this or not.

"Yes," said the Demon Lord, and stepped out of the pentagram. It effortlessly pulled the gun from Celluci's hand and tossed it out the window.

Celluci watched it go, there being nothing else he could do, then with lips a thin, pale line he bent over Vicki, ignoring the cold sweat that beaded his entire body, ignoring the terror that held his heart in an icy fist, ignoring everything but the one thing he could change. Fighting the knots out of the ties, he bound up her wrist with the first one he got free.

"It won't do any good," the Demon Lord observed. With all attention focused on Vicki, it sidled sideways, whirled around, and dove for the grimoire.

Henry got there first, scooped up the book, and backed away with it. To his surprise, the Demon Lord snarled but let him go. "You have no power," he realized. "You're in this world without power."

"The invocation is not finished," the Demon Lord admitted, its eyes still on the book, ''until the woman dies.''

''Then the invocation will never be finished.'' Brute strength forced the bindings off her legs and Celluci threw the ties across the room with unnecessary force.

''It will be finished very soon.'' the Demon Lord pointed out. ''She is dying,''

''No she isn't,'' Celluci growled, easing Vicki's limp body over onto her back.

Yes, I am. Vicki wished she could feel the hand cupping her face, but she hadn't been able to feel anything for some time. Her eyes itched, but she didn't have the strength to blink. She wished it wasn't happening this way. But she'd given it her best shot. Time to rest.

Then the Demon Lord raised its head and looked directly at her, its expression gloating and openly triumphant.

When she died, it won.

The hell it wins. She grabbed onto what life she had left and shook it, hard. *I am not going to die. I am not going to die!*

''I am . . . not . . . going to die. . . .''

''That's what I said.'' Celluci didn't bother to smile. Neither of them would have believed it. ''Listen.''

Through the glassless window, up from the street, she could hear sirens growing closer.

''Cavalry?'' she asked.

He nodded. ''I called in an *officer down* when I reached the building—the place felt like it was under siege. There'll be an ambulance with them. I don't care how much blood you've lost, they can replace it.''

''Concussed, too. . . .''

''Your head's hard enough to take it. You're not going to die.'' He half turned to face the Demon Lord, throwing his conviction over his shoulder at it.

It smiled unpleasantly. ''All mortals die in time. I will, of course, try to make it sooner than later.''

''Over my dead body,'' Celluci snarled.

''No need.'' Henry shook his head. ''It can't kill her or it would have the moment it left the pentagram. Her death is tied to the invocation and it can't affect the invocation. All it can do is wait.

"If you stay," he told it, moving closer, "you'll be fighting every moment. We can't destroy you, but without all your power you'll have no easy time of it."

The Demon Lord watched him move, eyes narrowed.

No, Vicki realized, *it isn't watching him, it's watching the grimoire.*

"So what do you suggest?" it scoffed. "That I surrender? Time is all I need, and time I have in abundance."

Vicki pushed at Celluci's arm, moving him out of his protective position. "A deal. . . . You want . . . the grimoire." If only her tongue wasn't so damned thick. "Go. . . . Break the invocation . . . it's yours."

"In time, I will take the grimoire. You have no idea of how to truly use the knowledge it contains." It made no effort to hide its desire as it stared at the book fo demonic lore. "There is nothing in your deal for me."

"Power freely given has more strength than that taken by force." Coreen went deep red as the two men and the Demon Lord turned to stare at her. "Well, it does. Everyone knows it."

"And power freely given is not a power often seen where you come from." Henry added, nodding slowly. The girl had brought up an important point. "It could be the makings of a major coup."

"The name . . . written on the . . . city." The demonkind had proven they were not without ambition.

"Upstart, grasping." The Demon Lord ground out a number of other words in a language that sound like a cat fight and its aspect began to slip again.

"Why wait for this world when you can have another now?" Henry prodded. "You want the grimoire. With it you can control others of your kind. Defeat your enemies. . . ."

"Yessss."

"We give it freely if in exchange you break the invocation and return where you came from. He who called you is no more. Nothing holds you here. Why wait when you can rule?"

With an effort the Demon Lord maintained its shape,

holding out hands that were no longer quite hands. "Give it to me. I will make your bargain."

"Swear it on your name."

"I ssso sssswear."

"And that you'll never use the book against human-kind," Coreen added in a rush, before Henry could move.

"It holdsss knowledge only to be usssed againssst de-monkind."

Her lower lip went out. "Swear it anyway. On your name."

"I ssswear. I sssswear."

Henry took a step forward and placed the book on what remained of the Demon Lord's hands. Grimoire and De-mon Lord disappeared.

Vicki stared to giggle.

Celluci looked down at her and frowned. "What?" he snapped.

"I was just . . . wondering . . . what you're going to . . . put in . . . your report."

* * *

"I saw Henry." Tony finished off the last of the gelatin and put the bowl back on the tray. "He came and told me what happened. Said I had a right to know. He's pretty cool. I think he was checking me out."

"Probably," Vicki agreed. "You know a dangerous amount about him."

Tony shrugged. "I'm no threat. Don't matter to me what time a guy gets up."

"Doesn't matter."

He grinned. "That's what I said."

The nurse's shoes squeaked softly against the floor as she came into the room. "Visiting hours are over. You can come again tomorrow."

Tony glanced from the nurse to Vicki and heaved him-self to his feet. He paused in the doorway and looked back. "Save me the gelatin."

Vicki grimaced. "It's all yours," she promised.

The nurse puttered about for a few moments, rearranged the blankets, checked the IV drip and bandage that covered Vicki's left arm from hand to elbow. On her way out, she ran into Mike Celluci on his way in.

"I'm sorry." Drawing herself up to her full height, she blocked the door. "But visiting hours are over."

Celluci gently moved her aside and, as she started to bristle, flashed his badge. "Police business,' he said, and closed the door.

He shook his head at heavy purple circles under Vicki's eyes, clicked his tongue at the IV drip, bent down, kissed her, and said without straightening, "You look like shit."

"Actually, I'm feeling much better." She reached up and pushed the curl of hair back off his forehead. "Yesterday, I *felt* like shit. And speaking of yesterday, where were you?"

"Writing up my report." He threw himself into the chair Tony had pulled up beside the bed. "Sure, you can laugh. That's one part of police work you should be glad you're free of."

It didn't hurt as much as it used to. In time, she suspected, it would hardly hurt at all. "What did you say?"

"I told the truth." He grinned at her expression. "Okay, not *all* of it."

"And Norman?"

"He got away while I was trying to keep you alive. Fortunately the chief remembers you through rose colored glasses and thinks that's a sufficient excuse. There's a country wide APB out on him." He shrugged. "It won't do my arrest record any good, but the killings will stop and I figure he got what was coming to him."

Vicki wasn't sure that she agreed so she kept silent. It smacked too much of an eye for an eye. *And the whole world ends up blind.*

"Your new boyfriend's a little shy."

She had to grin at the tone. "I told you. He's a writer. He's used to being alone."

"Sure. And I've told you, you're a lousy liar. But I owe him for taking care of that . . . teenager, so I'll let it go for now."

Vicki's grin twisted. Coreen had no idea she'd finally her vampire and that said vampire had *convinced* her that much of what had happened, hadn't. According to Coreen, Henry's version had left out both the lesser demon and the Demon Lord and had placed all the blame on Norman Birdwell. In a way, Norman was at last getting the recognition he craved.

She reached over with her good arm and poked him in the thigh. "That teenager, as you call her, just paid me a decent wage for that little dustup, so I'll thank you to speak of her with more respect."

Celluci grimaced. "Vicki, she's an airhead. I have no idea how he kept her quiet about, well, you know . . ." He couldn't say it, that would make it too real. ". . . but I shuddered to think of her getting to the press. And now," he heaved himself to his feet and headed for the door. "I'll get out of here so you can get some sleep."

Sleep was a long time coming. She palmed the pills they tried to give her and lay listening to the hospital grow quiet.

It was close to 1:00 when the door opened again.

"You're awake," he said softly.

She nodded, aware he could see her even if she couldn't see him.

"Were you waiting for me?"

She tried to keep her tone light. "Well, I didn't think you'd be here during regular visiting hours." She felt his weight settle on the side of the bed.

"I wasn't sure you'd want to see me."

"Why not?"

"Well, you can't exactly have pleasant memories of the time we shared."

"Not many, no." Some of the memories she found very pleasant, but Vicki wasn't sure she wanted to remind him of that just now. With four hundred and fifty years of experience, he had enough cards already.

Henry frowned, secure in the darkness. She said one thing, but her scent. . . .

"It must have been difficult for you to get in here."

"Hospitals have few shadows," he admitted. "I had hoped I could see you after you got out. . . ?"

"Sure." Would he understand what she was offering? Did she? "We can have dinner."

She couldn't see him smile, but she heard the laugh then felt the cool pressure of his fingers around her hand. "Do you believe in destiny?" he asked.

"I believe in truth. I believe in justice. I believe in my friends. I believe in myself." She hadn't for a while, but now she did again. "And I believe in vampires."

His lips brushed against the skin of her wrist, and the warm touch of his breath when he spoke stood every hair on her body on end.

"Good enough."